Yugen

By

Huckleberry Rahr

ISBN eBook: 978-1-959981-67-1
ISBN paperback: 978-1-959981-68-8

Editor: Weslee Imrisek
Developmental Editor: Dulaine Roode
Developmental Editor: Angela Grimes
Cover Art: Getcovers.com
Formatting: Huckleberry Rahr

Books in the Pebble Stone Series

1: Xenagogue

2: Yugen

3: Zephyr

Books by Huckleberry Rahr

- Jade Stone Chronicles
  - Wolf Healer
  - Epsilon
  - Alphas
  - Traitor
  - Pack
  - Battlefield
  - Pack Present
- Pebble Stone Chronicles
  - Xenagogue
  - Yugen
  - Zephyr
- Ember Savita Chronicles
  - Veiled Phoenix
  - Moonstone Phoenix
  - Battle Phoenix
- Hidden Magic Series (working titles...)
  - The Aura of The Chameleon
  - The Chameleon's Duplicity
  - Truth Exposed
- The Search – Short Story, eBook only

Acknowledgements

Every time a new book comes out, a new ball of joy blossoms into a flower in my soul. I love sharing these stories with anyone who enjoys reading them.

I have dreams of eBooks, paperbacks, and eventually audiobooks and maybe one day seeing all my books on screens.

I wouldn't be here without Wes Imrisek, Angela Grimes, Elizabeth Daly, Kay Wyatt, Maris Gellings, and Dulaine Roode. Beyond this fantastic crew, who jump in to read, critique, edit, and make sure Pebble's story maintains the integrity and story line from Jade's story, they are also always there to help me brainstorm and pivot, when the story needs that.

Outside of the specifics of the story, I'd like to mention Lawrence Henry and Quinn Ward, people always there to lift me when I need that extra push all of us writers need. I truly believe I've curated the best of the best in the writing world!

To The Readers

Yugen is the second book in the Pebble Stone Chronicles. This trilogy can be read as a separate series from the Jade Stone Chronicles. That said, there are spoilers in this series since it takes place after the end of Jade's books.

Chapter 1 – Paradigm Shift

"**P**ebble, sweetie, you're ready." Mom's warm gaze searched my face.

As amazing as my parents were, I knew they couldn't lead two packs. Everything was happening so fast. Somewhere deep down, under my fear and apprehension, I knew she was right.

Hadn't I helped my sister Jade with the ghost of her former girlfriend when no one else had been able to for over a decade? Wasn't I the person so many of the pack came to? And, to top it all off, wasn't I, Pebble Stone, the only person in recorded history, a young child, bitten by a werewolf, able to survive to adulthood, and not let the wolf take over?

Despite my words to encourage myself, a lump of unease grew, and I knew I had to banish it.

Mom squeezed my hands. "The Tennessee pack needs us, and—I fear—not in the short term. It's time for you to step up. You've been training for this. I wouldn't ask you to step up so soon if I didn't think you were ready."

Slowly, I nodded, barely understanding her words.

I pulled my hands from Mom's and stepped back, the enormity of it all threatening to swamp my senses. The kitchen narrowed as my vision tunneled down to just my mom's face. As I reached for the counter, everything started to spin. *Am I ready for this? Am I ready to fully take on the alpha mantle?* Mom sounded so certain. *But am I?*

Bumping into the large island, I slipped into one of the stools and gaped at my parents. I wasn't sure if they understood what they were asking of me. Again, I repeated the words of strength, who I was, and why I could do this. I had to believe in me, too.

Then my body tensed as the full implication of her words slammed into me. I was going to become the alpha of the Wisconsin werewolf pack. Not after I graduated college. Not in ten years or a few years. Not once I found a partner to help me lead ... but today.

I'm only eighteen ... and alone.

My hands shook and my mouth went dry. *I'm a freshman. Will I have to stop my studies? Will I have to give up my dreams until I figure out how to .... be alpha?*

My mind hyper-focused on who I had been for the last few months and what my future held. Everything was about to change. *Who am I anymore?*

A surge of power and warmth filled my body as my wolf gave her opinion. This was our destiny, our future. She'd believed in this potential a lot longer than I had. Just because our future was happening now didn't mean we weren't prepared.

Looking up at my parents, I knew they were right ... my wolf was right. I could do this. Moreover, Mom and Dad couldn't help out the Tennessee pack if they were worried about me or Wisconsin and our pack. They needed to lead as the Tennessee alphas until another wolf came forward to be alpha. They couldn't do that and continue to lead the Wisconsin pack ... it was too much to ask of anyone. They needed me.

But am I ready?

Again, my mind stuttered. Everything around me went out of focus as I tried to justify how I, an eighteen-year-old, was good enough to lead such a prestigious pack.

I swallowed, trying to stop my body from trembling. Bracing myself, I momentarily closed my eyes. *I have to be ready ... everyone needs me to be.* Finally, I met Mom's gaze, trying to be as strong as I could be. "Do I need to drop out of college? Move back home?"

Mom's face softened. "You don't need to leave college. It would be simpler for you if you lived here, but I think you can live in the dorms over the week and stay here on the weekends."

Dad nodded. "I don't think this is our first concern. Let's assume you're staying in the dorms. You can always change your mind later or decide to split your time as you need."

A hysterical laugh bubbled out of me. Focusing on where I'd sleep seemed so much better than any of the other things we had to do. "Okay, right. What do we do first?"

I searched the counter for paper to write on, but everything was put away.

Mom rubbed her face. "I need to head down as quickly as I can. We just got the call, and I can't put this off. Their people are worried. They need leadership right away. Everything needed to run the pack—money, security, order, you know, everything—needs to be sorted out and dealt with. Though each pack runs on its own, there's a system within the alpha council ... since they don't have anyone, me and Dad can get them sorted."

Cold dread washed through me, but I just nodded. Though my body was numb, the more I thought about the coming days and weeks, as the feeling returned, my insides would probably twist and cramp with worry. There was always my wolf and my sister's pack to lean on and ask questions if need be.

Working to keep my voice steady, I said, "Okay. You and Dad have trained me. I can do this." I wasn't sure if I was trying to convince them or me.

Dad wrapped an arm around me, and I was thankful he was still pack, and could still soothe. Even if he wasn't, the touch of wolf would always help another. "Of course you can, Applesauce. We both have faith in you."

"But." My mind whirled as I tried to piece together all the things that had to happen. "Shouldn't we tell the pack before we make the switch? Do they need to be here? I had to pull Trista in myself, and I pulled in Piper and Julez. Are we going to call a meeting? Do I move each wolf in one by one?"

That got me laughing again. Of course we'd have a pack meeting, we always had one. And this was *so much bigger* than so many of the other things we called meetings for. What were Mom and Dad going to do? Send out an email? *Hey, just so you know, we left, and you have a new alpha. Great working with you. Lots of love, Us!*

I slapped my hands over my mouth, then rubbed my face. Taking in a slow breath, I tried using some of Mom's breathing techniques, but the giggles kept erupting out of me as I imagined all the responses from the pack members.

Mom's eyebrow rose. "Yes. There will be a meeting on Sunday. But, sweetie, there are ways to shift the pack without having to do it wolf by wolf. We don't need them here." Her mouth tightened as I tried to stop laughing, the emotion taking me over. As much as I knew it wasn't the right reaction, I liked it better than the overwhelming feelings from before. "I figured the three of us can drive down to Chicago on Saturday, have lunch, then you and Dad can come back up here."

The shock that they weren't traveling down to Tennessee together sobered me up. "Wait, only you're heading down?"

"Yes. They need someone right away and it's our winter break. I have the easiest freedom of movement. Dad needs to get some things sorted out at work for an extended remote project. This also gives us a few days as a family before we need to pull in the pack. He'll fly out Monday once everything is set."

The thought of the pack soothed me. "I'll also have all of the pack to help me. I won't be alone, even if I'm the only alpha."

"That's right, Applesauce. Tanner, Clare, Allison. You have so many good people in this pack. Lean on them when you need help. They all love you."

While I was having my mini-laughing attack, someone brewed chamomile tea. Probably a good idea. It would be nice and calming. After taking a few sips, my body began to relax. "So, tomorrow Mom packs up her things, and on Saturday we all go to Chicago. When *do* I get the pack?" I tapped my head. "You know, up here?"

Mom smirked. "Now."

Chapter 2 – A Slight Wrinkle

I was surrounded by wolves, an ocean of my people. A bear ran through them, roaring. *Is that Dayna? Why is she here? Didn't this already happen?* She looked amused. She ran past me. I snapped my head up and saw a bird. *Is that a black swan? Or ... is it a goose?*

I jerked awake. Groggy, I forced myself out of bed and to the kitchen. It was my last weekend with Mom.

Mom packed and got ready to leave on Saturday. She hummed and moved about the house as if floating. I'd rarely seen her looking so ... free. Meanwhile, I felt like my head was full of bees. There was a muffled buzzing, like I was in a busy bus station. I wasn't sure which, bees or a bus, but it was distracting.

My low level headache steadily grew worse as the minutes passed. I stumbled to the kitchen for water. Mom dashed by and suggested I head to the gym to exercise. At first, I thought she'd lost it, but as I ran, then worked through a weight routine Dad had set up for me, my body relaxed into the familiar motions, and my head stopped buzzing.

During a hot shower, it all started to come back—a tsunami of the impressions and emotions of thousands of people. Well, there were only seventeen wolves in the pack besides me, so, seventeen people, but that was so much more than the three I woke up with yesterday morning. It felt like they all fought for center stage in my psyche.

Am I really strong enough to do this? My body trembled at the thought. What if I don't say anything and harm myself? *Did Mom and Dad make a mistake?* If they did, I may be messing up the Tennessee pack by keeping my parents here.

Once out of the shower, hands shaking, I slipped on an old pair of soft jeans and a sweatshirt that said, *Caffeine Loading, Please Wait ...* Rubbing my temples, I knew I needed help. My parents would help, but I had other options who may not be so busy ... ones who may remember being where I was without it feeling like ancient history. I needed help from younger alphas.

After a few seconds of debate, I sat on the edge of my bed and called José, a California alpha, one of my sister's best friends, and someone who felt like a brother and mentor to me.

"Pebble?" His voice was groggy. I checked my watch and saw it was nine. So, seven in the morning in California. Probably right about his wake up time, if not too early. Guilt warred with my pounding head, but I really needed his help.

"Sorry, José. I forgot how early it was there. Happy New Year's. Is today a work day, or do you get today off?"

He groaned. "Is that why you called?" There was the sound of movement, like he was getting out of bed.

Is Bevin asleep? Did I disturb everyone? Gods, I'm an idiot. "No, I just ... do you have a couple of minutes?"

"Yeah, I'm usually asleep right now." He yawned. "I have to get to work eventually, but I have about twenty more minutes of sleep. I can shift that to you ... assuming this is important. *Is* it important?"

"Did you hear about the Tennessee alphas?"

He sighed. "I heard there was an attack. Regional offices are very secretive. No one wants their territory invaded. Even though all the *leaders* are mostly on friendly terms, everyone is still pretty hush-hush. I think even more so with us being so new."

Did I say the wrong word? Gods, I was scattered! We always spoke in code when on the phone. A habit we were taught to follow from a young age.

The buzzing in my head got louder. I tried to sort it out. I realized Julez and Piper were both really happy. I squeezed my eyes shut. They'd planned on taking Spruce to a water park hotel at Wisconsin Dells for a few days. They were probably doing a morning ... something, with the kid. Spruce liked getting up early, and splashing around would be fun.

"Pebble? Are you still there?"

My breathing got choppy. "Yeah ... I just. Give me a sec." Easton was also emoting. I wasn't sure why. Was he happy or frustrated? I finally shook my head. "Okay, here's my question. Do you wake up with the feeling like there's a hive of bees in your head and how do you deal with it?"

"Is this your focus group? Piper, Julez, and that new person? What's her name? Trish?"

"Trista. And no. The Tennessee leaders weren't just attacked, José, it was bad. Really bad. Mom and Dad are heading down to take over until they can find a new ... um ... there wasn't a back-up leader. I have no idea why they don't have someone like Tanner or Clare, but they don't."

"Whoa. Hold up. Are you telling me Hazel gave you the ... um ... whole department?" He suddenly didn't sound tired.

"I don't know how much this needs to be on the down low. I mean, after the leadership meeting on Sunday there'll be no way, but yeah."

"When? Didn't this just go down Wednesday night or Thursday morning?"

I flopped back on my bed. His voice was intermixing with the grand central station of emotions in my head. "Yes. Mom gave me everyone yesterday. It wasn't so bad, but I'm guessing everyone was more subdued. There seems to be much more going on right now. I know I can ask Mom, but she's focused on packing and moving and taking over down-south. Our very own 'family emergency.' I don't want to distract her or have her worried I'm in over my head."

"I get it. When I started getting direct reports, it was gradual. I had time to adjust. I didn't get a sports team all at one time. Sit cross-legged on your bed and close your eyes. Think about how we train new employees for going out and dealing with large projects, breaking it down into manageable steps." He was talking about training new wolves with intense scents and sounds, compartmentalizing them into easier bits to deal with. "Now, for this, we can't ignore our people. We are the leaders, and what our people are telling us—whether or not they know the communication is there—*is* important. However, we don't need to experience it constantly."

"Okay, I'm with you so far and in complete agreement." I smiled. "No creating a big incinerator and destroying it all ... got it."

José chuckled. "Now, think of a malleable wall, maybe something like a wood fence with small slats. Put that around the information from your people."

"So, think of the individuals as some sort of animal, say wolves, in my head," José snorted at this, but I continued, "sort of like Jade's mental landscape, then fence them in. Make a section for them separate from me, but accessible."

José paused and I thought I heard him hum softly. "Yeah, that should work. Give it a try and let me know the results."

Sinking into myself, I tried to imagine my pack as wolves, then I gated them off. I wanted to hear them but not be overwhelmed by them. It was better, but the pressure still stung, and I groaned.

"You can do this Pebble." José's voice soothed me, and I felt my muscles relax.

Right, I was the alpha. I reinforced the fence, making the area a bit bigger but the separation taller, thicker, stronger.

A knot of tension in the back of my neck released and I moaned. "Gods above, that is so much better. My head is my own again. Thank you, José."

"Of course. This won't be your only hurdle, but I'm glad I could help." There was a pause. "I wonder why your parents didn't tell you anything like this when the transfer happened."

The pounding in my head began to recede and I groaned. "Probably because their minds are in a million places, and they just didn't think about it. It's another reason I came to you, I don't want to add stress to them." Though, Mom was anything but stressed right now … at least not about the Wisconsin pack. Her mind was already south, in Tennessee.

"Well, I'm glad I could help with the first of many challenges ahead of you, young one."

Despite his warning that there would be more challenges, a fact I was sure to be true, I felt much better. I had one more day with my parents, and that included lunch in Chicago. I saw nothing but blue skies looking ahead, at least for the remainder of winter break. There was time to acclimate to everything before heading back to the dorms and classes.

"Give my nieces and nephews kisses, as well as their parents. Bye José."

"Bye, Pebble. And remember, we're all here to help. We know what you're going through and all love you lots." After hanging up, I slid my phone into a pocket.

Finally feeling stable, I went to the kitchen. I heard Mom and Dad moving around in the bedroom, opening and shutting drawers, talking about what to take and what to leave. Scrounging in the refrigerator, I got out the ingredients to make fried potatoes and eggs and poured a mug of coffee as I got to work. Once the food was done, both Mom and Dad appeared, ready to eat.

"How're you doing, Applesauce? Mom said you looked haggard this morning. Did the workout and shower help?"

I stood to refill my coffee and get more potatoes. "I was feeling overwhelmed ... you know, with this," I tapped my head, "but I called José. I knew I could talk to you, but since you're busy packing and figuring out the logistics of moving to Tennessee, I decided to see what he'd have to say."

Mom's face tightened. "You told him about the alphas."

Dad moved to rub her back, looking less concerned.

"I did and he'd already heard about the attack. He knows not to tell everyone."

She rubbed her face and nodded, leaning into Dad's touch. "That's true." She let out a sigh. "I'm sorry, Pebble. Leaving our home ... it's a lot. We should've spent more time explaining things. It's been so long since I had a large number of new wolves, it's just second nature to me. And by Sunday all the alphas will know, then all the other wolves, and the secret will be completely out of the bag. Okay, okay." She nodded, then smiled wide. "It's been so long since my mind was this ... quiet. I just don't know what to do with myself. But, sweetie, you're okay? The transfer is usually slower."

I told them about José's suggestion, and Mom loved it. "Sounds perfect."

The rest of the day was a scramble of packing and stuffing everything into our largest van. Mom would drive that the next day with Dad, and I would take a smaller car. Then, after lunch, Dad and I would return home.

The hour and a half drive itself to Chicago was pleasant. The further south we drove, the more traffic we encountered, but never enough to impede our trip. We decided to eat at a nice steakhouse just north of the city. We got off the interstate at Rosemont, near O'Hare airport, and found a sit down restaurant.

Though it was midday on a Saturday, we were near the airport and the place was expectedly crowded. Without a reservation, we almost gave up when we were finally led through the maze of tables, people, and servers dashing about, to a table by a window in the back.

What José had said helped, but I still had a lot to focus on with the emotions of the pack. The normal werewolf issues of filtering all the emotions of the travelers in the restaurant, and the stress of the servers, a skill I'd had my whole life, suddenly became work. Staring at my feet as we shuffled to our table, I sat and finally scanned the room.

The place was crowded, but apparently most of the people there were small groups. We ended up sitting at a table that could seat six people. I thought it was interesting, but there were a lot of smaller groups eating.

Mom placed her hands on the menu as if she were going to pick it up, then she saw something over my shoulder and smiled wide. "Isn't that Dayna over there?

We met her at Thanksgiving. Don't you go to college with her? I wonder what she's doing here?"

With a sense of foreboding, I turned. Two tables over I saw Dayna, smiling and waving. She sat with her parents, as well as some other adults. And to my utter dread and prediction I realized if Dayna was here, then that meant .... Next to her, with a scowl on her face, sat Luna, glaring at me as if it were my fault we'd both ended up at the same restaurant.

Chapter 3 – A Chance Encounter

A cold dread slammed into me as I turned back to the table and picked up my menu. My hands trembled. There were already so many things going on inside and around me, and this was the last thing I needed.

"Aren't you going to go over and say 'hi'? You two were thick as thieves on Thanksgiving." Mom tilted her head and sniffed. "Sweetie, what's wrong?" Then she rubbed her head. "It's so weird not having your emotions in here to read. I know you're upset, but I can't decipher the finer details of what's going on inside you."

I tried to smile. "Well, you haven't had me in your head since I returned from California, so this isn't that different."

"Right, but you haven't seemed so ... upset." Her eyes bored into me, like if she could, she'd read my mind.

Thank the gods she couldn't. I didn't want her to know how unhappy I was to see Luna. I had finally gotten away from her—the semester was over, our science trip ended, New Year's had come and gone, and we were finally at winter break. Yes, according to my wolf, Luna was my mate, but obviously that couldn't be my only option. Luna had free will and she'd decided 'no.'

End of story. Time to relax away from the prickly red head who could shift into a mean and scary goose.

The server approached in crisp black slacks and a pristine white button down shirt. "Hi, my name is Delilus." She placed water in front of each of us. "Would you like anything to drink?"

Dad shook his head. "Water is fine for me."

Mom and I both agreed.

Delilus smiled wide. "Sounds great. Do you need a few minutes to look over the menu? Can I get you an appetizer?"

I searched my parents' faces. "I'm ready." They both nodded. "I'll have the calamari and a ribeye sandwich with a salad on the side."

Mom's eyes skimmed down the menu. "I'll have the shrimp appetizer and the house hamburger with the works."

Dad hadn't even picked up the menu. "Ribs. A full rack."

"And an appetizer for you, sir?"

"Hmm," Dad looked over at another server carrying out a tower of onion rings. "I'll have one of those."

"Sounds perfect. I'll get these in right away."

One of my eyebrows rose. "Donuts for lunch?"

"Vegetable donuts." His smile was devious.

Smiling back, I sipped my water and tried to relax. Just because I knew people sitting behind me didn't mean any of them would intrude on my family meal. We'd only had a quick breakfast before leaving, and this would be my last meal with Mom for a long time. "How long do you think you'll be in Tennessee?"

"I don't know. Finding someone else to take over will be a challenge."

"I'm going to miss you," I said softly, but she would be able to hear me, even with all the noise of the restaurant. It was a werewolf superpower. Even Luna, the cantankerous one, would be able to hear with her cobra chicken hearing.

Stop thinking about Luna! You're here with your family, not her.

Mom reached over and squeezed my hand. "I'm going to miss you too, sweetie, but I know you'll do great."

"Do you know why that pa—um, Tennessee branch doesn't have someone like Tanner or Clare?"

Dad rubbed the back of his neck. "They did. A guy named Ronny. He left eight or nine years ago. I'm trying to think. It may have been longer."

The time frame couldn't be a coincidence. "Isn't that when the California group ... when Jade and crew started forming their group? But he didn't join them. I would know if there was a Ronny out there."

"No," Dad said. "He had a kid, trans like Bevin or Maddy, also from Tennessee. If you remember, Maddy's family left Tennessee because the group had trouble with her transition. Ronny's kid was younger. He decided since he was strong, he'd move ... somewhere, I don't remember where. He may not have told anyone. His job had a second location; he transferred. Decided to strike out on his own."

"Wait." My mind whirled. So much information. "They had another—" I looked around at the other tables not that far off. "Leader. You're telling me, if Ronny was found, you two could come home?"

Mom shook her head. "It's not that easy. He left for a reason. He may not want to return."

I leaned back and tried to stop thinking about me and my situation. This person left to protect his kid. I had to respect that. "Well, all I know is, the Tennessee pack doesn't know what's about to hit them. They'll learn to be better people with you two at the helm."

That got both Mom and Dad smiling.

Our appetizers arrived. With them, Dayna and her dad, Norman. They sat down in two of the empty seats.

"Hi, Pebble, Hazel, River. How are you doing?" Dayna sounded excited to see us.

It took everything in me not to turn and check if Luna was still glaring at me. "I'm good. You?"

"Oh, we're great. I assume you're here for a similar reason to us."

I raised my eyebrow, but Mom, ever more diplomatic, answered. "Good food?"

Norman laughed. "No, Luna's parents, my brother, Stew, and his wife, flew out for Christmas and New Year's. My brother didn't get to have Thanksgiving with the family, but that doesn't mean I don't like to see him once in a while."

Mom and Dad smiled wide. Dad said, "It's great that you got to see family. Are they headed home, then?"

"Yes, that was the plan, but we're thinking about delaying the flight a day or two."

The bite of calamari I'd taken got caught in my throat and I started coughing. I sipped some water, hoping to not make too much of a scene.

"—your flight?" Mom asked once I could pick up the conversation again.

"Yes, well, Luna told us some of what happened on the trip. We all planned on just ignoring it, at least for now, but since you're here, and Luna's parents are here, we were wondering if, once you're done eating, you could meet us at Kennedy Park. I guess there's something

Luna's mom, Serena, would like to determine. It would clear up a bunch of things ... at least, that's what she thinks."

I eyed Dayna. "She wants to meet me? Hasn't Luna decided to just, I don't know, walk away? Aren't we past all this?" My heart pounded in my chest. This was not how I wanted today to go.

Dayna shrugged. "I'm just here to steal some of your appetizer. It looks great. I ordered the onion rings, which weren't." She put action to words, and I laughed.

Curious, I stole one of Dad's onion rings, and had to agree, the calamari was much better.

Once they left, Mom gazed at me. "What did I miss?"

I leaned back and sighed. After returning from my school trip, I only had the opportunity to tell Dad the story. When we'd finished our run, Mom had dropped the bomb about the Tennessee pack, and everything else had taken a backseat. "The premonition I kept having since Jade's wedding ... with the phantom in my dorm room telling me to find it? Well, it was Luna. I figured it out on the Colorado school trip."

Mom considered me. "Is this a good thing or a bad thing?"

"It's a 'thing' thing. But it's also not the end. My, um," my head bobbed back and forth, then I checked to make sure there weren't people too close before leaning in. Mom mirrored me so we were mere inches apart. My voice was so low, I could barely hear my words. "My wolf thinks Luna's my mate."

Mom's face hardened, then she reached out, rubbing my cheek with the back of her fingers. "No wonder you've been so stressed. Things have been piling on you left and right. This could be such an amazing thing, sweetie—"

The sides of my mouth smiled, though I doubted it reached my eyes. "I think the stress is a family trait right now. As for the rest, I don't know. Maybe it was all just wrong. Maybe I'm wrong." I regretted the words as soon as I said them. "No, I didn't mean that. I just ... I think I'm meant to do this alone. It's fine, I have everyone else back in Madison to support me. Don't worry."

Dad grunted, his hand resting on my arm.

"Do you need to talk about this, sweetie?" Mom's voice held such tenderness, I feared I would start tearing up.

"Not right now. I just want to get back to Wisconsin, find a good book, and read for the next couple of weeks."

Dad squeezed my arm, and Mom smiled. Then she shot a glance at the other table and nodded. "So, after you found out about the phantom, not being someone willing to lie, you told Luna the truth. And now she's told *her* Mom, and here we are."

Dad chuckled. "And here we are."

Our meals were delivered, and we thanked the server.

The buzzing in my head threatened to overwhelm me again as my focus shifted away from the fence holding everyone in the pack to Luna and her mom, the meal, and Mom leaving. A shiver traced its way down my back as the pain grew.

Gods, I don't want to deal with Luna right now! "We could always not meet up with the others."

Mom's brow rose and she became the teacher, though her eyes were soft with love. "And will that help your situation in the long run?"

Knowing there was no way to avoid her, I dug into my meal. I needed all the calories I could get.

The food was good, but all I could think about was that I really didn't need Luna's negativity on top of everything else that was happening.

After we'd finished eating, we caravaned over to the park. There were a surprising number of people there considering it was January and cold.

The grass was covered in snow, but the walkways were clear. Kids sledded down a large hill, squealing and screaming with glee. Majestic trees, bare of leaves, scattered the lawns, though, so close to the holidays, there were lights everywhere.

As we walked, I couldn't stop myself from glancing at Luna, my stomach clenching every time I saw her auburn hair blowing in the slight breeze. When she gazed around the park, watching the birds overhead, a peaceful look came over her face, serene, pretty.

Shocked at how different she appeared, I missed my step and almost fell, Dad catching me at the last second.

Once I caught my balance, I noticed Luna glaring at me, her typical look back. I was surprised at the regret I felt at her harder stare.

We found a semi-private place, each group walking together but separate. There were evergreen trees blocking the other people and we couldn't hear much of what they said, letting us know they wouldn't be able to hear us. This gave us freedom to speak.

When we finally stopped, Luna scoffed, apparently ready to leave. *Why didn't my wolf decide Dayna was my life partner?* Not that I had feelings for Dayna, but at least she was nice.

Mom rubbed her hands together. "Okay. I don't have a plane to catch, but I do have a long way to drive. Can I ask what this is about?"

Luna's mom—*what was her name? Oh, yeah, Serena*—looked a lot like Luna. She was a bit shorter but had the same auburn hair. She stood rigid and gave me a cold look. "My daughter told me a story about how yours is trying to mate with her. Some werewolf thing. I'm here to stop it, once and for all. Geese partner for life. We know who we'll match up with right away. It's in our auras. So, I'm going to watch as they shake hands, prove this is all poppycock, then go home to Maine. Then, I'll expect you to keep *her* away from Luna or I'll take out a restraining order."

Norman gasped, focus jumping between Serena and his brother. "Serena, no. That's going too far."

Dayna's jaw had dropped at her aunt's spiteful words and her eyes widened to the size of saucers.

My jaw clenched and it took everything I had not to snap back. Behind me, I could hear Mom and Dad shuffle, but for now this was my fight. I couldn't see their reaction, but if they were going to trust me to lead, it had to start now.

My eyes narrowed on Serena. Were all geese this awful? They were nasty in bird form. I guess it only made sense they were also mean in human form, but where was the tact?

"How about we all just leave, and I avoid Luna without the aura test?" I really liked this idea better, and I smiled. If I were being honest, who wanted to spend their life surrounded by geese? This childhood joke was no longer funny.

"Sounds good to me," Luna agreed.

Of course she agreed. It was the first thing she was agreeable on in a while. If only she could agree with me about everything else.

Dad placed a hand on my back and spoke softly ... just for me. "Applesauce. You know your wolf has never led you wrong. This will only take a moment. Then it'll be over. It won't even hurt."

"Much," I mumbled grumpily.

He chuckled.

Feeling defeated, I trudged the few steps to Luna. Her face was a mask of indifference. I lifted my hand. For several seconds she just gazed at me as if I were the enemy. With an eye roll, she reached out and we shook.

This wasn't the first time we'd touched, so I wasn't surprised when nothing happened. I was hoping to hear: *'Gadzooks! Eureka! I knew it! It was all a lie! Never look at or speak with my child again!'* Even if she called me a floozy, I'd probably be okay with it.

Serena sucked in air, then spoke in a low, almost pleasant voice. "I can't believe it." Her eyes widened, then narrowed.

Luna's eyes widened and she jerked her head in her mom's direction. "What?"

"This is why you need to learn to read auras, Luna." Her mom tsked and shook her head. "If you had, you'd know."

Luna's face stiffened. "What?"

I swallowed my own question. There was no way I'd echo Luna.

"It's true. Your auras. They match."

Chapter 4 – A Decision

Luna's jaw clenched. She squeezed my hand harder, and I narrowed my eyes on her. "You're wrong, Mom." Her voice snapped out, tight and insistent. The cinnamon scent of annoyance mixed with gingery shock wafted from her. She hid her shock well. I saw none of it in her expression.

"No, I'm not." Serena sounded exasperated. Her husband—I couldn't remember his name—moved up to rub her shoulders. "You're just unwilling to look. I've taught you how to read auras, you just refuse to do it. You told me you were dive-bombing this girl all semester, and only her?"

Luna blushed and my jaw dropped as my suspicion was confirmed. "It was you? All those times a goose attacked me on campus? It wasn't random wild birds?"

One of Luna's shoulders rose. "It's just ... no. It was me."

"Why me?"

"Because," she snapped out, then her mouth twisted up in a sneer and she didn't say more.

A huge smile blossomed on Serena's face. "Because, Pebble. That's the goose's version of pulling one's ponytail in elementary school. We're not the most socially aware group. We're more comfortable with our own."

A gust of cold wind chilled my still open mouth. After slowly closing it, I cleared my throat and said, disbelief dripping from my words, "You're saying, on some level, Luna knew this too ... and *likes* me?"

It was too much. I tried to pull my hand from hers, but she was holding on tight.

"No," Luna said sternly. "That isn't what it means. You annoyed me at the start of the year. That's all." Her head snapped down, as if she just noticed our hands connected. She ripped her hand away and stalked over to her dad, her dark red hair whipping around her head in the breeze.

Dayna stood by her parents laughing. "Okay," she giggled. "What happens now?"

"Well," Serena said slowly. "It's the start of winter break. Auras never lie. Though I believe in free choice, I also think that we should give the kids time to discover what all of this means outside the stress of school. So, in my opinion, Luna should return with Pebble and spend time with her and the pack."

Luna's mouth dropped open and her eyes turned their stormy attention to her mom, but before she could speak, both my hands flew up. "I'm sorry. A few seconds ago you were threatening me and now you want me to host your daughter for winter break because of a light show? What am I missing?"

Serena's head tilted as if she were considering me. "Auras are a bit more than a light show, dear. They've never lied. As much as your premonition from your wolf telling you that Luna is your mate is enough to convince you, well, the auras are enough to convince me. We all have our weird," her hands waved in the air, "mumbo jumbo, and this is mine. And, well, I don't know if Luna will ever become furry, but if she does, I'd like for her to figure out what it means to be a werewolf."

"What do you mean, 'figure out what it means to be a werewolf'?" Luna's blue eyes, the shade of the ocean before a storm, were huge and most of her bluster had vanished.

"Well, my darling child. If you're going to be Pebble's mate, help her run the pack one day, you're going to have to become a werewolf."

Luna started shaking her head, fast. "I don't want to lose the skies. I love flying. Why would I give it up to be with her?" She waved a hand at me. "Be a mammal and run on the ground? I love being a goose."

"And terrorizing the innocent," I mumbled. Before anyone could remark, I added with a grunt, "No one said you'd lose your current animal. I *did* tell you my sister was a shifter swan." *Wait, why am I encouraging her? I don't want her to join me, do I?*

"Yes, but then you passed out. You're also adopted. I assumed she was from one of the shifter families. Everything about you is weird."

"Careful," Dad said.

"I know." *So many secrets.* Mirroring Luna's hard stare, I was tempted to tell her to go home and leave me to my winter break. I had enough to worry about with my parents leaving. I didn't need to add her to the mix. Dad's hand on my shoulder felt like a stream of calm through my body and I took a steadying breath.

"My family," I vaguely waved my hand behind me towards my parents, "are wolves ... all of them. As it goes, my sister has more than one animal. The swan is one of them."

Dayna started to bounce. "I want to have more than one animal." She turned towards her parents. "I want to be a wolf ... gods above." Turning, her gaze found mine. "I've always wanted to be a wolf."

Norman chuckled. "That's true. She used to draw wolves and plaster them all over her room. But, Dayna, this isn't about you. This is about Luna."

A smile spread on her face, but her eyes looked sad.

Luna noticed. "What? Spit it out."

"It's nothing."

"No, what is going on inside that blue-haired head of yours?"

"This is about you, cuz. I just ..." She sighed at Luna's glare. "If they can make you a wolf, why not me? You know I don't plan on joining the sleuth, they're too ..." Her words faltered.

A laugh barked out of Luna, almost causing me to fall on my butt. It was such a foreign sound. "So stodgy? So stick-in-the-mud and stuck in their ways?"

I remembered Luna wasn't supposed to know about them because she hadn't shifted to a bear. Her family had also been exiled because her dad had fallen in love with a shifter goose. In the end, I understood her animosity.

Dayna shrugged. "They're ... traditional, let's say. And Pebble, who is amazing, will one day run the pack. And, apparently, you, my favorite cousin, will help her. I mean, how fantastic is that?"

My head started hurting again with the buzz of the pack. The control I'd learned was starting to slip. I rubbed my temples and turned to face my parents. "Mom, Dad, can we just agree to their demands and go home? Once

Dayna attends a pack meeting, she'll change her mind." Though my parents chuckled, neither said anything. Right, I'm the alpha, not them. Turning back, Dayna looked confused. "Okay, here's the deal, I'm not going to be the alpha 'one day' in the future—"

That got everyone talking.

Luna rolled her eyes, of course. "I should've known you'd mess it up. Typical. What did you do this time?"

Her words would not hurt me ... they wouldn't. I blinked. My eyes were moist from the cool wind, nothing more.

Dayna's face fell. "Oh, no! Why not?"

The others' voices were lost in everyone speaking.

I finally whistled. It was loud enough to hurt sensitive ears. "If you'd let me finish. Sonnara save me from people who don't let a person get a thought out." To ensure I had their attention, I met each of their gazes, one by one. This was it, the first time I announced this to a group. "I'm alpha right now. I took over yesterday."

The silence that followed was almost as deafening as the noise had been a moment ago. Everyone's intense stares, along with their vanilla tea scent of amazement mixed with ginger scent of shock, began to make me feel like I was sinking in quicksand. I wasn't sure which I craved more, the noise or the silence. I took a calming breath. "We're here to send Mom off. She's needed elsewhere for an extended period. Dad will follow on Monday, after he gets things in order at work."

Luna leaned in. "So, if we head back to Madison—"

"Stolzburg," I interrupted.

She shook her head. "Whatever. Stolzburg. If I return, I'll be made a wolf and thrust into a leadership position right away?"

I don't need her help. She'll make things harder and worse. I have enough on my plate right now.

Though I wasn't talking to my wolf, I could almost feel her chuckle. *A goose is good at finding what hides in the grass waiting to strike when you're not ready.*

I locked my muscles, unwilling to let anything show. A premonition now was not something I wanted to share. The pressure of everyone's attention pushed on me as well as Luna's last question. *Will she be my mate and leader ... ha!*

My jaw clenched at the gleam in her eye. For the first time, I was thankful for the group projects we'd been forced to endure together during first semester. I knew what sort of power-hungry group member she was ... and how she didn't work well with others. "Sort of. You'll need to be trained and would be in a probationary alpha position."

"But it would probably help you to have a partner's support?"

My shoulders slumped. *Why is she so smart? Can't she just go back home with her parents? I've already jumped through the mental hoops figuring out how to do this myself.* With a sigh, I had to admit the truth to both of us. "Yeah, probably."

Luna glared.

Serena stepped forward. "Why don't we all come up to Stolzburg, take a look around, spend a few days, and see what happens? Nothing needs to be decided today."

A flock of geese? My sister is going to have a laugh at this. Slowly unclenching my jaw, I knew I had to be the bigger person, so I forced what I hoped was a pleasant smile. The pack den was plenty big enough for all of these people.

"Fine," Luna snapped. "We can go back north. But don't expect much."

Like that would be hard.

Dayna narrowed her eyes playfully. "Can I come, too?"

Like a weight had been lifted, my smile finally felt genuine. If anyone could control Luna, it was Dayna. "Of course."

As we turned towards the cars, my dream of a winter break spent reading on the couch slowly faded—replaced by a lumbering bear and a honking goose.

Chapter 5 – Welcome To My Home

We stood in the park's parking lot by our cars. The others had headed out to pack. Mom gave me a big hug goodbye. "You did great, sweetie. And you'll be a fantastic alpha, I know you will. I'm so proud of you."

I squeezed her harder. "I wish I had longer before I had to test your assertion. I'm going to miss you."

"I know, but you're ready."

Holding back my tears, I stepped back. "But are the Tennessee wolves ready for you?"

Behind me, Dad chuckled. "Let's let Mom hit the road. She has a long journey."

I turned and headed to the car, giving them a few last minutes of privacy. Dad would be joining Mom in a few days, but they didn't spend much time apart. I unlocked the car and slipped behind the wheel, securing my seat belt.

With a small thump, my head hit the seat rest behind me. I closed my eyes and breathed slowly. *I can't believe I'm spending my winter break with Luna of all people. Not Fern, not Hollis, but that goose shifter bully.* A groan jerked my attention to the steering wheel, which I clutched tightly enough I was in danger of damaging. "Sonnara help me!"

After a few minutes, Dad joined me. "Ready?"

"To spend the next couple hours trying to pretend none of this happened? Absolutely."

He chuckled. *The idea of a goose joining the pack is probably the best dad joke ever. I bet he's cackling on the inside.* "And then you need to set up some guest rooms."

I started up the car, giving it a minute to warm up before I navigated to I-294, which would take me to I-90 and home. "I'm still processing that. Spending my winter break with Dayna sounds fine, fun even. I like her. Add in

Luna, then things change, gets stressful." There was more traffic now, so I focused on it before I added, "And then Luna's parents? I wonder how long they're going to stay?"

Dad's citrusy amusement filled the car. "Just think of Serena at the pack meeting tomorrow morning. The pack is going to have a field day knowing we're actually bringing a real goose to the house this time."

A smile crossed my face. "Do you think the geese do anything like our pack meetings?"

"Maybe, but it'd be much more ..." He trailed off.

"Loud," I suggested with a snort.

"Exactly." His eyes almost glowed. "I can't decide if I'd want to witness it or am glad I don't know anything about it."

"Everything I've read about geese suggests they're territorial and friendly to their own kind, or their own gaggle. When Luna is with Dayna, she's almost nice. Maybe when it's *just* the geese they're pleasant?" Despite it being my own argument, I couldn't imagine it.

"Maybe. You'll have to tell me, if you ever figure it out." Dad gave me a sidelong look, and I sighed.

We drove in silence for a few minutes, and Dad pulled out his phone. His focus intensified as he started typing away.

Needing to drive, I couldn't see what he was doing, but curiosity nibbled at me. "What are you doing?"

"Texting with Tyler. I know that Serena and Stew are probably what they appear to be, a shifter goose and a werebear. Coach Nelson does a great job at keeping info on his people. That said—"

"You have trust issues." A snarl rumbled from my gut. "I should've thought of that."

"You're young, and in all honesty, it's probably fine. I told Tyler to let us know if there is an issue. He'll probably not get back to us."

"Us?"

"Of course, Applesauce. You're the alpha. I told him to report to both of us."

Feeling a bit better, I changed the subject. "What about the Tennessee pack? Do they have the same kind of pack meetings that we do? Do you even know?"

"Well, that I can't tell you. We wolves are so secretive, it's a blessing and a curse. It's why most people in the pack don't really know much about how many packs there are, where they are, who the alphas are, how the other packs are run, and so forth. Part of that is safety. Part of that is habit. Mom and I have pushed for more sharing amongst the packs, but in the end, each pack is its own entity, and each alpha wants to run their 'family,' so to speak, in their own way."

"Okay, I got all that. So why do you know about Tennessee?" I asked. "Wait, did you and Mom call and ask a bunch of questions? Gather information before the big move?"

Dad gave me an impressed look. "Good, now you're thinking. Never approach a new situation without figuring out everything you can in advance. But no. Once I tell you, you'll kick yourself, but that's okay. It's been a long day."

I wanted to close my eyes and think. *What am I missing?* But I was driving, and that wasn't an option. "Was it when Bevin and José went out there to learn from the alphas? Did they get some of this information?"

For a few moments Dad just watched the scenery fly by. Then he shook his head. "No, but that's good thinking. Though the boys learned from each of the packs, for the most part, they were given a 'public' view of how things were run. Nothing too secretive. I guess if a meeting needed to be held it would've happened, but I wasn't told of anything like that."

"Okay, not them." I switched lanes, navigating around a car with a mattress strapped to its roof. It drove about twenty under the speed limit. "Gods, they're going to cause an accident." Once I got past them, I moved out of the left lane, not wanting to anger the cars driving twenty over the speed limit. *These speedy drivers don't even have a wereanimal to help them heal if they get into an accident.*

As I drove, Dad just sat patiently, waiting for me to return to the conversation. We neared the interstate exchange. It felt a bit like a weird choreographed dance with cars and roads until I was finally heading north towards home. Once I had cruise control on, I sighed. "Okay, tell me."

Dad's gaze shifted from the traffic to me. "Do you remember your cousin Dillan, Aunt Allison and Uncle Jackson's son? Now granted, he moved out there when you were nine, and he's only come home maybe two or three times. And, I don't think he talks about living in Tennessee when he's home. But, yeah, Dillan landed out there." Dad watched me as he said all this to gauge my reaction.

Nope, won't kick myself for that one. I had no idea Dillan was in that pack.

My face scrunched up. "He's in Tennessee? I thought he lived in Florida. Didn't we talk about visiting him once and going to Orlando? Are the Tennessee and Florida packs friendly? It seems like they're always connected."

"No, not Florida. The Floridian pack is run a lot like ours, despite the state. You know the alphas went to college with me and Mom and are good friends of ours."

"I did know that." My shoulders relaxed as the number of cars decreased.

He nodded. "Well, the Tennessee alphas were old-school wolves, arrogant, and close minded. Of all the alphas, they were the ones who were the least supportive of the California pack. Their comment was something on the lines of, 'Well, at least we can send all of those people to where they belong.'"

A shiver ran down my back. "And that's where you and Mom are going?"

"We're hoping the whole pack isn't like that. If they are … I don't know. We'll either whip them into shape or disband the pack." Dad sounded determined. "There's nothing demanding that a pack remain in that state. If they're all sticks-in-the-mud, they can relocate to other packs or become lone wolves."

His words were stern ... final. "So, you *are* planning on returning, right?"

"That's the plan, Applesauce. I think you'll make an amazing alpha, but I figure, outside of this Luna and Dayna fiasco, the next couple of months will be quiet and boring. You won't even notice you're the head of the most amazing werewolf pack in the world. Mom and I will return. Collect all the Wisconsin miscreants back ... at least for the short term. And you'll go back to just being a student."

We arrived at our pack den and started freshening up four guest rooms. Dayna's parents hadn't said they'd be joining the group, but it'd just be our luck that we were caught unawares.

We decided to put all the guests on the second floor. That way, if the wolves got to be overwhelming, they could really get away.

Once that was done, Dad called and ordered Thai food. Neither of us were in the mood to cook.

As he put in the order, I set the dining room table. I really wanted everything to run smoothly once the horde of guests arrived.

"Okay, Applesauce, I'm off. I should be back in about a half-hour with the food. If you start to feel stressed, just remember, it's one of your favorite meals. That should cheer you up."

"Wait, Tanner's coming over to make chocolate shakes?"

Dad barked out a laugh and headed out the door.

I flopped into a chair, taking a few seconds alone to relax. Dayna had texted me saying they were getting off the interstate and shouldn't be long.

It'll be a race between them and Dad.

My phone rang. Checking the display, I answered it. "Hollis! How are you?"

"Wow, it's been like two days. You sound like we haven't seen each other in weeks." She sounded amused.

"Oh, well a lot has happened here, and it *feels* like it's been longer than a couple of days." I looked down at my watch, as if it would tell me Hollis was lying. "Really, only a couple of days? Are you sure?"

"Pebble? Are you okay?"

I sighed. "I am. A family emergency came up and my parents are heading out of town. It's been a mad dash of getting them packed and out of here."

"Wait, what? Details." she demanded.

One of the first things Mom did was come up with a story to tell her department. She'd be missing the spring semester, so it had to be good. "Yeah, my great aunt in Tennessee fell down the stairs."

Hollis gasped. "Oh, no! Is she okay?"

"Yes and no. She's been living on her own and now has a broken leg and two broken arms. They don't think she can function without an aide. She refuses to go into any sort of facility."

There was a frustrated groan over the line. "Oh, my God, Pebble. That's awful! I can't imagine. That would be the worst."

I felt bad telling Hollis the lie, but she didn't know the truth. "I agree. Anyway, she doesn't trust any of the care centers. Thinks they'll steal all her money and ignore her needs."

"Ah, got it. And your parents are the best option?" Hollis sounded as dazed as I had felt Thursday.

"Yeah, pretty much. They're hoping they can get it straightened out and return soon, but they doubt it'll be before classes start, otherwise I may have been going, too." There was a small gasp before I continued. "Mom didn't want to risk it."

"Sounds like you need the night out with a friend." She sounded so hopeful. I thought back to our discussion about her not wanting to spend too much time at home, and guilt slammed into me. Gods, too many things to do.

"I do! I really do." I could hear the desperation in my voice. I didn't want to tell her about all the guests coming. How would *that* go over? "But not tonight. Mom left, but Dad needs to go in to work on Monday to finish some stuff off. How about Monday night after he leaves?" Part of me settled at the idea of being a normal teen for just one night. I ignored the niggling part of my brain yelling at me that I had guests coming and planning a night out was ridiculous.

"Great! Pick me up at six. Dinner, maybe a movie, dancing at the union, maybe bowling. We'll figure something out."

I heard a car pull up. "Perfect. I have to go. Dad's here with the food, and I'm starving."

"You're always starving. Okay, I'll see you Monday at six. Don't be late."

"I won't."

I stood and headed to the door, opening it before Luna could ring the doorbell. Her eyes were wide. "You live here? This is where you grew up?"

Gritting my teeth, I refused to roll my eyes. *No, Luna, I didn't grow up a pauper, despite what you may think.*

I forced a smile. "It is. Welcome to the Wisconsin werewolf pack home." I swung my arm to welcome them in. With six of them and their bags, they were quite the crew.

Dayna followed her. "It seems bigger when there isn't a pack of wolves and all their cars."

Luna whipped around. "Wait, you've been here before?"

"Well, yeah. Finals week, I ran with the pack. It's hard to run with them without coming here. I thought I told you about that."

Luna's top lip curled in a sneer. "I thought you said a park. Didn't you mention running in a park?" She squinted. "No, that was Thanksgiving." She scoffed. "You mammals are shifting and running all over the place, how am I supposed to keep track?"

Dayna laughed. "This from the person who randomly flies all over the place? Really?"

"Flying is elegant, Dayna. I keep trying to explain this to you. And I've seen where you live, and you told me about the sleuth. But this place ... it could be a five-star resort ... you know, if it had an exercise room and a pool. Or at least one of those things."

I snorted. "Are you ever satisfied? I mean, life must be really frustrating for you, always looking for things to pick apart."

She turned to me, face flat. "You don't have to worry about what makes me satisfied."

"Whatever." With deliberation, I shifted my gaze to Dayna. "Dayna, would you like to see where you'll be staying?" I then looked to Luna's parents. "Mr. and Mrs. Zweck, welcome to our home. Can I show you to a room? Dad should be back in about five to ten minutes with Thai food, so you have time to get a bit settled, wash up if you want."

Luna's mom smiled. "That would be lovely, dear, and do call me Serena."

Better than 'mom.' I bit back a manic laugh the thought caused. *Her all-in acceptance of me is so different from Luna's.* Was it to help Luna adjust? Was it because she married a werebear, so she knew what it was like going against the shifter geese ways? Maybe what she saw with the auras really adjusted her perspective somehow. *But isn't a 'mate' an option?*

I shifted to Dayna's parents. We were going to have a full house. "Norman, Kelly, it's nice to see you here." They'd already asked me to call them by their first names at Thanksgiving. "Welcome to our home. If you'll follow me."

"Thank you, Pebble."

From my periphery, I saw Luna roll her eyes. It took a bit of effort, but I stopped myself from reacting. "Can I help you with your luggage?"

Stew shook his head. "We only brought a small bag. We wanted to see what a wolf pack house looked like and maybe, if possible, if Luna does become a wolf, see that. Otherwise, we're needed back home this next week. We can't stay too long."

A cold shiver ran down my spine. My brain shorted out for a moment before it screamed, 'No!' *I don't need a second alpha. The idea of running the pack terrifies me, but a lot of things are scary. That doesn't mean they're not worth doing.*

Kelly smiled. "Same. We plan on heading back to Chicago on Monday."

Same? What? What were we talking about ... wolves. Luna ... and Dayna. Two more wolves in the pack. First my creating them, then my spending winter break training them. A shiver ran down my spine.

"Sounds great." *Did my voice sound weird? Keep it together, Pebble!* "Dad and I thought setting all of you up on the second floor would be best." I led them up the stairs, pointing out the major house features along the way.

Once on the second floor, we started down the hall past the library. "Tomorrow morning, we've scheduled a full pack meeting. Just to warn you, there will be a lot of wolves here. If you want to get some separation, the pack members rarely come up here."

"Smart. You're giving us our own bit of territory in which to escape," Norman said thoughtfully.

I patted the first door. "Serena, Stew, this will be your room. Norman and Kelly, I have you two across the hall. Both these rooms have en suite bathrooms. There are bathrooms between these rooms and the next ones over." I pointed to the shut door. "Dayna, you can have that room, leaving this one for you, Luna." I indicated the last door. "Those rooms don't have en suites, so you're stuck with the public bathroom."

Kelly placed a hand on Dayna's arm. "If it's all the same, I think we should switch with Dayna. We're only here for a few days. If she's staying any longer, it makes sense for her to have the better room."

"Are you sure?" I shrugged, eyebrows raised, and hands held out in question. This was up to them, not me.

"Absolutely," Norman said.

"Us, too," Serena said, giving me a wink.

I was dumbfounded. Where was the woman who started out threatening me? She'd gone from terrifying to sweet too fast for my liking.

Once everyone knew where their room was, I headed back down to the kitchen to find drinks. It didn't take long for the others to join me. "Do you want something to drink or a quick tour?"

Serena smiled. "Why not a tour? We've been sitting for almost two hours."

"You've seen the upstairs. If we'd turned right instead of left, we'd've gotten to the office for the alphas."

One of Luna's eyebrows shot up. "I have an office? Like, I could come here and do school work?"

"No!" Everyone's gazes snapped to me, and I saw Luna smirk. I took a second to get control of myself before I kicked her out of the house, mate be damned. "The office is for pack business. Until you *are* pack, have chosen that life, and have been trained, you are just a guest. You've made it very clear that you don't like any of this." My hand flew out to indicate everything.

"That's because I'm not giving up my wings because of something your wolf decided." Her voice dripped vitriol.

Serena's mouth opened, but Stew placed a hand on her shoulder, stopping her.

"And that's another thing. You get these ideas in your head and don't listen to anyone about anything. No one, literally, no one, has said anything about you losing your wings. Quite the contrary. But your only focus is on that." I shook my head. "I'm done repeating myself. You're an adult. You'll have to make up your own mind. As long as you're here, the room I gave you before is yours." I waved to where her bags were. "Most of the family have rooms on this floor. If you, or Dayna, want to claim a first floor room in the future ... assuming you join the pack, that can be arranged."

"You know I'm ready to join." Dayna mumbled low, smiling sheepishly when I shot her a look.

"As for doing school work," I sighed, ready for this to be over, "that's more easily done in the library or the basement."

Luna scoffed. "Do you have dungeons down there?"

"No, but now that you're here, I'm considering it."

Dayna, her dad, and Luna's dad chuckled.

I took a calming breath. *I may have to brush up on relaxing techniques.* "The basement was designed for the younger generation. On full moon nights, parents can leave their kids there to be watched by older kids or non-wolf spouses. There is also a second kitchen, more bedrooms, games, and study areas. It's a hang-out for teens and young adults."

Dayna went to the top of the stairs, turned on the light, and looked down. "Cool. It's like the lounge at the dorms, only with food."

"Yep," I agreed. "Now if you'll follow me into the living room." They did. "Down that hall, the one under where you all are staying, are the family rooms. For now, I'll be the only one staying there. Well, Dad too, but he's leaving on Monday."

Norman nodded. "This room looks like it could hold a lot of people."

"Yeah. If we head down this hallway, this door leads to the pack's meeting room."

"Whoa." Dayna gaped, her head swinging around. "This room is huge. I love the couches and comfortable seats all over the place. It looks massive ... it could hold ..." She faltered.

I smiled. "It can hold a werewolf pack and give them room to spread out. You'll see it tomorrow morning. As you can see, we came through this entrance, as do most, but this is the front of the room. There's another door in the back. If we head that way we can check out the back yard and the woods."

Early January wasn't normally a time to show off outdoor accommodations, but we all had some type of animal to keep us warm. I didn't suggest we get our coats since we weren't going to be out long and the other door to the backyard led into the dining room.

"Wow, this yard is great!" Stew stepped out, his voice booming loud. "I can see why this land is so valuable to your pack. You have a full forest in which you can run. And you said you've had some of the bears run with you?"

Dayna wrapped an arm around her uncle. "I ran last month, silly. It was great."

Serena pointed to the privacy walls. "That's right, you can't shift with clothes on. Geese are so much more civilized. I do like that you give some privacy to your pack members."

I quirked a smile, determined to only be amused by Serena's snobbery. "I'm glad you approve." The sound of tires crunching up the driveway stopped my next thought. "The building over there." I pointed at the barn. "That's our gym. It's large enough for the full pack to work out at the same time, though we usually don't do that. Dad usually sets up exercise plans for each pack member that lasts four to six months. He updates them regularly to ensure we're all staying fit mentally, physically, and in top fighting form."

Norman's brows knit. "Fighting form? Is he ... are you worried about fighting? About being attacked?"

"No, not really. However, there are rogue wolves out there, and I'd rather know how to defend myself than worry about being caught defenseless."

He nodded. "Okay, that makes sense. The other werecreatures don't have as many rogue elements. I mean, there are some, but not that many."

"I wonder why that is," I mused. "What is it about wolves that has so many more of my kind out there causing havoc and mayhem?"

Kelly chuckled. "There are just more of you. The other weres are more regulated because the numbers are so much smaller. Also, since wolves are one of the only animals that have such a strong calling to the moon, that need to shift has probably caused more accidental bites."

I nodded. "That makes sense. If werebears don't have to shift with the moon, then a lone bear has more control."

"Exactly," Dayna's mom said, smiling at me. "I mean, that's just my guess. I don't know for sure."

Luna huffed. "Okay, first of all, when I said you didn't have a gym, you didn't correct me. That looks like a really big gym. Second, we all heard the car and it's cold out here. When are we going inside to eat? You are the worst host ever."

Chapter 6 – What's Good For The Goose …

My stomach quivered with excitement at the smell of all the good food. I was so ready to sit down and dig in. Dad had placed all the food on platters, so everyone could see what he'd bought. Everything was lined up down the center of the table, ready for us when we walked in the sliding door.

As people found seats, I walked towards the kitchen, itching to sit and eat. But I was the host and represented the family. "We have soda, water, coffee, or tea. What does everyone want?"

Once everyone made their requests, I turned on the coffee maker and started searching the huge industrial sized kitchen. The coffee maker was fast, so it didn't take long to pour three mugs of coffee.

Back in the dining room, I could finally sit. Despite my body wanting to relax, I stood for a moment, gazing at the table, and all the people who joined us. Normally I sat next to Dad, but tonight, the group left the seat at the head of the table for me, the one across from Dad—Mom's seat. A cold chill played across my shoulders and down my arms as the implications sunk in. *I'm the alpha ... that's my seat now.*

My throat dry, I tried to swallow. I forced my feet to move, as I made my way to the seat. The scent of the Thai food, sinking into my soul, battling my numb uncertainty. Once I sat, Dad smiled and winked.

The plates were passed around and I dug in, knowing the food would ground me. Thai cuisine was the family's go-to for celebrations and when we were stressed. It was my main comfort food ... not that any of our guests knew that.

I had just sampled the different tastes when Luna made a satisfied sound then put down her fork. "Can we really discuss this? I mean, yes, Mom, you said you saw something in our auras, but that can be faulty, right? It's a potential, not an absolute. The idea that Pebble and I are destined to be mates ... that's just not possible."

I sipped my coffee, another flavor of home. All I wanted to do was be a kid a little longer. "In the end, mates are a suggestion, not an absolute. We have free choice. You can always go home with your parents on Monday, Luna, no harm, no foul. Leadership is a choice." I picked up my fork and continued to eat, trying to ignore Luna's glare. *Please choose this.*

Most of the others around the table looked at me in an array of interest. Finally Norman nodded. "That makes sense. We always think of our 'chosen' as a done deal, but how many people don't find that special someone and go on to live perfectly happy lives?" He reached over and squeezed his wife's hand.

Serena leaned forward. "Pretty words, but the two of you are young. Yes, Luna, you *could* come home with us on Monday, but I think you should stay here until school starts." Luna started to bristle, but her mom just held up a hand. "I think both you and Dayna should stay. You can't know your future if you're always running from it."

What is she running from? She always acts like she's paving a future she's planned out her whole life. But she's running?

"Of course, we're staying!" Dayna said, lifting a fork of Pad Thai.

Luna's eyes narrowed. "I don't run from my future." Her voice cut through the room like a scalpel. "I chose this college because it's a good one. I'm studying biology,

Dayna's debating biology or physical education. Either way, we wanted to go to the same school and we both decided to go here."

Serena nodded. "I know dear."

"Then why did you say I'm running?"

"Because you've avoided meeting anyone. You refuse to be your warm wonderful self with new people. You're pushing everyone away, like a nervous gosling."

Luna ... warm and wonderful? I guess if you're her mom, maybe. My mind boggled at the thought. *Would I want her to be warm and wonderful to me?* I shook my head, uncertain where that thought came from.

"Fine, I'll sleep on it and go to that stupid meeting. I can't see how sitting in and listening to dozens of wolves yapping will make me want to be part of them more."

My jaw tightened at the word she used, and I saw her smirk. *I have to control my reactions. I can't let her get to me.*

Dayna sighed. "Does this mean we're not going to become wolves?"

Luna sneered. "You *really* want to become a wolf? I thought you were just playing in the park. You can turn into a bear, why would you want to do more? Or less? Isn't a wolf weaker than a bear?"

"Gah! It's always about status with you. It's more than strength, I want the community, a pack. The sleuth is really old-fashioned, and in all honesty, they don't have what the wolves do. The bears come together for big events, but nothing more. This pack gets together all the time. I've been hearing about them for years. It's why I always wished I was born a wolf, not a bear. The kids all played together, then they get to run together." Her eyes, bright with wonder, turned to me. "You even all went to the same school district, right? Not like us who were scattered all over."

I smiled at her exuberance. "Yeah, just about everyone in the pack lives in this neighborhood. It's a thing. We love being a family, and it's easier if we're close."

"That." Dayna pointed at me. "I want that. They know each other, live close to each other, support each other, they're a family. They're young, hip, and fun."

Luna snapped her focus from Dayna to me. "And does she only get a chance at becoming a wolf if I go along with this ... malarkey, too?"

I opened my mouth to answer. I wasn't sure what I'd say. On the one hand, I didn't want to bite anyone or add anyone to my already crowded headspace. On the other, why would I force Luna into doing something she didn't want to do? Hadn't I already explained this needed to be her choice, not anyone else's? Had she listened to me at all?

Stew placed a hand on her arm. "Luna, what's wrong? You used to ask to run in the woods with me all the time. You wanted to roar as a bear. Now's your chance to become something new and you're ready to throw it away ... and why? Because you're following your attitude?

Please tell me there is some of me in there and it isn't all—" He faltered, not ending his thought.

There was a lightness to Luna when she looked at her Dad. "I did want to shift into a bear, and the thought of running with you ... it sounds ... *sounded* amazing. But what if I become a wolf and I'm ... what's the word? Submissive? Would I even qualify to help lead?"

Oh, is that what this is all about? "Do you know what a submissive is?"

"Yes." She snapped. "It's a weak wolf who can't do anything. A dud."

Across from me, Dad's face hardened. I sipped my coffee. "The submissive wolf is the heart of the pack. A pack without a submissive, or several, tends to not function well. Some of my favorite pack members are submissives. Honestly, I wouldn't have been upset if that's what I was. They give the pack purpose and keep the wolves with higher emotions calm, human, happy."

Dayna laughed. "Oh, don't worry Luna, that won't be you."

The others around Luna chuckled.

"Okay," Luna said. "But there are more wolves in a pack than alpha and submissive. What if you do," her hand waved, "whatever it is you do, and I'm just a wolf?" There was a bit to her voice, but a woodsy scent emanated from her, giving away her determination.

Everyone at the table turned to me, including Dad, who smiled at me encouragingly. I wanted to roll my eyes. "A pack only needs one alpha to lead. I am, at this moment, the sole leader of the Wisconsin werewolf pack. Though Dad is here, it's only for another day or two, and for all intents and purposes, he's a visiting wolf, not part of the pack."

That got the heat off me. I worried someone would pull a muscle as everyone swung around to gape. For his part, Dad just smirked and winked. "Don't worry, I got permission from the local alpha to be here. I did my due diligence."

I barked out a laugh. "Technically, you didn't. But I'll let it slide." Between the two of us, some of the tension eased. With Luna, I hadn't even realized what had built between us. "Anyway," I continued, "If I found a partner, human, werewolf, or other non-wolf shifter, they would be my partner. I would hope that they would help me in all aspects of running the pack, save maybe two."

Before I could continue, Luna scoffed. "And what are those? Are you power hungry or something?"

Do not kick her out ... do not kick her out.

Dayna sighed. "You know, Luna, she's going to kick you out if you don't stop. I can't believe she hasn't already."

I smiled at her, then turned to the goose shifter. "That's exactly it." I leaned back and sipped my coffee. I was glad for the Thai food, but at this rate I'd need to be eating it her whole visit. Once she looked ready to listen, I gave a curt nod and put my coffee mug down. "If my partner is an alpha level wolf, they'll have an alpha mantle and can help with all aspects of what I can do, including when the power is needed. Usually, the power isn't needed, and they can help. If they don't have it and it's needed, they can't. It's pretty much as simple as that."

Brow furrowing, Luna tilted her head. "What's an alpha mantle?"

"It's our power. I keep it pushed down ... hidden so to speak. When I release it, just about anyone can feel it, sometimes even humans. It's intense."

"And you're saying, I could have this power?" Despite the argumentative tone, and the eyebrow raise, her citrusy scent told me she was excited.

I sighed. "You're making me not want to offer this to you. Power is a responsibility."

"I know that, Pebble. I'm just getting all the facts before I make a decision. It's a wise practice, if you didn't know."

My jaw hurt from clenching it so hard. "Very well. Do you have other questions? Because if you don't, we could finish our meal, and you could sleep on it. Decide tomorrow after the pack meeting."

Luna grunted. "Whatever."

Serena shook her head. "She'll come around, don't worry. It takes time, but it'll get better."

With effort, I kept my face blank. I couldn't imagine the amount of time I'd have to wait before Luna Zweck became pleasant towards me ... a year, a decade, a century ... more time than I had.

I waited a few seconds before going back to my food. It was a bit cold but still tasted wonderful.

Before my first plate was done—because I was already mapping out my second—Dayna put down her fork. "Just so you know, I don't have to sleep on it. Regardless of what Luna decides, if you'll have me, I want to become a werewolf."

I put my fork down and gazed at her, my eyebrows raised, her face alight with hope. "Really? I hadn't picked that up."

The tension in the room dropped as everyone laughed.

Chapter 7 – A Gathering

I woke up early on Sunday, changed into exercise clothes, and headed into the kitchen to grab a water bottle. The house was quiet. I was so used to Mom waking up before me, it took a second to realize what was missing, and then a wave of sadness washed through me.

There had been other times she'd been away. She and Dad had visited Jade and Owen in California without me or had visited one of the other packs, but this felt different.

A weight of change and responsibility settled on my shoulders. It was as if I were beginning a new normal.

Shaking my head, I dismissed the thoughts. *She's not gone forever, Pebble. Suck it up.*

The pack meeting was earlier than usual. We wanted to let everyone have time to get things done during the day if they wanted. I only had a few hours to get ready.

The buzz started in my head, and I had to reinforce the fence. The damn wolves kept trying to escape and I wanted my head to be my own. I took a minute to breathe, hoping if I were centered it would help.

Shaking off the melancholy of missing Mom and the stress of the pack, I found a bottle and turned. Dayna and her dad, Norman, stood on the far side of the kitchen. Jerking with surprise, I realized I had to get my game face on. Even in the safety of my own home, people shouldn't be able to sneak up on me, especially those who weren't pack.

As always, a smile played across Dayna's face. "Hiya Pebble. It's a bit cold for shorts and a halter top, don't you think? I mean, I usually don't judge, but there *is* snow on the ground." Dayna winked.

I pointed to the stairs I hadn't shown them the night before. "Those lead to the barn. I'm going to run, get in one of those torture ... er, exercise routines I told you about. The ones my Dad loves to put together. Then I'm off to shower, eat, and prepare for the meeting. Well, I've mostly already prepared, just, you know, mentally set myself up to fully lead this one. It'll be my first as alpha."

Dayna nodded. "The one and only. You'll be amazing, you know. I have full confidence in you." Her words warmed me. She gazed out the window towards the barn. "As for your current activities, that's great. I was wondering if anyone used the gym if it involved snow travel."

I laughed. "The underground passage is preferable in extreme weather. When I get back, I'll start breakfast for everyone, but until then, coffee is made, and if you want something else, feel free to poke around." I listed off several of the options we had and where to find them, including pre-made breakfast casseroles that just needed to be thrown in the oven..

Norman nodded. "Don't worry about us, we'll manage. Go, have a few minutes alone before this place fills."

With a wave, I headed off.

The gym had a few private rooms for yoga or if someone wanted to watch an exercise video. In the center were some machines and free weights. Circling all of it was a quarter mile track. Along the wall, at the foot of the stairs, lay some stretching mats and a white board where Dad posted pack stats. Not everyone in the pack worked out here regularly, but if they wanted, they could be added to the list.

Under the board was a desk. I found my small book, checked my calendar and mentally mapped out what I wanted to do. I started off with a ten-minute run. Once warmed up, I did twenty minutes of arm weights in a circuit.

Originally I had debated a longer weights set, but midway through I altered my plan. First, we had guests, and I figured I should get back to the kitchen and start cooking. Second, as more people in the pack woke up, they were thinking about why we were having a meeting. As they thought about the pack and us, their ping on my mind was stronger than anything I'd felt before. The cardio helped more than the weights, and I decided to hit the track again.

As I stretched my muscles in a second run, I let myself move as fast as I could. Our gym was one of the few places I just let myself run. I heard footsteps on the stairs. I took a slow inhale.

Luna. I'd recognize that scent anywhere. My heart beat faster, before my mind caught up and frustration hit. My moment of solitude was good and over.

I debated ending my run a few minutes early, then decided I wouldn't let her affect my activities, not to mention, it would be rude. *If she wants to utilize this area, that's her choice. She's an adult. I'm an adult. We can each do our thing separately. This gym is very much big enough.*

After a few minutes, Luna caught up to me. "Whoa, you have some speed, alpha-girl."

I just focused on my form, thinking of the lessons my brother Owen had taught me. He always wanted me to push for more. Finally, I decided I was being rude and despite enjoying the feeling, I knew I needed to stop. "We have animals in us, speed comes with the package. Not only that, I've been training most of my life."

Luna started to breathe harder. "Why aren't you on the track team? You'd be the star. Hell, you could go to the Olympics."

I cut my eyes to her but continued for a few seconds. "You seem to be keeping up with me."

"But not for long, you've been at this pace for how long?" As Luna slowed, I started to match her speed. "No, keep going. I want to watch."

Whatever. I had about two minutes left and really wanted to get two miles in under ten minutes. It wasn't my fastest—but it was close—and it was a way to end my workout.

When I got done, I updated my book with my run time and distance, excited by making my goal, then moved to the mats to stretch. I watched Luna run. She had good form, but if she relaxed into her stride, she'd move faster. My guess was, she didn't want my advice. After her run, like me, she headed to the weights.

Once my muscles were stretched, I entered my stats into my book and headed back up to the kitchen. Someone had made more coffee, and it smelled like there was something baking in the oven. My stomach growled its approval. Since I didn't see, hear, or smell anyone, I filled a mug with coffee, and headed off to my room to grab clothes, and then to shower.

Just like last time, the heat of the shower relaxed me, and for a moment I forgot to keep up my mental guard. I had a moment of being almost overwhelmed with the emotions of everyone in the pack. Are they thinking about us, the alphas, the pack den, coming in for the meeting, or something personal to them? Their focus on us ... and in a way me, was making all of it more intense.

I placed my hands on the walls of the shower, supporting myself, and closed my eyes. I reinforced the mental fencing around the pack of wolves, playing and rough-housing. In my mind they all looked to be having fun, but I needed their excitement to be over there, and not taking over my mind.

Would an electric fence work better? Or putting them in a different mental world? Or planet? Could I even do that?

A sense of peace flowed through me once I'd managed the mindscape.

With my equilibrium back in place, I sent a mental 'thank-you' to José, then finished my shower, and dressed. I wore black jeans and a long-sleeve black shirt with a stylized multi-colored calico cat sauntering off to the right. Underneath it read, *It's Like Herding Cats.* It had been a birthday gift from Jade last year.

Back in the kitchen, Stew moved around the huge room like he owned the place. I smiled at him. "Are you enjoying yourself?"

"This kitchen is amazing. Your Dad said to make myself at home ... and I hope this is okay." He slid a mug of coffee to me and decided even if I didn't completely approve of his cooking, I'd have forgiven him.

"Yeah, whatever you're doing smells amazing. What *are* you making?"

"Well, I have several loaves of bread pudding baking in the oven., They'll be done in a couple of minutes. Then I made a ham and cheese scramble for on the side."

"Gods, it all smells great. But ... what about that?" I pointed to a huge pot on the far stove.

"Oh! Well, you've invited, what, a dozen or two wolves over for a mid-morning meeting?"

"Seventeen. With me, the pack has eighteen people. But it'll feel bigger. We're a rowdy lot."

"Right." He said. "But with your dad, me and mine, which is another six, that's twenty-five, right?"

I did some quick calculations, and realized he was right, and nodded. "Though, there may be more if kids or spouses come."

His smile widened. "My point exactly! Two dozen or more people. And none of them, outside of a select few, have tried my award-winning chili." His face lit up as his brows waggled.

My eyes widened. "Your chili has won awards?"

"No." Luna came up from the underground passage, her clothes sweaty. "He claims it has, but he's never actually competed." She kissed Stew on the cheek.

For a moment my mind short-circuited ... Luna could be affectionate? I sipped my coffee to cover my shock.

Stew smirked at his daughter. "But ..."

"But," she sighed dramatically, "your chili is very good. I'm glad you're making it." She sauntered off towards the stairs that led to her room. "I'll also throw together some cornbread. Can't have one without the other? Right?"

Dad walked out from the hallway, dressed, but otherwise looking mostly like a zombie. He fell into a stool. "Smells good."

Stew got him a coffee as well. "Thanks." He downed most of it in his first sip. "Gods, why are we having the meeting so early?"

I laughed. "Because we want the pack to have most of the day to do their things ... and you to be able to finish getting ready to leave. Remember?" I leaned towards him, wondering how much his groggy mind comprehended. "You're leaving tomorrow. Have you packed? Are you ready? Do you know who you are, yet?"

"I know, I know." He sighed. "Smells great in here. As soon as I leave, you bring in a ringer. Making stew, Stew?"

The other man laughed. "Never! It'd be too ridiculous, even for me. I'm making chili."

Dad's eyes narrowed. "Isn't that just a variation of stew?"

"Depends," Stew said, eyebrow raising. "Do you want to eat it later?"

Throwing his head back, Dad laughed.

Before the pack overwhelmed the house, I got the guests settled in the meeting room. To make things simple, I gave them the spot in the front, nearest the stage, farthest from the door. It was the area I usually sat ... though for now I'd be leading the meetings, not sitting in the audience. My hands felt numb, and I oscillated between shaking them out and rubbing my thumb against my fingers.

Luna and Dayna sat in the center row of the three sets of loveseats in front of Dayna's parents. Luna's parents sat behind them.

Once they were settled, I went out to greet the pack members as they showed up. Some asked about Mom. No one knew she wasn't somewhere in the pack den, but me and Dad just evaded the questions.

"Just go sit, we can't get to that amazing-smelling food if we don't start the meeting!"

Tanner narrowed his eyes. "None of you cooked that. Okay, but I'll need to know the chef before I trust anything out of that kitchen. I thought it was just you Stones. Or is Hazel finishing up? She can cook." He looked like he was about to shift direction to the kitchen, but Easton stopped him before we could.

"Dad, meeting. I'm starving. If you go wandering, this will never end."

Janet, Bevin's mom, shook her head. "I can't believe everyone is here this early. Then again, if you'd told us about the food ... Who's cooking? Is it Hazel? Where is she?"

Fred gazed at us, always too perceptive. "Come on, let's just give them a chance to explain everything once."

Over and over, everyone had something to say. It didn't take long to get everyone settled.

The few non-werewolf family members hung out in different areas of the house. We debated inviting them to the meeting but felt that would put the pack on edge. With the bears in the meeting room, there was already enough for the pack to be distracted about, then there was the main topic, which was going to stress them out. They could rehash with family members later, letting the new chain of command really sink in.

Monica, Tanner's wife, was in the kitchen, socializing with Helen, Piper's mom, one of our regular non-wolf cooks. When Helen smelled the chili, she immediately started prepping sides. She loved playing in the kitchen as much as anyone I knew.

I stood outside the door with Dad, about to enter the meeting room. *This is it. The first meeting I'll be running as alpha.* I had to get my nerves under control, or everyone would know right away from my scent.

Dad gave me a one-arm hug. "You got this, Applesauce. I'll be just off to the side, your biggest supporter."

After one last deep breath, I opened the door.

The talk in the room washed over me. It was so familiar to every other meeting, it cleansed me of my fears. For a moment everything felt ... normal.

I smiled up at Dad, and we each walked up onto the stage.

When I got to the center, everyone quieted down. "Hi, everyone. Happy New Year!"

A wave of good wishes echoed throughout the room and a smile grew on my face. These were my family, my pack. *Why was I so worried?* I searched the wolves filling the space. I picked out a few of the friendlier faces, people who would always support me. Piper, Julez, Trista, probably even Tanner. Then I sought out the submissive wolves, the heart holding us together like glue. Their jobs would be critical today, Aunt Allison, Chris, and Andy. Their smiles were infectious. As I looked around, I decided probably everyone was someone I could count on in the end.

Mom and Dad were right. This was the best pack ever.

"Today's meeting is a big one. I have a lot of news to share with you."

Chris, Chloe's dad, and the most curious and outspoken wolf, stood. "You? You're running the meeting? Not River?"

I tilted my head and raised both my brows. "You know I'll answer all your questions if you just let me talk. Obviously, Dad is right there and hasn't said a word."

Chris's eyes narrowed. "Is this a training exercise?"

Andy, Chris's husband, yanked on his arm. "Personally, I want to get to that delicious-smelling chili. We'll never get there with you asking a million questions, love." Andy turned to me. "Can you imagine living with him *and* Chloe? They're both like this all the time, you know."

Laughter bubbled up everywhere. I cut my eyes over to the guests and saw even they seemed amused.

"Okay, so now that we've established that I'm the one talking, and not my dad. I'm glad we've all passed the first test of perception." I waited a beat to let another wave of citrusy amusement pass. "On to the serious part of the meeting, because we have urgent and important news."

That got everyone's attention. People sat up. Clare, in the back, always quick to read a situation, narrowed her eyes. *Did she already guess what's going on? Did José talk with his mom? He wouldn't have done that ... would he?*

"On New Year's Eve into New Year's Day, there was an attack in Tennessee."

In the back, Clare nodded. "The alphas. This is about them."

Like observers of a tennis match, everyone turned from me to her, then back.

"It is. What isn't being talked about is that the alphas didn't survive." The gasps and small chatter only lasted a moment before I continued. "We haven't gotten all the news on how the attack went down, but we plan on finding out."

Tanner snarled. "That pack is a mess. They don't have anyone else strong enough—" His head whipped around. "Where is Hazel?" Then his eyes shut. "No."

Tensing my muscles almost as if someone were about to punch me, I knew what was going to happen next. Slowly, as if on cue, the members of the pack shut their eyes.

At all times, I could sense the emotional state of the pack. Any pack member, if they focused on their alpha, could get a basic sense of who their leader was ... where they were.

Chris shot up again. "Pebble, you're the alpha!"

I held up my hands. "If you'll let me continue. The Tennessee alphas didn't survive. And as Tanner said, their pack didn't have anyone else strong enough to lead. They needed leaders. Mom *and* Dad have volunteered. Dad is staying until Monday to get things closed up at work."

Andy shook his head. "Is this permanent?"

"No." I stood tall. "We are a strong and, frankly, amazing pack. We are in a unique position that Mom and Dad could step up to help as a stop-gap until Tennessee finds a new alpha or alphas. Once that happens," I shot Dad a quirky smile, "I should be able to go back to being just a student again."

"Wait." Chris eyed Dad. "That means he's a lone wolf? Did he ask permission to enter our territory?" Chris tried to hold a hard expression, but a smile spread across his face as he spoke. "Join our meeting? Did he follow our protocols?"

The questions broke some of the tension and pack members around the room laughed and gasped comedically in turn. "Not right away, but he brought me Thai food last night, so I forgave the time delay."

Aunt Allison snorted. "Well, as long as he bribed you with your favorite, I guess we can forgive him for his trespassing."

Dad guffawed and everyone else laughed.

Smiling, I continued. "At first I was as worried as you about becoming alpha so early in my training ... and alone."

It was Clare's turn to stand. "You are *not* alone, Pebble. First of all, you've been working hard to learn the ropes. We all know how smart and strong you are. We've all seen it. If you need help or advice you have me, Tanner, Allison, hell, you have Chris, if you're willing to wade through his questions."

Tanner nodded, his deep voice reverberating through the room. "Clare is right. You *are* ready." His voice brooked no question. "We are a strong pack, and you are a strong leader. None of us are worried."

Warmth filled me as I gazed at all the faces in the crowd. "Again, the arrangement isn't forever. Once Mom and Dad have Tennessee—" A pain stabbed into my head.

My hand shot up, rubbing, and I squatted down, looking to Dad. He raced over, kneeling behind me, and wrapping me in his arms, just as the premonition hit.

I looked over a field of lush green grass. The sky was blue with white clouds. I heard a rustling and when I looked down, a huge open mouth with sharp teeth shot up towards me, ready to bite.

With a start, I jerked back. Only Dad behind me kept me from falling. "What was it? What did you see?"

Everyone in the audience—well, most of them—knew exactly what had just happened. There was an overwhelming scent of sandalwood from their concern filling the room, punctuated by a few spots of minty confusion.

I shook my head. "Help me up."

Dad did, but his dark eyes were full of questions. When I gazed out at the pack, so were theirs. I sighed. "Let me see if I can determine what that meant on my own, first. Then we can spread the gossip. I'll tell Chris; he always gets the news to everyone faster than if I say it here and now." That got everyone chuckling, though the worry was still there. A few people, our guests and new pack members, like Trista, just looked confused. They didn't know about the premonitions at all. *Oh, well.*

After one more cleansing breath, I smiled. "The other part of our agenda is, well, a premonition I had over the summer. It repeated throughout the semester." I held up my hands. "Yes, I know this is new. I've never had recurring premonitions before. I'm not sure if it's because it had to do with me, or because it was really important, and I wasn't 'getting' it."

This got everyone's attention. My premonitions were always hard to decipher.

"Apparently, I have a mate." A stillness took over the room. "And this person was someone I didn't know. She's not a wolf."

Andy raised his hand. "Will you turn them? Like I was turned? Does she want to become a wolf?"

I looked over at Luna. This wasn't the first time we'd had visitors to one of our meetings. It wasn't a regular occurrence, but the pack trusted us and were patient with our news. They knew if there were strangers, they would be introduced in time.

Before the meeting, I had asked if Luna wanted to speak for herself and she said 'no.' I told her I'd be speaking for her then. This was her chance to change her mind.

Luna's eyes narrowed, then I could almost hear her growl. She stood and walked up to stand next to me, a woodsy chamomile scent wafting off her. Determination and acceptance. Interesting. "I've been asking myself the same things." She smiled. "Hi, my name is Luna Zweck, and I'm a goose shifter."

The room had the tension of the calm before the storm. Everyone stared at her, their eyes getting wider. Then Piper started to giggle.

As the laughter grew, Luna turned to me. "What's going on? Do they think I'm joking?" I could almost see her feathers being ruffled.

"I've told you the stories about geese in this family. No one here knew there were goose shifters, and the idea that I went so far as to find a mate that *is* a goose, it's like the checkmate on the goose game we've always played. Everyone has been watching the goose games for years. It's a real thing around here."

Luna smirked. "So, I get to be the queen goose. I like it. It may make sticking around worth it."

I groaned, not liking the idea of her being the queen.

In the back, Clare said, barely holding in her laughter, "Oh, my gods. This is the best thing I've heard all year. Please tell me it's true."

I shook my head. "It's the fourth day of the year—that's a pretty low bar. But yes, it's true."

"Fine," Clare said, shaking her head and biting her bottom lip. "The best thing from *last year*. Hell, since Jade was attacked!"

Tanner sniffed. "The others aren't geese, are they? Wait, no ... humans? I don't smell anything. Are they geese? Did you bring a flock of geese to the meeting? What are you planning, Pebble?"

The werebears had a soap that could cover their scent. Though they hadn't been using the shower products, I asked them to use it for this meeting. I figured it would be easier than having four bears with their scent in the meeting.

"They aren't human, they're werebears. I asked them to use the soap so that their scent wouldn't disrupt the meeting."

Everyone stilled for a moment before talking erupted everywhere. I let them gossip for a moment, before reeling them in. "Luna is considering joining the pack. But Dayna, who is a werebear, has dreamt of being a wolf her whole life. We may get two new members to our pack."

Tanner grunted. "What is it with kids today and their dual animals? Why isn't having one enough?"

Dayna turned to him. "If you were a bear, you'd dream of being a wolf too, trust me. And this meeting is the most fun I've had in a while."

Julez stood. "River, what do you think of all this? Adding two new wolves and everything else?" Her voice sounded amused and flabbergasted all in one.

Dad held up both his hands and shrugged. "I'm just a lone wolf observing. This isn't my rodeo; I'm not in charge of the chaos."

"Dad, that was awful. Can you stick to one metaphor?"

He grinned. "You can't make me. Now, are we done yet?" He gave me a wicked grin. "Man, I've wanted to be the one to say that for years!"

I gave him a death look, and he threw his head back and laughed. Ignoring him, I faced the wolves again—a much nicer group—and sighed. After years of Jade and her weird epsilon ways, not to mention being the first pack to know about werepanthers and werebears and to have werepanthers as members—not that we still did—the Wisconsin pack knew how to take things in stride. As always, my people were supportive, and it warmed me. With the smells wafting in from the kitchen, I wasn't going to accomplish much more. "Stew, Luna's dad made his award-winning chili and Luna made cornbread."

Luna, still on stage, scoffed. "The only awards are in his imagination ... but it does taste good."

"And I believe Helen has been prepping sides," I added, thinking about the last thing I saw in the kitchen. Stew's eyes widened, as if offended, but I didn't give him time to object. I had more to say. "I was hoping after we ate, we could take a run. If you don't have time, no worries, but I'd like to head out with a group prior to next week's full moon. That way we can all stretch out our muscles."

The call of food got the room cleared out in record time more than the thought of getting furry.

Chapter 8 – Coming To Fruition

During the meeting, Helen had been busy. She'd grated sharp cheddar cheese, diced jalapenos, onions, tomatoes, measured out a few herbs, and arranged each of these ingredients on four boards. She also spread around the board some chips, chunks of French bread, slices of lime, and crackers.

Searching the area, I saw boards placed on the kitchen island, one on the kitchen table, one in the dining room, and the last in the living room. Next to the boards sat plates piled with cornbread. Bowls and spoons for the chili, as well as drinks were scattered in the kitchen for easy flow.

When Stew saw what she'd done, his irritation turned into amusement. "Okay, I won't roar too much at the intrusion. People can try my creation first. It doesn't need all this, but it's nice for mix-ins." He smiled and scooped his own bowl.

I ended up in the dining room with Dad, Tanner, Clare, and several others. I wasn't sure where the bears and geese ended up, but figured they found their own corner of the house. It was big enough for everyone.

"Gods above, this chili is great." I could feel my soul warm with the spicy flavors. I hoped there would be leftovers. Given time, the spices would be amazing. Despite how good the cornbread tasted, I wasn't going to tell Luna. She had a big enough ego.

Tanner grunted. "It's good. And you said Luna made this?" He held up the cornbread. "Finally, someone else who can cook."

"But you waited for me to leave?" Dad whined from my other side.

The pack's search for people who could cook was as deeply rooted as their jokes about geese, especially Dad's.

The contented enjoyment from the pack reverberated through my mind, warming me more. Part of me swore I could feel my wolf purr in pleasure. She'd been yearning for this, her proper place in the pack.

Once everyone had eaten, Monica said she'd be on clean-up duty. "All of you go out and run. You need to move, or you'll all be useless blobs for the rest of the day."

The group went out in pairs and groups of threes to change. Dad pulled me aside. "I'm going to hang back with the cleaning crew. I think it'd be confusing to have me run with all of you."

The idea of not having him or Mom run hurt something deep inside, but it made sense. I nodded. "Yeah, I get it." I flung my arms around him in a big hug. "Gods, I'm going to miss you. I wish we could have one more run together."

"I know. Maybe tonight if there's time. If not, I'll be back before you know it and we can all run as a family." He leaned down and kissed my forehead. "Before you head out, and while everyone is busy, can you tell me what you saw?"

We had about twenty minutes before the run. The wave of wolves shifting always took time. I pulled him into the hallway with the meeting room. "It wasn't big. It was a field ... full of grass, maybe wild grass, or hay? And a creature leapt out at me, mouth wide, ready to strike and bite me."

Dad's head tilted. "What kind of creature?"

I closed my eyes and thought about the mouth, the teeth, the strike. My heart started pounding faster. "It was ... I think it was a snake."

He nodded. "It may not matter, but the kind of snake could be important."

I grunted. "Green ... like grass."

His eyes shut, but then he shrugged. "Okay, so, in some place, here or Tennessee, there is a snake in the grass. Some sort of traitor. You'd been talking about Mom at the time, but we were in a pack meeting here. So, a warning." His face tightened. "But for who?"

I sighed, "Isn't that always the question? My guess would be you and Mom. The timing would be right, and we know that pack has its issues. Maybe the alpha assassinations were planned internally?"

He sighed. "You know you never go into an investigation with preconceived notions. Don't try to assume one way or another, Applesauce. We'll be careful," he tapped my nose, "but you need to be watchful as well."

With Dad's warning and my premonition on my mind, I headed off to find Luna and Dayna. They were standing in the living room. "Are you two ready to face the wolves?"

Dayna's eyes twinkled. "You know I am. I'm ready to sign on. I love your pack. That meeting was everything I'd hoped it would be. When is the next?"

My shoulders drooped. I just survived my first and she was ready for another? "Really? You want *more* of them?"

"Heck yeah! Bring it, alpha! And running with all of you last month was fun, but that meeting was a hoot!"

I bit my cheek to stop myself from laughing at the word 'hoot'.

Serena smiled tightly. "It was an informative meeting. Your control over your people is ... interesting. I'm guessing you'll get more disciplined as time moves forward?"

It took that control and discipline she didn't think I had not to laugh in her face. "Actually, that was a pretty average meeting. That's how wolves are. We're a family, not a company. We lead, we don't demand silence, if that's what you expected."

Her mouth tightened and she gave a curt nod. I could smell jasmine and lilac on her. She felt smug and superior.

Luna shook her head. "It was fine, Mom. It felt like most of our classrooms. Controlled chaos." Her eyes cut to me. "No wonder you never flinch around the ... others." The way she said 'others' made me feel like she had a less complimentary word she wanted to say, but there were too many adults around.

"Back to the matter at hand." We needed to stay on topic. "Who's heading out for the run? I really need to get a feel of running as alpha, but if any of you want to come out with us, you're more than welcome."

Stew smiled, and it warmed the coolness that his wife's words inspired. "I think it should only be Dayna and Luna. Let them get a feel of being part of your pack. Us oldies will hang back, help with clean up, maybe see if your dad can play poker."

I smiled at the joy in his last words. I had a feeling he was a ringer at cards. "Sounds good." Glancing at Luna and Dayna I said, "Ladies, shall we head out?"

Yugen

Dayna squealed happily and Luna sighed.

The joy of the pack surged through me as I let the wolf out. She flowed over me almost before I thought 'wolf.'

There was pain, but the close relationship I had with my animal-half meant both aspects felt natural. The wolf's need to have her moment always superseded any hurt. This time, I also had seventeen points of excitement and anticipation exploding in my mind, as my pack was ready to stretch their legs and run. Though the pack's emotions took up a piece of my headspace, instinct took over, and my mental load felt easier.

I trotted around the privacy barrier into the main back yard, my paws sinking into the sloshy snow. I howled to Sonnara, the sun god, since it was near noon, and not a night run. My song was echoed by my pack. A roar reverberated behind me, and a huge brown bear smiled at me, eyes sparkling as she ran past towards the trees. A honk from above had my head snapping up, and I saw a goose.

In my head, a stabbing pain threatened to take me under. I snarled. *You are not doing this now. I get it. This is the second recurring premonition. I'm not that dense. You don't need to be so persistent, wolf. Just run!*

And we did. Behind me I heard the pack following as we cut through the snow, over fallen logs, and into the woods.

Around me, it almost felt like I could follow the location of every wolf in the pack. More so than when in human form, I knew where each member ran. Clare stubbed her paw. Julez snapped at Trista. Chris and Andy played, racing and bounding back and forth. Their antics amused me, but my wolf knew how to juggle their information separate from our own.

Why can't we do this in both forms?

A bubble of amusement filled me. *An acorn is just a tree before it blooms.*

As always, helpful.

Though this run wasn't about a hunt, the image of us running, and a deer to our right flashed through my mind. The image was from above, as if from the sky. A quick look, and I realized Luna still tracked our progress.

Is this an alpha thing? Is there more Dad and Mom haven't told me? Is this a me thing? Is this a goose thing? What's going on? I had so many questions ... I just had to figure out who to ask.

I turned and signaled the pack to split up. Tanner and Clare would help with the take down.

The wind was wrong, so the pack was confused.

I wasn't sure of the exact location of the deer. *Can I do what Luna did?* With Jade, I imagine a door. This time, I put an 'L' on the door and knocked. Nothing happened.

Grr. What is going on? Is there some alpha secret I need to drag out of Dad?

Maybe ... *I feel ridiculous.* Rolling my eyes, though no one saw, I tried to think at Luna, *are we heading in the right direction?*

Another image of us running, angled a bit off, popped in my head, and I nearly tripped. Amusement followed the image, and I snarled.

The deer was dashing away.

I adjusted our path, then the wind shifted. The pack caught the scent.

We were off.

The majority of the pack took pursuit to wear the animal down. Three of us circled to pounce.

Once we were in position, Clare and I leaped high, Tanner went in low. As alpha, I got first taste. I took two bites before backing up. The others got in, giving tribute to the animal that gave its life to us.

Dayna was the last in. We turned and ran to the river, thankfully not frozen. As cold as it was, the water was refreshing after the run. Then it was a quick run back home.

I had to find Dad. Why were there so many secrets?

Chapter 9 – Decision Made

Closing my eyes, I mentally whispered to my wolf, *'human.'* The shift began, and the feeling of emerging from my cocoon rolled over me. The shift wasn't the fastest in the pack, as my wolf loved to be dominant. She loved to run, and the feeling of the wind in her fur, the ground under her paws, and the power of being on four legs. But, in the end, she knew it was time. In a breath, I had hands and feet.

I panted for a moment, readjusting my mindset as cold winter air filled my lungs, and leaned back to a kneeling position. A shiver ran from my head to my toes as I settled into my skin. The feeling of the pack as the pain of their shifts hit them occupied a chunk of my brain. With a small push, I reinforced my mental fence. *Gods, I hope that gets to be automatic soon.* Once it was all settled, I stood to find my clothes before my skin chilled too much from the winter temperatures.

In another area of my mind, I thought I could feel Luna's irritation.

Damn it. I need to talk to Dad before she finds me.

Slipping in the side door, I headed up the back steps to his office, then texted him to meet me there. It occurred to me as I waited that this was now *my* office. A shiver ran down my spine, and I rubbed my hands together to warm them. *So many changes.*

"Hiya, Applesauce. Is everything okay? How did the run go?"

I released a big gush of air. "Can you shut the door?" The office was soundproof and what we were discussing wasn't common knowledge. If it was, he or Mom would have told me about it already.

"What happened?" His jovial attitude morphed into something more concerned.

"Nothing, I mean, something happened, but it isn't as scary as you may think. It's just, Dad, what haven't you told me about alphas?"

He sank into the seat across the desk from me. "I'm not sure what you mean. You'll have to be more specific."

"Dad," I snapped out. "I need to know if what happened is me ... or if it's an alpha thing. Please, don't be coy."

His jaw tightened and he rubbed his face. "Pebble, I need to know what happened to you to know if it was personal or general. You and your sister seem to pick up an oddity of the month. Keeping ahead of the two of you has been a full-time job. So, if you don't tell me what happened, I can't explain if it's you, something general, or something we need to research."

I huffed out a growl. He wasn't wrong, but this time felt different, like it was bigger than me. "I saw the woods from Luna's point of view. Not, like, constantly, but ... I don't know, a snapshot? It was like she sent me an image. I *think* I sent her a question, but again, I don't know." There wasn't a scent of confusion or befuddlement filling the room. It wasn't surprising to him, just unexpected. "This wasn't a me thing or even a goose thing, was it?"

"No." Dad sighed. "True alpha mates can exchange small amounts of information. Some impressions, images, maybe a word here and there. Usually, touch is needed, but not always with strong alphas. It also usually needs time to build up. Luna hasn't even accepted the idea of getting a wolf yet, much less the whole alpha package. I thought I had time to discuss this with you." He huffed out a laugh. "I should've known, Applesauce. You don't do anything the normal way, do you?"

"If Luna decides to leave, not join the pack, will this connection go away?"

My stomach twisted. I wasn't sure anymore if I wanted this or not. The idea of our being linked deeper than regular pack bonds scared me. *How close would we get? Will she continue hating me the whole time?*

I stood. "Okay, I think I understand. Though I wish I'd known before it happened. I need to talk to Luna about this."

When we opened the door, Luna and her mom stood outside the door. I sighed. "Oh, hi." Even I reveled in my brilliance.

Luna sneered. "We need to talk. Mom wants to be there." She eyed Dad. "I'm guessing you do too?"

Dad shrugged. "No need. Pebble is alpha, and from the sound of it, you're her mate. I'm sure the two of you can figure out anything that needs to happen. I have friends to say goodbye to and then packing to finish up. Lots to do and little time to get it done in." He gave a small head bow and slipped away.

I turned on my heel and returned to the seat behind the desk. "Close the door, please. The room is soundproof. I'm not one hundred percent sure what you want to talk about, but if I'm right, we'll be discussing pack secrets. Having you here, Serena, is already breaking some rules."

Tension filled the room. Luna glared as she snapped out, "What happened out there?"

I leaned back, willing my muscles to relax. Wishing again the phantom premonition related to someone I got along with. Thinking about the number of secrets in our world and how many I still didn't know, how much I would miss my parents, if I could just lead the pack alone, a lot of things, I rubbed my face then sat up. I debated playing dumb but decided there was no reason. "So, it didn't initiate with you?"

Since Luna didn't have a wolf, this possibility was the only reason I allowed Serena to join us. *Could the geese have a similar ability?*

That got her attention. She shot her mom a quick glance. Serena shook her head before Luna returned her glare to me. "You said a word in my head. I was flying above the hunt wondering why you didn't go after the deer. Then you changed direction. Then I thought I heard your voice in my head, the word 'direction.' It wasn't, of course, that would be impossible. But then you shifted and got your target."

My head started to pound. Would anything with Luna be simple? "Just so you know, this is as new to me as it is to you. That's what I was just asking my dad about. There is lore in the werewolf society that no one talks about. Apparently, alphas, *true alpha pairs* can send images and sometimes words back and forth. He didn't think we'd get there for weeks if not months and then only if you'd become a wolf. Oh, and apparently in the early stages it needs us to be touching."

A look of dubious doubt came over Luna's face. A cinnamon and cumin scent filled the room. "We did something that shouldn't be possible?"

"From what I understand, yes."

"And if I become a wolf, that could get stronger?"

I smiled warily. "Are you asking if you could cheat off my test papers if we were in the same class?"

She snorted. *'As if.'* The words were as clear as day.

Though I heard the words, her mouth didn't move. "I heard that."

The side of her mouth twitched, and her scent turned citrusy with amusement. It was the first smile I'd seen from her all day. "We'll have to figure that out. But our connection is the most convincing thing I've experienced yet."

Serena's face stiffened. "Luna, I told you your auras matched. Why does this wolf thing convince you more than the goose auras? I've picked out pairs your whole life."

"Right, but that's goose mumbo-jumbo. You know, as much as I love most things about goose life, I've always thought that auras were ... not scientific." The last was said with disdain. "Only a few people can see auras. But Pebble spoke in my mind."

"And you sent me images of what you saw."

Luna gaped at me. "I did no such thing."

"The wind was in the wrong direction. We couldn't scent the deer. We only knew to go that way because of the scene you saw from above." I needed more coffee to help with my headache. "Your view of us and the deer let me know first about the deer and then how to adjust our approach."

A tremor traveled down her body. "Okay, right. Mental connection ... with you ... city girl."

"Does that help you make up your mind one way or the other? Do you know if you want to become a wolf or head back to Maine?"

"How often do you have those pack meetings?" Her lip twitched in a sneer, but her scent gave away her amusement.

A laugh barked out of me. "Often ... like all the time. I think it's an excuse for everyone to feast together."

Chapter 10 – Family Connections

Back in the living room, Trista ran up to me. Her words almost were lost on me as a slight red glow surrounded her. Shaking my head, I focused on her exuberance. "The run was amazing. You're going to make the best alpha ever! I can't wait until the full moon next week! Joining the pack ... I mean, going home for the last run really showed me how much I enjoy being part of this group."

Again there was something niggling in the back of my mind. It was harder to figure out with the high emotions of the pack swirling all around. Everyone was excited and sad about Dad's new adventure. I saw him making the rounds and several wolves had tears in their eyes.

I smiled and accepted the hug Trista offered. "Thank you for your support. I hope you had a good time with your family." While she was away, I could feel her happiness and stress, but she'd kept her emotions locked down. Wolves connected to me couldn't hide everything, but unless I was focused on them, or there was a big emotion, I didn't know ... at least that was how it was supposed to work. Once I was used to having the full pack, that was how it would be.

Her face fell and her citrusy, excited scent shifted to an almond incense ... the subject made her tense. "We can talk about that later, right? Not now."

"Okay, yeah. If that's what you want."

"It is. Anyway, I have to head back to my apartment. School, you know. Lots of homework. I know your university doesn't start up for, like, ever, but my school, gah! Anyway, later, Pebble."

She spun and was off before I knew what to say.

Behind me, Luna scoffed. "Wow, that one's a piece of work, isn't she?"

Closing my eyes briefly, I turned. "What does that mean? Or are you talking about me again?" It occurred to me that Luna, too, had a bit of a red tinge around her. I rubbed my eyes. "You know what, never mind. I'm really tired. I need a moment alone. I'm going to my room. I'll be back in a bit. Let me know if you need me."

'As if I'd ever need you.' She hadn't said the words out loud, but I heard them. After rolling her eyes, she sashayed off towards the kitchen.

In my room, I pulled out my phone and called Jade. She picked up right away. "Pebble!"

Her voice centered me, and I relaxed onto my bed. "It's good to hear your voice, sis."

"We usually talk on Sundays. But after I heard how busy a day you were going to have, I didn't expect this."

In the background I heard shuffling. "Yeah. I know. The den is still full of the pack, but I needed a moment of downtime ... and sister time. So much has happened." My voice dropped to almost a whisper at the end as I tried to catalog everything.

There was a snort. "Did you really run the meeting?" Owen's voice came over the line, making me laugh.

"I did, and Dad complained that it went too long. He sounded like us on a long car ride."

Both Jade and Owen laughed. Owen choked out, "I bet he's been waiting for years to get one of us back."

"Pretty much. His grin was devious." Their voices soothed me. "I miss you both. Why can't you be here instead of there? You know kids love snow, right?"

They laughed, as I intended. "Is there anything specific you need?" Jade sounded concerned.

Eyes shut, I thought about everything that had happened. "Actually, I think I need to ask Bev a question

... one of those secret ones. I probably should've called him or José. I just miss hearing your voices."

Bevin's soothing voice replaced Jade's. "I'm taking you to my and José's room. He's right behind me."

"Hola, Pebble." José said. For some reason, of all the people in California, José was the one who could relax me the most ... even over the phone.

I could hear a click, then Bevin said, "Okay, it's just the three of us. What's up?"

"First, I need to tell you about Luna." It didn't take long.

"So, she was promoted without your input?" Bevin asked, sounding incredulous.

My head hit the wall behind me. "Yes, and as much as I'd love to discuss that, there are bigger issues." They both grunted. "I asked Dad about this, but, well, Luna sent an image to me ... you know, wirelessly, during a ... well, we were out running. And apparently I sent a word back to her. I was on the ground and she ... well, wasn't. She's like Jade, her third position, but different."

There was a pause, then José chuckled. "You and your sister. If we had all three of the Stone siblings living together and all five of the kiddos, the house may implode. Can any of you go any amount of time without something weird and different happening to one of you? I just can't imagine."

Bevin laughed softly. "Did Luna agree to the promotion, then?"

"That's just it, not really. We don't get along. She doesn't like ... well, I don't know that she likes anyone. Actually, no. She likes her cousin, but *everyone* likes Dayna. Dayna is amazing."

Bevin sighed. "And this is your partner? Your actual ... person, like me and José?"

I could hear what sounded like a slap and Bevin huffed out a laugh. José said, "Bev, they shared thoughts, only leaders like us can do that. And it sounds like they weren't even touching. Gods, the two of you will be strong. When you two marry ... *if* you two marry, I'm sitting in the back row. Maybe in a different state."

That got Bevin laughing.

"I'm just hoping for cordial potential friendship. I think you're jumping *way* ahead of yourself there, José." My ears rang with the partial lie, and I rubbed my face. Apparently, deep down, I wanted more than that. Maybe if I ever had time to really stop and think about everything, I could work it out, but I didn't see that happening any time soon.

"Maybe, but your inner self doesn't usually make that kind of mistake,"—mentally I replaced 'usually' with 'never.' My wolf had never made a mistake that I could remember— "and if you're making mental connections ... I'm sticking to my conclusion."

Bevin made a sound of agreement. "José's not wrong. Give it time. You're a strong woman and are at the start of being an amazing leader. We're so proud of you. I know you're not one of my sisters, but you feel like one.

Continue our legacy out in the cold tundra. Just know, we all believe in you, and you can call whenever you need us."

Though the lightness of the conversation made me feel better, I still felt a bit like I was drowning. "Thanks, guys. That means a lot."

José hummed. "I can hear your hesitancy. We can believe in you until the cows come home, and where we are that will be a long time, but you're going to have to start believing in yourself. We can't do it for you."

I flopped back on my pillows. "I know. And for the most part I do. It's just ... it's a lot. But you're right. I have you, and my parents, and all the amazing people here." I sat up as something occurred to me. "You know, maybe if I play my cards right I can get more chocolate shakes from Tanner."

A laugh burst over the line from both of them. José managed to say, "You're going to be just fine."

After saying goodbye, I hung up and headed out. My steps felt lighter and my soul less burdened.

With a tiny smirk, I made my way back into the gaggle of wolves. Some of the pack had left, though most were still milling about. I found my Dad with Aunt Allison, Uncle Jackson, and Tanner in the dining room. I wrapped my arms around Dad in a hug. "Do you think, once all the riff-raff have left, we can go for a run, just the two of us? I missed having you out there."

He tilted his head back and smiled. "I think stretching my legs before tomorrow's flight to Tennessee sounds perfect."

The wind ruffled my fur as I ran over the slushy ground. Next to me, Dad kept pace, the two of us practically flying through the woods, leaping over downed trees, and navigating through the trees.

This last outing wasn't about hunting, it was about the run, moving our bodies, and bonding one last time before he left.

An image flashed through my mind, and I stumbled on the root of a tree. My stomach churned and nausea gurgled up my throat. I paused and I realized the image, or series of a few images, like photos, were of two wolves, both gray, though one almost looked black. Dad's wolf had black streaks, making him almost look like the river he was named for. It always amused me that his name and his wolf matched.

Closing my eyes, I saw my own stumble in the flashes of sight sent to me. Dad rubbed against me, his touch brought calm, centering me enough to be able to run again.

I gazed up and saw a goose flying above me. When we had set out, I wanted this to be a run for just me and Dad. Though it was interesting to see what we looked like from above, I didn't need to be followed by Luna. The tension and pressure I'd finally begun to release built in my muscles again.

Dad snuffled, and I shot him a glance, but quickly looked away, not wanting to trip and fall again. My mind whirled because, like Luna and Trista before, there was a subtle redness about him, almost a glow. I wondered if this was something to do with my new alpha status. I'd have to look more closely at the rest of the pack. If others were red, I may have to go back to asking questions, like, what does red mean?

Maybe I should carry a small notebook and write down my questions. I ran, checking to see if it was just Dad or other things around the woods. Nothing else seemed weird. *Maybe it's just the wolves. Or me?*

Chapter 11 – Care For A Quick Bite?

Sweat dripped from my forehead as I sat on the mat, legs crossed and thought about the day ahead of me. Today, I would purposely bite two people as a wolf. I'd avoided sinking my teeth into humans since I was five and accidentally turned two people who had scared me. I'd been homeschooled for years to teach me this was something to avoid. One of the basic rules I'd defined my life around had been: don't bite anyone.

And today, this time, I'll be turning two people on purpose.

A shiver ran down my spine at the thought, and bile rose to the back of my throat.

It's okay to bite people in this situation. They want it, and I'm the alpha.

The first rule of being a wolf was not to bite humans, not get their flavor and become addicted. That would make a werewolf a rogue. The only caveat, the only loophole, was when someone wanted to join the ranks.

The buzzing of the pack began to invade my mind as I spiraled. *Control, I need control. Nothing I'm doing today is wrong.*

Hand trembling, I pulled out my phone. The display flashed seven a.m.. *Five in the morning in California.* Desperate, I texted Jade. *When you wake up, give me a call. I cut our call short yesterday, and I could use a few minutes of sister time.*

It wasn't unheard of for her to be up this early, so I waited a few seconds, but when she didn't call or text, I pushed myself up and headed to my book to record my workout. Then I traced the design of a flower on the front of the book. For years it had always been ice cream based, but I found this one and loved it.

If Dad doesn't get back in the next month or so, who will create the next plan? I know we all tease him about these, but they're what keeps everyone safe. It's one of my connections to him. Despite the teasing ... I don't want to lose this.

Every time I turned around, I found another change. Something I, as the alpha, would have to figure out. *At some point, probably later today, I'll need to find a notebook. I keep mentally adding items to a list of things to do. It's about time I actually write it down. I don't want the pack to lose any of its greatness with the absence of my parents.*

After a few moments, I realized I stood frozen. I'd let myself fixate on my parents again and how I would live up to their legacy. *Remember José's words. Everyone can believe in me, but it only counts if I believe in me, too.*

Not wanting to wallow, I shook myself and took a deep breath. "You can do this, Pebble," I whispered before heading back to the main house.

Stew was at it again, cooking up a feast. *Is there a blueness about him, or is that coming in from the sun reflecting off the window? Why is my mind playing tricks on me?* "You do know you don't have to cook for us ... not that I'm complaining. It smells amazing in here."

"Have you really ever checked this kitchen out? It's a dream of a room. Kids today, totally spoiled!" He waggled his brows at me. "Anyway, you said we'd get started at eight. I assume everyone needs to eat. Breakfast sandwiches will be ready in about a half hour." He handed me a mug of coffee and it made me smile. He felt like any other pack member taking over the kitchen. His actions grounded me better than anything else I'd done. His eyes twinkled as if he knew the effect his actions had on me. "How long were you over in the barn? I didn't even realize you were up. And I thought I was an early riser. Do you want water?"

I smiled at him. "Just under an hour. I drank water while I was there, but yeah, I'll have another glass before I head off to shower." I put action to words since he was doing so much. "Are you worried about Luna? You seem in such good spirits."

"Should I be worried? Do you have a history of failed attempts?"

"No." A laugh bubbled out of me, sounding only a little manic. "But this isn't something I've done a lot." I finished my water and put the glass in the sink. I was ready for the ambrosia that was coffee. "And Aunt Allison will be here. She's our pack medic."

He smiled, then sipped his own coffee. "Good, good. I like that woman. Everyone in the pack seems great."

There was a natural lull, and Stew went back to cooking as I headed off to change. I knew I'd need to scrub down again after the biting, but I wanted to clean off the sweat and grime of the barn. After a quick shower, I dressed in a UW-Madison sweatshirt and sweatpants.

My phone rang, and relief washed through me when I saw my sister's name. I answered it. "Jade!"

"Hiya, sis, everything okay?"

"I don't have a ton of time, but here's the situation." In as few words as I could, I filled her in on what I'd skipped over in our quick discussion the day before. I couldn't believe how much I'd missed and what all had happened until I started telling her.

"Gods above, Pebble, you've done so much. I'd heard some of the goings-on, but ... that's a lot." I blinked back tears at her words. Everyone had been supportive, but it was nice hearing her sympathy. There were few people I'd want that from, but Jade was high on the list. "Good job with running that meeting. And you're hiring two new people to the company today?" A small laugh bubbled from me at the thought of Luna being 'promoted.'

"Yeah, that's the plan." I hadn't told her about my connection with Luna. I figured the boys knew and that was good enough.

Jade snorted. "I still can't believe that for all these years I didn't have to strip for that aspect. Just think what else Luna may bring to your branch."

I groaned thinking about how I'd learned Luna was a shifter. She'd become a goose in front of me, without taking off her clothes. Apparently, that was another difference between shifters and wereanimals. When Jade found out, she was both thrilled and annoyed at the years she hadn't known. "Has Owen told work yet?"

Our brother worked for a secret branch of the government that worked with werewolves and shifter swans; it was how Jade had ended up with her third animal. He was the trainer.

"No, we're still deciding the best route. But that's for a later discussion. Back to you." My stomach twisted. "Do you remember when Owen got his second promotion?"

"I was too young. I had just been brought up from Joliet, not even adopted."

I could almost feel Jade's sigh. "Just remember, this isn't like a normal promotion, it has to be ... more. Like, *kill* them with kindness, if you know what I mean. This is an extreme interview."

Nodding, I rubbed my eyes. "So, more than normal, because they'll want to stay at their current position."

"Exactly!" Jade laughed. "This is almost fun. The other thing, Owen was out for over a day, healing and adjusting."

"Gods, once again, I wish you were here." I heard the whine in my voice. "Jade, can I do this? You know I spent the last dozen years focused on not biting." It wasn't until the words were out that I realized I hadn't shifted to code.

Her voice softened. "You are strong and amazing. Mom and Dad wouldn't have trusted you otherwise. I know today will be hard, but it should be hard. That said, you'll be amazing. Don't forget you'll have Dad to lean on, and Aunt Allison, and the others. Don't worry, sis, you're going to shine. Just be your brilliant self, okay?"

I sniffled, trying not to cry. Her words were exactly what I needed. "Got it."

"You've got this. And if you need more cheerleading, just call. I'll put you on video and have Owen do a routine."

The absurdity of the thought made me laugh. "Gods, thank you. I wish you were here. The candidates will want to know if they've received the new position ... you know, right away. And I won't be able to tell them, not before next week Tuesday with the full moon."

There was a pause. "You know, I've been talking with the others, and we've been planning. I may be able to come up next weekend. I'm not working because of the kiddos, who are amazing, by the way. I'll send some videos. But on the weekends, the boys dote over them. They feel they don't get enough time with them during the week. I could fly out Saturday, maybe stay until Monday."

I wanted to yell my excitement. "That would be ... Jade, I would love it if you could do that. I know it's not for a week, but I'd really appreciate it if you could carve out that time for me, if it's at all possible. Who knows, five days as top dog, so to speak, the company may be a chaotic mess. Or, you know, I may personally be perfecting my underwater basket weaving."

She laughed. "You know you can perfect anything you put your mind to. Of course, you'd need a pool to perfect that. And you'd need a love of weaving." We both laughed. "I'll text you later, sis. Love you lots."

"Love you, too."

Once the call ended, I slipped the phone into the sweatshirt pocket and headed to the bathroom to wash my face. I didn't need the others to see how emotional I'd been.

Back in the main area of the house, the others were at the kitchen table and island, eating. I took a plate from the pile, stacked two sandwiches on it, filled a mug with coffee, and took an empty seat at the island. It was my usual location, where I'd sat ever since I was big enough to imitate Jade and didn't have to join the table proper.

"So, will we be wolves by tonight?" Dayna asked my dad, her face alight with excitement. I shook my head when I realized, unlike Dad and Luna, there was a tinge of green around her.

Gods above, what's wrong with me. Is this about stress? Did I hit my head and don't remember?

Dad shot me a look—right, alpha. I silently thanked Jade for the call. "No. In all likelihood, you won't wake up until tomorrow."

Everyone gaped at me. The spicy scents of anger and frustration hit me first, then the undertone of minty confusion. I rubbed my nose before I sneezed. "This has all happened really fast. Part of what I wanted to do this morning was discuss everything with you."

Norman nodded. "It has been a mad dash to get here. Please, tell us what's going to happen."

Was that orange around him? I rubbed my eyes and decided I had to put whatever I was seeing into a box. Dad had a flight soon and needed to do a few things at work, so I'd call Bevin and ask him about it later. Now wasn't the time.

"If everyone in the room were just norms, you know, normal, simple, plain Jane, humans, all I would need to do is bite you. A bite doesn't guarantee you become a wolf. Not even a severe bite. However, the more of my saliva that mixes with the blood, the better the chances."

Years ago, Jade found the body of someone she thought was dead, mauled by a werewolf. She realized the person was alive, just really close to death. He also didn't have a seed of a wolf in him. *I can't imagine having her ability to be able to tell all those things. It's just fantastic!*

Luna looked like she was mentally taking notes. *Is this what she's like in class? What the professors see?* "So, you bite us, we bleed, then we're wolves. Anything else?"

"Yes." I sipped my coffee, thinking of the best way to answer her. "Have you ever noticed there really aren't many people who have two animals?"

Serena leaned forward. "I was wondering about this. I know about shifters and wereanimals, but the idea of having two animals ... that seems ludicrous. I figured we would try this thing, you would fail, and we could move on. But then you said your sister has two animals."

Dad coughed and I smiled. "We said she had more than one, we didn't say two."

Kelly's mouth dropped open. "She has more than two?"

Sipping my coffee, I nodded at her. "You may also recognize that we all heal fast. Our beasts help us heal."

Stew nodded. "That they do. It's a great side benefit to the bear."

I finished one of my sandwiches. "So, between my aunt being a healer and my ... sister. Well, we know a lot about the topic. The thing is, shifters and wereanimals don't want their humans to sustain any injury. If I'm going to change you, I need to inflict enough damage that your beast can't 'heal' the werewolf seed before it can take root."

Dayna blanched. "Could I die?"

"No. Well, not really. First of all, I won't go that far, second of all, we'll have a couple of healers here to help."

Serena nodded and I noticed she, too, seemed to have a bit of red around her. I clenched my jaw, not wanting to think about that. "You've really planned."

It took me a second to continue speaking. *Did she think we'd just maul her daughter and walk away as if this were our first time as a pack doing this? How primitive does she think we are?* "I've also asked a few extra pack members because not only will the current animal in residence try to heal the wolf away, they may try to stop me before the seed can be planted."

Luna rolled her eyes. "Are you afraid of me honking or biting you?"

I barked out a laugh at the ludicrousness of it. "No, not even a little. A bear, however, can knock me around like a rag doll. I've play fought with Dayna, and I'd rather have a bit of back-up if her bear decides she doesn't want to share."

A bit of color drained from Dayna's face, and the other adults nodded, their faces contemplative.

As the group continued to talk, I finished off my breakfast. The food filled me, but I still needed more. Between my wolf and the morning exercise, calories were a must. That said, I figured I'd eat more after we got Luna and Dayna into the medical wing ... down the hall, past the meeting room.

Just after eight, Aunt Allison showed up with Uncle Jackson and Tanner. We waited a few more minutes for Helen, the only non-wolf who would witness the brutality of the day, but she was a nurse. I asked Tanner to come and help with a possible wild bear. I had no idea how Dayna would react to being bitten. She may think she wanted this, but that didn't mean her bear wanted to share space.

I smiled up at all of them. "I didn't know you were coming, Uncle Jackson." The warmth of family filled me.

"Since River is heading out later today, I figured I'd help in any way you need me and help him pack the taxi when it comes to take him away."

"Wanna make sure I'm good and gone?" Dad teased him.

"Pretty much. Hazel called and said the pack down there is—" He gazed around the room. "She wants you down there. My sister never exaggerates."

Dad grunted. "That's the truth."

"Okay," I said, clapping my hands. "Let's get the stretchers and everyone outside. I want to get this over with quickly. It's cold." I stared at the two of them. "I think Luna should go first, then Dayna."

Luna narrowed her eyes. "Why not just do both of us together?"

"It's below freezing and to have the best chance of working I'm going to ask that you wear exercise shorts and a tank top. Undies would be even better. Also, watching someone get mauled by a wolf, knowing you're next, isn't always fun. Considering my wolf only has one mouth and I can only do this one at a time." I shrugged. "I figured this is what you two would want. But do whatever you think is best."

"Fine." She snapped, stalking to the dining room. "Let's get this over with." Her ire oozed from her.

Living with her is going to be great ... just great, I thought to myself. Not for the first time, I wondered why my wolf thought she would be my perfect mate.

I looked at the parents. "The bite hurts. Having a couple of extra adults to help in case she squirms and to help carry her in would be good. Tanner will help, but Norman, Kelly, if you two can be on standby as well, that would be perfect."

Stew stepped forward, and I held up a hand. "It's really hard to see your own child get hurt. You two can help when it's Dayna's turn."

Dayna looked at me, eyes wide. "Can I watch?"

I shook my head. "I wouldn't. It isn't pretty and this *is* something you want."

Everyone else knew what to do. They'd all been part of something like this before. In reality, I was the only one who was new, and I refused to let them see me tremble.

I headed out and stripped. *'Wolf.'* A sense of glee washed through me as my humanity was cocooned away and my wolf emerged. For the first time since I woke up, a sense of calm about biting two people enveloped me. My wolf knew what she was doing.

I trotted in a few circles in the backyard, stretching my legs. Tanner and Aunt Allison brought the stretcher out and put it in the yard near the house. Finally, Luna came out. She wore a tankini.

"Don't dilly-dally, Pebble, it's cold out here." My instant reaction to Luna's command was washed away by my wolf's amusement. *Maybe if I stay in wolf form, our relationship will work better.*

Dad squatted next to me, raking his fingers through my fur, and a part of me calmed—both from the touch of wolf, and the feel of the pet. "Remember, this is about speed. You need to get in, bite her five or six times, make sure the bites are deep, but do *not* eat the meat. That is really important, Pebble. I know we've discussed this, but it's doubly important when it's humans."

We'd been over all of this before but repeating it in animal form was part of the process. It helped remind the animal soul what we were doing. That said, my wolf scoffed at how silly it all sounded. She knew the rules and human meat sounded gross.

Luna laid down, and before she was fully settled, I darted in. I bit her thigh twice, and she gasped. Then I gnawed just above her hip. Finally, I switched sides and got her other hip. Despite being human, there was a bird-like flavor in my mouth. I could almost taste feathers.

At some point in the biting, she passed out.

It seemed like my wolf almost sighed in pleasure. At my inquiring push, she said, *A building can't stand when its supports are far away.* Served me right to expect anything more from her.

Dad came over with a bucket of water. I lapped some up and tried to spit it out. There was a second bucket that I drank from. I appreciated the forethought of multiple buckets.

A tremor ran down my spine at the thought of biting another human. Everything about what I was doing went against years of training.

I saw movement and looked up. Stew came out with a new stretcher. "Hi, Pebble, it's just me. Allison said you did a great job with Luna. She doesn't know if it worked, but you did exactly what you were supposed to do. You were right to keep me away ... all that blood. It was ... a lot."

I stared at him, wondering if he thought I would answer. "Yes, I know, Dayna is my niece. I think I'll let Tanner and your pack watch over her. I hate to admit it but watching her get attacked would probably trigger something in me, too." He placed the stretcher down. "You don't need an upset bear when what you're doing is what we asked you to do." He gave a lopsided smile and headed inside.

Tanner, Uncle Jackson, and Helen came out. I tilted my head.

Tanner chuckled. "You're biting a bear, kiddo. Even in human form, if she fights back, you'll need three of us. I just hope three will be enough."

Dayna walked out in an outfit similar to Luna's and waved. "Uncle Stew said he wasn't joining us. He worries he'll go all big bad bear." She looked at the three men near the stretcher and laughed. "This is something I want. I don't know why everyone is so worried. I promise I'll be as passive as a lamb. You'll barely even know I'm participating." She blanched a bit at Luna's blood. "Except for the clean-up."

She dropped down on the stretcher and relaxed.

I could see the tension leaving Dayna's body. Before I could second-guess myself, I clamped down on her thigh. As Dad's previous words played out in my mind, I didn't want to lose focus or take too much time. There was almost a furry mammal taste to her. *Is this the bear or the human? Am I making up the idea of these flavors because I know they have the other animals?*

She twisted and punched my head, knocking me away. I spit out a chunk that had remained in my mouth, shivering in disgust. *Did I get too much in my mouth? Will I turn rogue?*

A low growl came from her direction. I snapped my head up. Her eyes glowed brown.

All three men had her pinned.

"Hurry," Dad snarled, his wolf in his voice, "she's gone primal. She'll shift in a minute."

Head pounding, I slammed my teeth down, making sure my saliva mixed in, in the same places I'd bitten Luna before. I moved as fast as I could. Thankfully, my wolf worked with calm precision.

Unlike Luna, Dayna twisted and fought, kicking at me.

She threw Uncle Jackson. He landed under the tree house with a grunt. I lunged, biting down on her shoulder, trying to incapacitate her arm. This was no longer about becoming a wolf, it was about survival.

Suddenly, her eyes widened, and she began to tremble. "It's me, I'll stop." And then she passed out.

Slowly, I backed away. She was more mangled than planned. Not only did I get her thigh and stomach, Dayna's arm was hanging loose. Everything looked much worse than I'd expected. Bile filled my throat, and I hacked.

Helen did a quick triage right there in the backyard. "She'll be okay. You did a lot of damage, but you had to, she was fighting hard ... or her animal was. That was terrifying." Helen's voice wavered, but her hands were steady. Her face had lost all color. She wasn't one to come out when we did anything in animal form or ask questions. This was probably more of the violent side than she was used to seeing.

Dad brought me the two buckets of water. I trembled as I washed my mouth out. Dad's arm encircled me. "You did great, Applesauce. I'm proud of you."

He had to help with the others, so after a few seconds he headed off to help Tanner carry Dayna away. Helen gave orders to keep her level as she tried to bandage the worst injuries.

I turned to Uncle Jackson, but Aunt Allison beat me to it. She ran to him as he sat up, chuckling. "That girl is strong. Are we sure she's not the next alpha strength wolf? Wow, I haven't been thrown like that since I used to fight with Hazel."

Once I knew he was okay, I called on my humanity and dressed, ready to shower and forget this experience had happened.

Inside, the house was somber, everyone unsure what to do next. I wanted my second shower to be as fast as the first, but I had to scrub to make sure all the blood was off me. Gazing at it, I shivered despite the heat of the water. No one had died, but as I looked at my feet, the pink swirls looked like a crime scene.

I rested my head on the shower wall, willing my body to relax. As I let down my guard, my hold on the rest of the pack fell. Stress surged through me. First it was Clare. A spike of worry embedded in my brain. As I focused on her, I realized she was at work, and it wasn't anything I had to worry about. Easton, too, sent waves of anxiety through our bonds. But Tanner was calm. If it were a pack emergency, he'd call his dad in.

My heart beat faster as Piper, Julez, Greg, even Andy had high emotions. Each of them sending signals my mind and body wanted to react to. Whimpering caught my attention ... who was suffering? Someone was hurt.

With an effort, I forced the walls back up. I had to figure out who needed me. *Is it someone close? Can I send Aunt Allison to help?*

As the pressure in my mind released, the sounds of distress increased. A tapping on the wall alerted me and my eyes snapped open. My body trembled. My fingernails beat a rhythm against the tile, a counterpoint to the near sobs. My sounds of distress.

Breathing slowly, I grabbed the shampoo and massaged it into my hair. The biting was over. My control was back. Everything would be okay.

It took a few soapings before everything rinsed clear. Once out of the shower and dry, I put on warm clothes, this time ready to keep them on for the rest of the day.

Back in the main room, Aunt Allison gazed at me intently, a yellow glow about her. "Both young women are doing great. I don't know when they'll wake up, but their bodies are healing. I have high hopes that next week during the full moon we'll have good news."

"Actually," I said, smiling, "Jade may come this weekend to help us learn sooner."

Dad narrowed his eyes. "With the babies? If she comes with my grandbabies and I'm not here—"

"No." I held up my hands. "Just her, maybe Brooke. The boys want some time to spoil the kids. They think Jade has all the fun since she's off work."

He chuckled. "That sounds like them. Okay, they all survive ... for now."

Aunt Allison beamed. "Well, that will make all of this much easier. We can wait until she gets here to confirm your brilliance." She came over and gave me a big hug. She whispered in my ear, so soft I didn't think the others could hear, "Are you okay?"

As a submissive, she could feel my emotions. She would've known about my breakdown in the shower. I nodded. "Yeah, I think so."

"Okay, but let's talk ... soon."

It didn't sound like I had a choice, but I loved spending time with her. "Love to."

She squeezed me again. I hadn't realized until that moment how much I needed it. Touch of family, of pack, and of a submissive wolf. It all helped me to feel centered. On top of it all, her confidence in me felt great.

Dad kissed my forehead. "Okay, Applesauce. I'm off to work for an hour, then I'm catching my plane. You'll be great ... you've *been* great. Heck, you are great!. You've done an amazing job so far. We'll keep in touch."

This was it. He was leaving. I wrapped my arms around him. "Love you, Dad."

He squeezed me back, tight enough to last weeks. "Love you, too."

Chapter 12 – A Gift From Down South

Through the living room window, I watched as Dad disappeared down the driveway. An arm wrapped around my shoulders, and I rested against Uncle Jackson. He leaned into me. "You're doing a wonderful job as alpha. I know this came on earlier than expected, but my sister put her trust in the right kid."

"Thanks. I already miss them both." I knew I had to be strong, but this was my uncle. If I could be a kid with anyone, it was him.

He kissed my head. "I know, but we all believe in you. Anytime you need us, just call."

Closing my eyes, I rested my head on his chest and took strength from him. I may have been his alpha, but he was my uncle, and he'd always support me. I wasn't alone. There were people closer than California who were willing and able to help.

I took a deep breath. "Okay, I'm good. I need to go check on my new pack mates."

He didn't release his hold. "You know they're going to be healing for the rest of the day, well into the night. If it's like Owen's experience, they won't wake until tomorrow. Allison is here, I'm here, their parents are here. There's nothing you can do."

"I know, and believe it or not, I have plans for tonight. I'm going out with Hollis. First, I'll have to explain to the parents why my being away isn't the end of the world, but then for one night, I can be a regular teen. Think of it, I can spend a few hours with her before returning to be the alpha and trainer for the remainder of winter break."

Uncle Jackson's hug got a little tighter. "I'm glad. You need to be a teen for a night ... maybe more. You know you don't have to be 'on' all the time. Now, get away from here, hang out with your friend. You have your cover story for Hollis. Everything should be a blast."

Dad finally disappeared from sight. I rotated and gave Uncle Jackson a proper hug. "Thanks, I needed to hear that before I faced the gauntlet."

He smiled, letting me know I had his support.

Slipping away, I headed to the medical room. Aunt Allison moved around, making sure Luna and Dayna were comfortable. They each had an IV attached to them, getting what I assumed was only fluids, though I wasn't sure. Serena and Norman sat in the two guest seats. Stew leaned against the wall by Luna's bed, Kelly next to Dayna's. The room wasn't big enough for this many people.

"Aunt Allison, do you think you'll be using any more of the equipment from this room?" I stood in the doorway. There wasn't even enough room for me to step in.

She turned and smiled. "Probably not. We brought the two ladies here because of the blood and their need for fluids. I don't want them to get dehydrated. Dayna was in a bit more need than Luna." Her words made me wince, though I tried to hide it. "I gave her a few stitches, but they're both past medical needs. My guess is the stitches will need to be removed before midnight ... maybe sooner. I'll maintain the saline throughout the day, but that's easily done."

"Since it's just us in the house, could we move them to the living room? I think it would be more comfortable for everyone."

Aunt Allison tilted her head. "That's not a bad idea. With five people worrying over them, seven if you include you and Jackson, this room is ready to burst."

I rubbed the back of my neck as I thought about the logistics. "Okay, I think Tanner is still here. I'll get him and Uncle Jackson to help with the move."

Stew shook his head. "There are six of us here now, isn't that enough?"

I considered everyone. "Yes, if there are two people on each end of the beds, we can move them. We are all strong enough." Everyone started to move. "However ..." They all paused. "If anyone doesn't hold the bed perfectly flat, Luna or Dayna could slide. I'd prefer extra hands to be there to make sure everyone stays where they're supposed to be."

Before they could argue, I headed out to find the other two men. It didn't take long to move the beds. As soon as we were all sitting on couches and recliners in the living room, Tanner took his leave. He wanted to spend the afternoon with his wife.

Gazing at all the stressed faces, I made an executive decision. "I'm going to order some food. Does anyone have something they'd prefer, or is pizza okay?"

Serena made a face but shrugged.

Stew, watching his wife, said, "Is there any decent Mexican food around here?"

"Yeah, I can order that. Before I do that, though, I have something I want to discuss with all of you."

A weight filled the room. Kelly slid a hand over to Norman's, then asked, "Is everything okay?"

I winced, realizing I could've worded that better. "Yes, it isn't that big a deal. Luna and Dayna are going to be healing for at least twelve hours. I've been ... going, for a few days. When they wake up, I'll be training them in the ways of the wolves."

A small smile played across Kelly's face. "You're going out tonight, aren't you? You want the night off to be a teen."

I slumped a bit. "Yes I am, and yes I do." I tensed, worried about their reactions. "But not until later. I figure I'll have lunch with all of you and leave in the early evening."

Stew gave me a small smile. "As long as we have your number and can call you back if things change, I think that's a great idea. Allison said she'd stay tonight to monitor them. You don't know medicine, so you really can't help. Go, enjoy your night off."

As hard as I tried to keep a blank face, I knew I smiled at them goofily. "Thank you. I'll get the food, and we can discuss what happens next."

"No." Uncle Jackson pushed me towards the door. "We can handle that, we're all adults, and I know about the food around here just as well as you do." There was a chorus of laughter in the room. "You can take a few hours off. I'm sure Hollis won't mind you being early."

A lightness filled me as the door clicked shut. I hadn't expected to be kicked out of my own house, but their reactions were amusing. First on my list was texting Hollis. It was cold, so I got into the Subaru Impreza and belted in as another car pulled up in the driveway. The light blue Toyota stopped a few feet behind my car and a young man, probably about my age, got out. I didn't think he noticed me sitting in the Subaru.

He had short, dark brown hair, and dark eyes, close to black. He wore a navy-blue button-down shirt over light khaki pants. He shut the door and turned, gazing around the property as if assessing the pack house's value. When he stopped rotating, he pulled out a phone as if trying to get his bearings. Before I remembered to ignore whatever had been going on, I saw a bit of green glowing tightly around him.

A moment later, I got a text from Mom, stopping me from agonizing over whatever it was that was wrong with me. *Pebble, I forgot to tell you, and this is important. Tilly and Rory, the alphas from Florida, said that their son is coming to visit.*

I looked at the teen again, deciding he may be who Mom spoke of. Huffing out a laugh, I texted her back. *Okay. Coming as in he's here?*

There was a moment while I watched the indicator that Mom typed. *Right. It's a bit of a story, but I'll let Conner explain. Do you have time?*

I sighed and got out of the car.

The guy jerked to look at me. "Whoa, I didn't see you there."

"Conner, right?" He had to be. He smelled like a wolf. The wind blew away from us, but I could still just make it out. And how many wolves would pop up here out of nowhere?

He slowly nodded, then looked down at his phone. "Yeah, and you're Pebble? My parents told me about you. You and Jade and Owen."

I wish my parents had told me about you. I tried not to show my frustration. Lifting my hand to shake, I said, "Mom told me you'd explain your sudden visit?"

"Oh. I thought you knew. I've been planning to transfer to UW-Madison for some time. They have the best engineering program around. Didn't they tell you?"

I squeezed my eyes shut for a moment. "It's been ... well, it's been a bit crazy around here. After Christmas, I went on a school field trip, which went until New Years. Then there was the Tennessee thing ... do you know about that?"

He shook his head. "I've been on the road since New Year's. I spent the night hanging out with my friends, then started my drive up here. I left on the second. I know it's only a two-day drive, but I stopped at a few places to see the sights." He sounded relaxed but his eyes had an intensity about them after I'd mentioned Tennessee.

I shook my head, trying to get my thoughts in order. "Okay, so, you're transferring to Madison. Are you staying in the dorms?"

"Yeah, but I was hoping to have a room here, too. I want to switch packs, at least for the next four to six years

... you know, until I graduate." He gave me a sheepish grin, which was completely charming.

"How long have you been a wolf?"

He ducked down. "December was my first shift."

Gods above, my pack will be getting a fourth new wolf since September, three in the span of a couple of days. "Okay. Before we go in, I need to tell you what you're going to find in there. It's ... well, it's a bit of a shock if you're not prepared."

As I spoke, his eyes widened. "They both will have two animals?" He shook his head. "And they're in the living room now, healing?" I just nodded, waiting for him to work it all out. "Wait, and you're the alpha?"

And there it was. "That I am."

"But you're my age."

"It's not unheard of. Do you still want to join?"

"I do, if you'll have me."

"Let's head in."

We walked in. I found everyone still in the living room. I narrowed my eyes. "What happened to Mexican food?"

Aunt Allison smiled. "I could feel your need for time. Well, no, your confusion, really. When I checked on you, I saw you speaking with—" She broke off, lifting her eyebrows in an opening for me to finish.

"Conner. This is Tilly and Rory's son. He is transferring to Madison for their engineering program. He had his first shift in December and wants to join the pack."

Uncle Jackson stood. "Fantastic. Have you brought him in yet?"

"Not yet, I thought I'd let him check out the house, get him a room. Then I'd welcome him in."

Serena sat forward. "Is the ceremony private?"

Conner beamed. "Now, this one I can answer. I've seen my parents do it before. No, you can watch if you want. It's pretty anticlimactic."

Stew leaned back and crossed his legs. It was the most relaxed I'd seen him since Luna had been bitten. "Then give us a show, Pebble. I assume this will be something you'll do with both the girls once they come to."

"Yeah, that's the plan. A whole slew of new wolves. A winter break of training." I shrugged. "What else does an alpha want to do on their time off?"

Conner gazed around the room. "I'm really good with training. I can help if you want. My parents always said I was a calming force in the family. They weren't happy that I was leaving the pack, but they understood my reasoning."

I narrowed my eyes at him when he said 'calming force.' Then I shot Aunt Allison a look. Her eyes were wide as she stared at the newcomer. "What exactly do you mean? Was it just a turn of phrase or did you actually calm people around you?"

He shrugged. "I don't know. The rest of the pack sometimes said they liked hanging out with me after stressful days. Said it was like walking in the woods, drinking tea, or taking a bath."

Leaning in, I sniffed. He smelled of sweat and his travels, and wolf, but there was an underlying scent of eucalyptus trees. It was soothing, maybe an undertone of citrus tea. I felt the muscles along my shoulders relax. It was a similar sensation to when Jade was around.

I pulled Conner to one of the open couches. "Sit with me for a few moments."

His eyes lit up. "Of course. Are you going to tell me why I'm weird?"

"Because you're a teen werewolf." My answer was instant, and the adults chuckled. I thought my aunt and uncle knew what I was suspecting, though the others probably had no idea. "As for the rest of it, maybe. I don't know how though. This seems impossible."

"What?" he asked, a laugh in his voice, a smile on his face. The citrus scent told me he was having fun.

"Let's start at the top. You said you just turned furry a few weeks ago."

"Yes."

"When you close your eyes, can you see your wolf? Speak with him?"

Instead of closing his eyes, his eyes widened. "Oh, my gods! Yes! Whenever I talked to anyone about that, they thought I was bonkers. I quickly learned to hide that ability. Mom and Dad suggested I wait a few days before bringing it up here. Can you do that?"

I shook my head. "No, I can't, but my sister can. It's an ability only a few werewolves have."

"That's so cool. So I'm not broken?"

"No. I'm guessing you're what we call an epsilon wolf."

His mouth dropped open. "No way. Really? The mythical epsilon?"

"Yep. And lucky for you, Jade is coming this weekend, and she can help you figure out some of this, but I also have a book in my room you should read. But first, let's get you a room."

He reached out for my arm. "Can you bring me into the pack first? I'd really like to be formally part of a pack that recognized me for what I am in like, minutes. That was fantastic."

Reaching up, I placed the heel of my hand on his forehead, letting my fingers drape over the crown of his head. My wolf whispered his name to me. "Conner Sebastian Wall, welcome to the Wisconsin pack."

I braced myself for the onslaught of his emotions and being in my mindscape. With the number of wolves I had, it wasn't as bad as the first wolf I'd picked up. Once I was able to concentrate on the room again, I winked at Conner who looked thrilled.

Standing, I spun towards the family wing. "Okay, I'm going to go get a room set up for you."

Uncle Jackson stood as well. "I'll help. Which room?"

"The one on the other side of Jade's. It's free and won't take much to get ready for a long-term guest or, possibly," I cut my eyes to Conner, "a permanent guest."

Conner leapt up. "I can help, too."

Aunt Allison patted the seat next to her. "Why don't you come speak with me? I'm one of the submissive wolves."

I could feel Conner's indecision. "It's okay, the room won't take too long. Talk with Aunt Allison. She's a good person to know."

As we headed down the hall, I heard her say, "So, engineering. Have you ever thought about medicine?"

Chapter 13 – The Flip Side

After Uncle Jackson and I got the room together, I sent a quick text to Jade, updating her on what she'd be doing this weekend. *Who knew our teasing you to write a training manual would be a real thing?*

It didn't take long for her to reply. *I can't believe there's another E in the world. I don't know if I feel put out that I'm not unique or thrilled to have someone to compare notes with. I'll have to spend some time this week thinking about where to start with Conner. It's been so long.*

That made me laugh. *Don't let the others hear you say that. They'll knock sense into you faster than you can run. I think this is amazing. I wonder how this is even possible. How are there two of you?*

The phone went silent, and I walked to the kitchen. There was food from a local Mexican restaurant, so I made a plate with tacos, rice, and beans. I sat at the counter, enjoying a few minutes of solitude.

Jade's reply finally came. *E isn't that unique. I'm glad there's another staff member there I can talk to. But less than a month out. You're right. I'll start writing some notes.*

Conner came into the kitchen, and I smiled up at him. "Are you hungry? Or do you want to see your room?"

"Room first. Allison showed me around the den, it's fantastic. It's so big. You have everything here."

A sense of pride filled me. I knew the California home was bigger, had more, but they'd built their den to be a place for all their pack members. Our home could house more than the family, but our town wasn't so expensive or big that people couldn't find standalone homes nearby.

"Not everything—we don't have a pool—but I love it, too."

He laughed. "I don't think I'd want to swim during a blizzard."

With a wink, I stood. "I don't know, the polar plunge is all the rage around here." His eyes bulged as I started to show him the family hall, and the room he'd be using.

"This is great. And next week I'll be able to run with the pack. I guess I'll be meeting everyone then." He bit his lower lip.

I shut my eyes. "I may be calling a pack meeting on Sunday. My sister is coming to town and I'm guessing everyone will want to see her. Not to mention the outcome of Dayna and Luna's bites. Now there's you. That's three items. That seems meeting worthy."

"A whole meeting? Isn't that extreme?" He sat on his bed hard.

I shrugged. "We have a lot of meetings here. It's an excuse to come together, socialize, and eat. I don't know what it was like down in Florida, but we're a social lot. *And* we may be a lot." I waggled my eyebrows at him.

A smile tugged at the side of his mouth. "Mom always wanted something like that, but the rest of the pack seemed to balk. It's interesting seeing how different packs run."

"I don't know that we've ever given the pack a choice. If they didn't like it, they could opt out ... of the pack that is. We want to make sure communication is always very transparent."

"I like it." He gazed around the room. It was pretty basic: a bed, dresser, desk, and small table for a lamp and to charge a phone. "How much freedom do I have in here to change things?"

"Ask Aunt Allison or Uncle Jackson where the hardware store is. You can paint, put up shelves. We have good Wi-Fi. Beyond that, talk with me first, but this is your room."

"Any color I want?"

The room had been Brooke's when she'd been training. In the time she'd spent living here, she'd painted the walls pink.

"Are you saying you don't like the color of the walls? Bubble gum isn't ... you?"

Amusement colored his expression. "I was thinking of a green with a dark gray on one wall. If I can paint the furniture, I'd like to cover the white with a light gray with black trim."

"Sounds good to me. We can always repaint later if we want. This is your domain, friend. Enjoy. And if you play your cards right, you'll even have some help."

"Great. Is there a reason you can't show me where things are, oh fearless leader?"

"Yep, I'm off to see a friend. We have plans." I checked my watch and saw it was almost five. Conner's visit ate away most of my 'seeing Hollis early' time. I didn't mind because meeting him had been fun. "I'm off for the night to be a teen sans wolf. Remember those days from your far-off past? But don't worry, I'll be here in the morning when you wake up. Let me get that book for you so you can start reading it. It'll give you something to obsess over ... trust me."

His eyes practically glowed at that. "Sounds great. Have fun tonight, Pebble. See you in the morning." He bit his lip. "And thanks. I'm really excited to be here. I was a bit worried heading up ... and then when I realized you were the alpha I had a moment of panic, but ... everything's going to be good, I can tell."

After I delivered the book, I found the others back in the living room. I hugged my aunt and uncle, and once again headed out. This time, I got to text Hollis I'd be early and managed to turn the car on and leave. No interruptions.

A giddy thrill surged through me as I drove down the driveway and headed to her house. *Tonight is going to be epic!*

When I pulled up in front of my friend's house, she waited on her porch, her blue and purple hair making her look like a frozen statue on the steps. She ran to the car and slipped in. "I am so glad you came early. About an hour ago, I debated calling or texting, but then my Dad and I started in on our 'discussion,' again. Gah! It just wouldn't end."

"Was it that, 'majoring in languages—not even linguistics—won't get you very far in life, Hollis, you need to think about your future.' or 'I have nothing against lesbians, Hollis, but I worry about your future, what if you want a family and kids, you're the best thing that's happened to me and mom,' discussion."

Hollis's head dropped back, and she groaned. "The second. Fern called and is going to come for a week to visit. They should be here tomorrow. We've been going round and round about it." As exciting as I thought that bit of news was, Hollis sighed. "They'll stay in the guest room, so it isn't like there's any issue, but it's like Dad needs to get all his objections out before Fern gets here."

I slapped Hollis on the arm. "When were you going to tell me about Fern? How long have you known?"

Hollis sat up, a smile taking over her face. Her scent shifted from a cayenne and mint combo—disgust and frustration—to citrus. She was excited. "Fern and I have been talking. They finally figured out a time with their parents that they could make it up here. At first, right after Christmas, their Dad was like, no way. But then on Friday, he *finally* relented. Fern said something came up at home and he actually agreed to them coming, insisted even. It was weird, I don't know. I don't understand any parents, they're all completely weird, if you ask me. You and I haven't had much time to talk in the last few days, and it was after our night out together on New Year's Eve."

"Fine, you survive ... this time." I navigated the streets, heading to campus. We hadn't discussed what we'd do, but Memorial Union had food and bowling as well as music. It gave us options, all in one spot.

She laughed. "What about you? Your dad left. Home alone? Will you be lonely?"

The idea that I'd be alone just about broke my head. I forgot I hadn't told Hollis about all the guests invading our territory. "Actually, my house is full right now. We have some family guests—"

"You have guests, and you made plans with me?"

By some miracle, I found a parking spot in the small lot. "Well, my Aunt Allison and Uncle Jackson are back home entertaining. It doesn't always have to be the punk teen, you know. They practically tossed me out on my butt."

That got Hollis to relax, chuckling as we headed into the union. "That annoying, huh? I mean, I get it. I've lived with you for a full semester, Stone."

There wasn't a long line to order burgers and fries. We added a side of cheese curds to share. At the table, I asked, "How is Fern? I haven't spoken to them since we left after finals. My winter break has been ... unexpected."

"Tell me about it. Your parents left you and now guests. How long are they staying?"

I ate some of the fried cheese, relishing the flavor and outside crunch of the melty cheese. It was so good. "It's unclear. Actually, another one just appeared on the doorstep today." Mouth full of fries, Hollis lifted an eyebrow to tell me to continue. "One of my mom's best friends' son from Florida just transferred up to Madison."

"Wait, your cousin's uncle's neighbor's brother's dog's owner? Really?" She shook her head. "What does that make us?" I laughed. "But, really, if you have this guy at home who's our age, why didn't you bring him? He's new to our campus, we could've shown him around."

This was why I loved Hollis. She would've rolled with just about anything. "He just drove up today. My aunt was also one of his mom's friends, so she wanted to spend time with him."

"Okay, you pass this time, but Wednesday, we should go out again. That way we can meet this person, you can see Fern, and we can ... maybe roller skate? I need to be active."

"I'll let you know. But there's a good chance that's a yes." I figured that Dayna and Luna would be sick of me after a day and a half of training. Well, at least Luna would be. She was always good at school, but I didn't think she'd love me teaching her. In all honesty, they'd probably relish some time to get away from me, but I didn't want to finalize plans before I spoke with them. I finished up my burger. "How's your mom?"

Hollis ate through her fries. "Good. She loves Fern. She tries to help when I argue with Dad, but that just makes him harder to reason with, so she lets me do my own thing. We've discussed this over ice cream."

I moaned. "Ice cream. We should get some ice cream."

Hollis laughed. "You are so easy. We just ate a huge meal. How about we bowl first?"

I sighed dramatically. "If we must."

With a wicked grin, Hollis added, "Loser pays!"

For the first time since my parents left, my body relaxed. I really needed a night to be a college coed, and Hollis knew how to bring me back to me.

Chapter 14 – Back To The Beginning

When I rolled over and looked at the clock, it was just after five in the morning. With the list of things I wanted to accomplish, I forced myself to get up and start the day. I changed into exercise clothes, then slogged to the living room. The couches were occupied by sleeping parents.

Trying to be quiet, I went to check on Luna. Her eyes were open. A quick scan of what I could see looked good. She was under covers, so her being awake precluded any checking of injuries.

She pushed herself up. "Why?" Her voice sounded like it came through an airhorn in the quiet of the house. My finger snapped to my mouth and my other hand shot out in a stop sign towards her. She immediately looked around the room and nodded. She started over, quieter. "Why am I in the living room?"

I matched her quiet tone. "It's Tuesday, early, but still Tuesday." Her eyes widened. "We wanted a comfortable spot for everyone to be able to monitor you and Dayna."

On the next cot, Dayna moaned. She spoke as quietly as we did. "It's about time someone woke up. Please tell me there's coffee."

"Not yet, but there can be. I can go get it started." I pointed down the hall. "Bathroom's that way."

Before leaving them, I made sure they could stand and move without toppling over. They both headed in the direction I had pointed and only then did I walk to the kitchen. Someone had prepped the coffee maker, so all I had to do was turn it on.

I dug in the freezer and found frozen waffles. After putting some in the toaster oven, I got out syrup and scrambled a bunch of eggs with diced ham and cheese.

When Luna returned from the bathroom, she poured some coffee and sat at the table. It didn't take long for the food to be done. By the time her plate was ready, Dayna was sitting next to her, sipping from her own mug.

Luna sighed. "Frozen waffles? We've been eating so well."

"I figured you two would be hungry. I want to get to the gym and exercise before everyone is up and expecting something from me. You're welcome to make anything else you want ... the kitchen is a free space."

Though I half-expected some sort of negative comment, Luna just stared at me blankly before she dug in.

Dayna started eating. "Gods above, I'm hungry."

"In theory, you have two animals now. You think you ate a lot before, but things are going to be way more intense now."

She leaned back and gaped at me. "I hadn't even considered that. So, does that mean you think it worked?"

"I have no idea. You could be hungry because you just woke up after being out of it for almost a full day and it's just your bear making you aware of her."

Dayna nodded. "Right. That makes sense. Okay, eat, exercise, shower, clean clothes."

I rubbed my face. "You want to exercise this morning?"

Her shoulder bobbed slightly. "I figured it was a pack thing. I mean, I don't have a book with a plan, not yet, but I can probably figure something out. My degree *is* in kinesthetics and high school physical education." She took another bite. "Well, that or biology. You know, decisions to make." She laughed. "Since your dad isn't here, I thought I might try to upkeep any of the plans that start to run out of details."

I grinned at her. "I don't know if I should be thrilled that the pack will continue to be strong, or resentful for not getting time off for good behavior."

Dayna smiled, and Luna sneered. "You are way too peppy. Why don't you go, and we'll meet you over at the gym when we're more—" She waved her hand at me, probably indicating my awake-ness, but didn't finish her thought.

Knowing I had a busy day ahead of me, I only did a quick ten-minute run before switching to strength training. It was a legs day, so I focused on squats, lunges, and leg raises. I interspersed my static training with active movement. After forty-five minutes, I dripped with sweat. Drinking from my water bottle, I wiped my face and then filled out my log-book.

I heard motions on the steps, and then Luna and Dayna showed up. "Hi, I'm about to go and shower. You two are welcome to enjoy the facilities."

Luna eyed me suspiciously. "Do you have some guidelines?"

"Not really. I ran and focused on my lower half, but you are welcome to do what you want. In the rooms, we have yoga, pilates, and tai-chi videos. If you are curious, you can look through the books; they're on the table. There are probably old books in the drawers, but since they're created for each person, that may not help very much." I turned to leave, but when I got to the stairs, I swung back. "We do have some basic werewolf training I want to start today, so don't overdo it."

After that, I returned to the kitchen, poured some coffee, and carried it to my room as I prepared for the day: shower and clean clothes.

After my shower, I saw I had a text from Trista. *Hi. I was wondering if you'd have time tonight. I'm a bit out of sorts. Thought we could hang out, talk.*

I flopped onto my bed, unsure what to say to her. As her alpha, I knew I should say 'yes.' If she needed some time to decompress and talk with me, that was part of my job. It was also Aunt Allison's job, or Andy's, or Chris's. But Trista didn't know them that well, at least not yet. That was one of my plans for after the next pack meeting on Sunday: get the submissive wolves and the new wolves connected.

Which reminded me ... I needed to send out an email to the pack about the meeting on Sunday. Too many things were coming up to not inform everyone.

I rubbed my temples. Food. Dayna and Luna's parents, who were leaving. Conner. *Gods above, how could I forget our newest pack member?*

I pushed myself up and headed to the kitchen. Making a mental list wasn't helping. *Why didn't I grab a notebook yet?* The only hope was to get some items completed, then actually write down the list. My mind spun with everything I had to do. No wonder my parents always seemed so distracted and busy.

The living room was empty. I assumed the adults had all headed up to get ready for the day, or sleep in a more comfortable bed. Since their daughters were awake, I leaned more towards the first. In the kitchen, Conner sat at the counter.

He turned, his face aglow with his cheer for the day. "Morning, sleepy-head."

I snorted. "I've woken up, cooked, exercised, then showered. I'm not sure the title fits."

One of his eyebrows shot up. "Well, okay then. Maybe *I'm* the sleepy-head, though I've never thought of eight as late before."

I chuckled. "Did you get something to eat? Are you thirsty?"

"I had a banana and toast. I'm good for now." His head tilted. "I was hoping to talk to you about the epsilon stuff. I know your sister will be here this weekend ... I just—what can you tell me?"

After filling my coffee, I stood across from him. "That may be enough, but you should start eating more. As for the epsilon stuff, well, I can tell you some of the things Jade can do."

"That would be great." His face lit up, and I needed sunglasses.

"Let's start with the internal stuff. You said you can talk with your wolf. Jade created a kind of mental landscape. In hers, she has a kind of camp scene, with woods, a fake fire, a cabin, and a pond out back. It gives her a place to go to talk to her animals. She can also pull other people in with her."

Conner's eyes widened. "Do you think I could do that?"

"I don't know. Why don't we go sit at the table, or in the living room? It's more comfortable there."

We ended up on a couch. Conner closed his eyes and breathed slowly. The scent of eucalyptus and citrus tea filled the area around him. A feeling of sitting on a warm beach by the ocean. A calm filled me, and I sank into the couch with a low moan.

After a few minutes, a smile blossomed on his face. "This is really cool." He waved his hand over his thigh. "Can you hold my hand?"

Dayna and Luna walked through the kitchen to the stairs. They looked over at the two of us, but I waved them off. With an indifferent shrug, Luna dashed up the stairs, barely making a sound. Dayna looked like she wanted to ask a question, but after a moment, followed her cousin.

Once they were gone, I placed my hand in Conners and closed my eyes. At first, nothing happened, then I felt a tickle travel up my arm. Then I was in paradise.

I gaped as I stood on a beach overlooking an ocean. Turning slowly I saw palm trees surrounding me and a raised square house on stilts off in the distance. Behind me, Conner stood, a huge smile taking up his face. A large black wolf with white paws and white tipped ears stood next to him. My gray wolf yipped and ran over to touch noses.

Conner laughed. "I ... this is amazing. I don't even know what to say or think about this. It gives me a place to think and learn. It's ... thank you, Pebble."

"Don't thank me yet. When I start using you to talk to my wolf, figure out what she's trying to tell me, you'll start to regret it. We'll see how long before you tuck tail and run back to Florida."

He laughed. "I can't imagine ever being annoyed with any of this. It's all amazing. And from everything I know about you ... you know, like all twelve or so hours, I'm totally in." He knelt in front of my wolf. "Are you being cryptic? Trying to confuse my alpha?" His mouth dropped open. "She says she is my alpha, and if you'd listen, you wouldn't be confused."

It was too much. I threw my head back and laughed. "Okay, all of this takes a lot of your energy. I'm guessing you didn't eat enough to hold me in here for long. Let's separate and get some food for you before you pass out."

His hands began to tremble as the shimmery vacuum sensation of moving back into my body washed through me. His eyes opened slowly, and he shook his head. "Did that ... Pebble? Did that really happen?"

"Yes, and now you need to eat."

This time, I knew I was feeding more people. I put three pounds of bacon on two trays into the oven. I prepped more scrambled eggs. Then I started on toast, coffee, and fruit. All of that should be enough to tide people over until at least mid-morning.

As I cooked, Conner sat and kept me company. "I don't think I'm as bad off as you say I am."

I gave him a flat look. "You were trembling in your mindscape. Are you telling me that you suddenly got energy from the air?" I continued to stare until he squirmed.

He pulled his hands from under his legs. "You saw that?"

"Look, I spent a lot of time seeing or hearing about my sister passing out because she pushed herself too hard while learning all the nifty things an epsilon can do. I know you want to know everything, experience everything, but, Conner, I want it all to be done safely."

He sighed. "Fair enough."

"Good. No more trying to hide things from me."

"Does that mean we're done with new skills for the day?"

My smile stretched across my face in an instant. "No. There are one or two other skills I'd love to see if you have. If you do ... well, that will just make life grand."

He narrowed his eyes, but didn't ask any more questions. And when I gave him food to eat, he ate it.

I wasn't sure if everyone came down because they were ready, or if it was the smell of bacon, but as I pulled it from the oven, the kitchen filled with people.

Luna entered first. "Who's he?" As tactful as always.

I opened my mouth to answer, but Conner beat me to it. "Hi, I'm Conner. I just moved up here from Florida. My parents were friends of Pebble's parents, as well as

Allison's in college." He went on to give a bit of his background.

Sitting back, Luna eyed me. "So, you're taking on more strays? Is he joining the training sessions?"

It was like our group projects all over again. Could she ever be pleasant? I already missed the hours of her unconsciousness. "Actually, he offered to help *with* the training. He's a child of werewolf alphas, he knows a lot about packs and werewolves. He may not know the specifics of this pack, but he knows the broad strokes."

Dayna leaned forward. "But there's more, isn't there? You were doing something with him this morning ... something weird. Was it training we'll be doing, too?"

Serena waved a piece of bacon, pointing at Conner. "It's that epsilon thing you mentioned last night, right? Is that what you were training?"

No one in the room reacted to the word 'epsilon.' Some non-wolves had heard about the elusive epsilon wolf and knew what they were, but apparently not this group. "No and yes. No, it won't be something I'm showing the two of you." I waved my fork towards Luna and Dayna. "Yes, because it was an epsilon thing. There are a few skills an epsilon has that other wolves don't. It isn't really known by many, wolf or otherwise. There isn't a book or manual of any kind ... yet. Over the last dozen years, my sister has been figuring out what she can do." I looked at each of them in turn. "She's the only other known epsilon out there. She left when I was pretty young. I don't know everything, but the bigger things I've seen or heard about."

"Like what?" Luna snapped.

My jaw clamped for a moment before I said, "Well, that's part of what we want to figure out. Are the things universal for epsilons or special for Jade. I want to take this slowly."

Luna continued to glare at me. With a huff, I went over to whisper in Connor's ear what I wanted him to do. I only chanced doing this because he had a plate full of food sitting in front of him and had already cleaned off another one. When I was done, I returned to my seat and braced myself.

This was Jade's specialty. She'd honed it to a scary degree. She could not only aim where her power went but to what extent it hit. When she used it, it wouldn't blanket … everywhere. With Conner, if he could figure it out, we'd all feel the effects.

Conner closed his eyes and took a deep breath.

Luna scoffed. "For goodness sakes, he isn't even doing anything. Is this great new ability the power of meditation? My gods, look at that," she waved her hand towards him, "it's like watching the most boring thing ever. He's just sitting there."

During her rant, I could feel the pressure and stress building within Conner. He worried it wouldn't work.

With his exhalation, a wave released from him. He'd pushed out a huge punch of epsilon calm. I hadn't even thought to tell him to moderate his level. Yawning, I picked up my coffee and took a sip. "Eat, Conner, before you pass out. You used too much energy."

At the kitchen table, Kelly's and Norman's heads were down, Norman snored softly. Stew tilted dangerously to the side. Serena yawned. Luna rested her head back, eyes closed, but I didn't think she was asleep, and Dayna drooped.

Dayna appeared to be trying to open her eyes back up. "What? What did he do to us?"

Fighting the effect as best I could, I smirked. "He calmed the masses."

Chapter 15 – Ducks In A Row

The scent of eucalyptus filled the room. As I sipped my coffee, I contemplated the smell. Whenever Jade put the calming smackdown on a room, it smelled of pine and our backyard, and everything good about a Wisconsin woods. I wondered if eucalyptus was a common smell where Conner was from.

Dayna shook her head. "What do you mean, 'calmed the masses'? Were we not calm?"

Conner gaped at me. "I had no idea I could do that. I just ... whoa."

I continued to eat while I waited for everyone to recover. Though Conner packed a punch, he was new to the epsilon game, and it only took a few minutes for the biggest hit to wear off. "Conner is an epsilon werewolf. There isn't much written down about what that means, since there are very few of them around. Actually, from what I understand, he's the second one alive right now that anyone knows about. They are rare."

Norman leaned forward. "Just two? The other is your sister, right?"

"Yeah, it's Jade."

"That's amazing. I mean, he comes here and lands in one of two places that can really help him."

I shrugged. "It's good. I don't know nearly as much as Jade, but I did watch as she muddled through a lot. I can help Conner with the basics and after that, Jade can help, even from afar."

We ate for a bit longer, then I got up to clear my plate. "Okay, we should start our training today. I want to make sure the two of you understand the basics of being part of a werewolf pack. We should also discuss how your life will change if the wolf took."

Luna slumped. "Gods, we have to wait until next Tuesday's full moon?"

I bit my lip and leaned back a little. Then tried to turn before they could read the indecision on my face.

The problem was the weird connection between me and Luna. Her eyes bored into me. "What?" she snapped. "What are you thinking, Pebble? There's a way, isn't there?"

"It's your sister, right?" Stew asked. "That's what you and your dad were talking about."

Luna continued to stare daggers into my back. I could feel it even as I gathered dishes to put into the dishwasher.

A shuffling sound preceded her standing in front of me. "Pebble." For once her voice wasn't harsh. Shocked, I looked into her face. "If we can know for sure now, why not? What aren't you telling us? Knowledge is power and all of that, right?"

I put the dirty dishes down and faced the table. Everyone stared at me, hope in their eyes. My focus shifted to Conner, who watched me with an interested expression. He had no idea that my next words would revolve around him once again.

With a sigh, I walked to the sink to wash my hands. "I don't know if it'll work."

Dayna gasped. "But there may be a way? Then our training would make more sense."

Drying my hands, I leaned on the counter. "Yeah, there *may* be a way, but it's a longshot." I looked at Conner again and his brow knit. "One of the epsilon abilities is reading people and their potential wolves." Chatter started around the table and Conner's jaw dropped.

"There's no way." Luna sneered, a twitch emphasizing her words on her upper lip.

I lifted my hands before anyone could say more. "Whoa. We have to remember that Conner didn't even know he *was* an epsilon wolf when he arrived yesterday. He may not be able to do this yet or at all. Jade is the only other epsilon, and we don't know if every epsilon can do the same things." As I spoke, Conner snapped his mouth shut, and a determined look hardened his face. Breathing slowly, I continued. "More than that, I'm the one leading him and I'm not an epsilon." My head fell back, and I gazed at the ceiling before looking back at Conner. "If nothing else, Jade will be here this weekend."

Waves of determination and disappointment crossed Conner's face as he realized he didn't know what to do and wasn't sure I could explain it to him. Finally, jaw set, he had the look of a person ready to conquer the impossible. Part of my analysis was reading his face, part was feeling his emotions through my alpha bond, and part was scent.

All morning I'd set and reset the fence between me and the pack. It was a work and school day, and there wasn't much to block. Some of what I'd done had been instinct.

I shook out my arms. Unlike the rest of the pack, there was a lot of emotion in the room. "We should go into the living room if we're going to try this out. We should bring food to help avoid Conner passing out."

The citrus scents of hope and excitement, the two variations mixing to tickle my nose, filled the room as everyone got up.

Conner sat on the couch with Luna and Dayna on either side of him. He gazed up at me. "Okay, I'm guessing this is like what I did before? I take one of their hands and ... imagine my wolf, um, traveling over to them?"

I checked my phone. As we walked into the living room, I'd texted Jade. She hadn't immediately texted back. I hadn't really expected it, but it would've been nice to have her explain this.

Of course she's not available. Of course I have to train an epsilon, a goose shifter, and a werebear a week after becoming alpha, when I barely understand what being an epsilon is myself. And is Jade available? No. Or my parents. Why would they be here? Just little old me. Great!

"I think so. If that doesn't work, I'll call Jade and hope she answers her phone."

Conner took Luna's hand and they both leaned back, closing their eyes. After a few moments, Luna tensed, then Conner tensed, then his eyes flew open. "Gods above, okay, that um ... okay, I'll have to try again. I just ... there's a goose, and she's mean. She's really mean."

Luna smirked and I tried to keep a blank face. "You did really good, Conner. You figured it out, which is half the battle. You should be able to speak with the goose, try to reason with it. Explain why you're there. If that doesn't work, we may not be able to get the information from Luna."

Do not laugh, Pebble. You cannot even crack a smile. If anyone can reason with a goose of all things, I'm sure it's Conner ... our brand-new epsilon wolf. This can do nothing but end well.

Luna's face tightened, her smirk falling away. "My goose will behave." Her smug jasmine scent shifted to a woodsy determination.

The two repeated the actions from before and once again, they both jerked. My guess was it related to the shock of Conner entering Luna and being startled at seeing the goose. Luna began to smell of eucalyptus and citrus tea. It wasn't as strong as Conner's scent, but it was there.

Dayna sniffed. "What do I smell? Conner smells like what the kitchen smelled like when we all felt woozy, but less. So does Luna. Is that normal?"

The others came over to sniff the area around the couch. "That's fascinating."

Conner took more time before he opened his eyes. When he did, he wobbled a bit, and I handed him a plate of food to eat. Between bites he beamed and said, "Luna has a beautiful red wolf with black paws and a white patch on her nose."

Luna's eyes widened and she took in a shaky breath. "Okay, so, this is all real then. I'll be a wolf in a week."

Conner nodded. "From what I could tell, she's really dominant. Both your animals had opinions about my being there."

Stew moved to kneel in front of her, slipping his hands into hers. "You okay? This is what you wanted, right?"

She nodded slightly. "Yeah, it is. It's just ... it's real now."

Before Conner took Dayna's hand I said, "Bears can be as mean and territorial as geese. Just be careful."

The four werebears chuckled, and Kelly leaned forward. "Pebble isn't wrong. Don't move too quickly around Dayna's bear."

Eyes wide, Conner stared at Dayna for a moment, whose mouth quirked up to the side, all cheer and goodwill. Then they both sank into the test. Though Dayna jerked when Conner made contact, he didn't show a reaction this time. *He must be figuring it all out.*

After a few minutes in which his epsilon scent perfumed the area around both of them, he opened his eyes and nearly collapsed. I noticed his hands trembled and realized despite the food, he'd done way too much. This was all new to him and he needed a lot more fuel. I stood to head to the kitchen to find him something to eat as he said, his words a bit slurred and soft, "Dayna's wolf is as brown as her bear."

I didn't make it to the kitchen for more food before Dayna yelped, "Conner! Gods, he passed out."

We got him settled on the couch. The others gathered around him while I got him a tray of snacks for when he woke up.

Luna's face scrunched up. "Is this something I need to worry about? Passing out?"

For a few seconds, I worked at not reacting. The idea that she was epsilon—a calming force—was so bonkers that the laughter fought to come out. Both Jade and Conner, from his stories, spoke of calming people even before the wolf came out. Luna could never be described that way. "I don't think so. This is a byproduct of using too much of the epsilon—" I tried to think of the word but finally shrugged, "power, I guess. Most wolves are just norms or wolves. We don't have much extra."

Dayna wrung her hands in her lap. "So, if we're wolves, are we expected to move into this house?" She looked around as if this were her new home ... or prison. The sour scent of her being overwhelmed surrounded her.

"No. You both have rooms upstairs, and you're welcome to keep them. You could also move into rooms down here if you'd prefer. There are a lot of rooms available. You could choose not to have a room here, if you don't want. You'll notice the lack of pack members in residence."

She pursed her mouth, then sighed. "Are you going to live here from now on?"

"Me?" My hand flew to my chest. "The pack den? I do live here. But if you are referring to during the school year, I hope not. I mean, things *could* get to the point that I spend more time here than the dorms, but the pack really doesn't need me living here full time. I'll probably spend weekends here, and full moon nights, but otherwise stay on campus. Don't forget, I have a phone, I can be contacted."

"What are the cons of the dorms?" Luna asked, leaning back. "I mean, beyond them being dorms."

This was the big question. "Excellent question. Your senses are going to be much better. Smell will probably be the worst. After you go wolfy, we'll spend time at the mall, maybe go to an emotional movie, do something with big feels. You need to learn what it's like to be around a lot of people, fast."

Dayna scoffed. "I did all of that when I got my bear. I'll be fine."

"No." I shook my head. "You forget, I saw what my sister went through with multiple animals. Well, not so much saw, but heard the stories. My brother also has more than one animal. I really have heard it all. It's not the same." I took a deep breath. I had to slow down. "You'll run faster, walk faster, hear better, it'll be like getting your first animal all over again."

Both Dayna and Luna paused, then Dayna nodded. "Okay. So, we need to go through training again. But, since we don't have our wolves yet, we should be fine, right?"

"I think so."

She smiled. "Our parents want to take us out for a goodbye dinner. They're leaving tomorrow morning. Would that be okay?"

"Of course. I mean, yes, I need to train you, but you don't have to ask permission beyond checking if I had anything planned, which I didn't."

Conner started to groan. "What happened?"

I explained about using too much of his ability without restocking with food. Then he started eating. The rest of the morning the four of us continued discussing expectations of pack life. There were some differences between Florida and Wisconsin, which was interesting, but for the most part, Conner helped train more than was trained.

At four, the group broke up. Conner went to read the werewolf history book some more, Dayna, Luna, and their parents headed out for their dinner, and I went to meet Trista to see what was wrong.

We met at an Italian restaurant. I wore jeans and a UW-Madison sweatshirt. Trista wore a navy-blue dress and she continued to have a bit of a red glow around her. *I need to call Bevin.* For a moment I thought about Julez's assertion that Trista thought we were dating, but her scent was nutty ... she was nervous, but not acting like she was nervous about a date.

I let the idea slide off me as we were shown a table.

The hostess brought us each menus and a glass of water. I picked up my menu but didn't immediately look at it. "How is everything, Trista? I didn't really get to speak with you at the pack meeting last weekend."

"Oh, well, it's okay, I guess." Her scent was a mixture of cinnamon annoyance and bergamot relief.

My eyes flowed over the menu offerings except I didn't really read anything. "Is anything wrong? Was your trip back home bad?"

It seemed like Tennessee was a hotbed of negativity for everyone. My mind drifted to my parents, and I wondered how they were doing with the new pack.

Trista put down her menu and sipped her water. "Home was ... fine."

As she started to speak, I had to pull my mind from imagining what the Tennessee pack was like and focus on her.

"My grandpa—I love him and all, but he's getting on in years."

I shook my head, focusing on her, not my parents and how much I missed them.

"Well," Trista continued, finally looking up, "he was diagnosed with cancer. My family, the ones I've been living with, they don't know if they can help support me anymore." She still held the combined scents of cinnamon and bergamot. *Maybe she was both annoyed and relieved with the situation? She was on her own, but not under the control of that part of the family?*

I thought about the time between Christmas and the big pack meeting. There hadn't been a spike in her emotions, though I'd been busy and maybe missed it.

Maybe she just knew how to bury her emotions so deep no one felt them ... even herself.

Reaching over, I gave her hand a quick squeeze. "I'm really sorry about all that. It's all so horrible. Did they give your grandpa a set amount of time? Do you feel like you should go back to Tennessee? Is school out of the picture for you, now?" Realizing how many questions I shot at her, I snapped my mouth shut. It was the last thing she needed.

I wonder why she didn't call or text me. Thinking about it, I decided it had to do with me being a new alpha to her, and maybe she wasn't ready to think of me that way. *I really need to get the new wolves connected with the submissive wolves. Trista should know that Aunt Allison, Chris, and Andy are also available and great people to help her out. Gods, what would my parents do?*

Trista picked up her napkin and dabbed at her eyes and looked down at our clasped hands. "I was told there wasn't enough room at the house—"

A stabbing pain was the only warning I had before the image of the snake took over my vision. It slithered through grass before it flew towards me, mouth open, teeth aiming for my—

With an effort, I pulled my mind from the snake. A shiver ran down my body. Trista's words brought me back to the here and now.

I forced myself to look into her eyes. She'd been looking down at our hands and missed whatever I'd done during the vision.

"—home. They need me to stay here. As for school, well, I'm paid up through the end of the year, so I don't have to drop out, at least not this year." Her focus had dropped back down, and she wouldn't look up from her hands which fidgeted with the napkin. If it weren't cloth, it would be in bits by now. "It's more the rest that I can't afford. My apartment, food, utilities. You know, living." She laughed, humorlessly. "Maybe I can live in my car."

I needed to call Dad and tell him about this premonition, but there were people in Wisconsin who needed me now ... *Trista* needed me. Trista was worried about her grandpa and school and where to live.

As her words seemed to dry up, she slumped. The server came over in a crisp pair of black pants, white button-down, and black pencil tie. "Hi, I'm Dor. I'll be your server this evening. Can I start you off with anything?"

Neither of us had looked over our menus. I had no idea what I wanted. "Can you give us a few more minutes?"

"I absolutely can. Be back in just a few." Dor headed off, stopping at another table to chat them up.

Without speaking, Trista and I each picked up our menus and started to look them over. By the time Dor returned, we each had something picked out.

"Sounds great, one meat lasagna, and one pasta with meatballs. I'll have your salads out in a moment."

Trista continued to stare down at the table. I sighed, the weight of alpha heavy on my shoulders. It was my responsibility to ensure my pack didn't suffer or end up homeless. "What are you going to do? You know that living in your car really isn't an option."

"I don't know. Do you have any suggestions?"

Pack house was supposed to be available to anyone in the pack. I just didn't feel comfortable with people I didn't know living there alone, without one of us. And though I just let Conner walk in and take a room practically across the hall from mine, he'd be living in the dorms once school began.

Closing my eyes, I made the decision to move back home. *No more dorms for me.* "You're one of us. You could always move into ... you know, home. I remember Mom telling you that when we first met."

Her eyes widened and started to water. "I could do that? For real? I didn't think that offer was for real. Oh, my gods, Pebble, you're a lifesaver. If I could have a room and not have to worry about rent ... it would be amazing."

Part of me felt at peace for helping her. Another part felt the weight of responsibility wrap tight around me.

Chapter 16 – A Run

Since the day I first came home to pack house at the age of five, I had had the same room. When I first moved in, we'd painted it. At the start of high school, my parents bought me a new oak bedroom set, and I've done a bit of redecorating over the years. But all in all, this room has always been my safe place.

I sat in the center of my bed, thinking about the last week. Everything had happened so fast. My trip to

Colorado ended seven short days ago. We were seven days into this new year. Seven days, and in that time both my parents had left, I had four new pack members living in the pack den, I needed to train, both myself and my new pack members. And in just under three weeks, school would begin.

Leaning my head on the wall behind me, I closed my eyes and breathed. *I can do this. It may feel overwhelming, but it's all within my wheelhouse.*

Once I felt centered, I slid my phone from my pocket and navigated to text Dad. *When you wake your lazy butt up, we should talk. Love you lots.*

Annoyance flashed through my mind. I closed my eyes and pinpointed on Luna. Looking over the fence at my mental flock of wolves, they all were ... being. There were emotions, normal day-to-day ups and downs. I could tap into any one of them. There wouldn't be communication like an epsilon could do, but the emotions all seemed stable.

Groaning, the inevitability of the situation was inescapable. I needed to join everyone in the kitchen and figure out what was happening.

Time to leave my sanctuary.

I'd already exercised, showered, and had a mug of coffee. I raided my dresser and closet for jeans, shirt, and a sweater.

As I headed to the kitchen, I saw a bunch of suitcases stacked in the living room. Dayna and Luna's parents were leaving today.

In the kitchen, I found ... everyone. Stew handed me a plate with pancakes. A second plate had eggs, sausage, and toast. My stomach growled. "Gods, why aren't *you* moving in?"

He chuckled as I sat at the table and started to eat.

A few bites in, I looked around. Trista sat at the counter, ignoring everyone. With a sigh, I realized I couldn't just ignore everyone and eat ... I had to work. "Trista, have you met Dayna, Luna, and Conner, our new pack mates?"

Slowly, Trista looked up from her plate. "Yeah, I saw them at the meeting on Sunday."

Before I could say anything, Luna scoffed. "Conner wasn't even at that meeting. How daft are you?"

Trista's face hardened. "I meant I saw you and ... the other one."

"Her name is Dayna. Is that so hard?" Luna snapped.

Okay, that was sharp, but still within the bounds of okay.

I could feel Trista's anger at being reprimanded as her face scrunched up. "Do you know the names of all the people who were at that meeting?"

Luna glared. "No, but I will after the meeting on Sunday. I wasn't sure I was joining at the last meeting, I know now. How long have *you* been part of this pack?"

Trista sneered. "Well, you must be better with names than me."

Putting down my fork, I rubbed my face. *How would my parents handle something like this? It's gone too far. I need to stop it. Are they dealing with fights like this in Tennessee?*

A knife stabbed my head. I whimpered at the pain. *A shadow of a bird flies through the air. No matter how much I squint, I can't tell any details beyond: bird. Suddenly it splits in half, becoming two birds. One flies away, disappearing into the distance. The other drops to the ground, then launches, carrying a snake in its talons.*

I shivered, rubbing my temples.

Once my head cleared, I opened my eyes. Most of the others in the kitchen were eating, not paying attention to me. Luna glared at me. *Gods save me, what did I do this time? Will my life ever go back to being easy?* "What the hell was that, Pebble?"

Everyone stopped moving and a quiet fell over the kitchen. "I don't know what you're asking, Luna."

She tapped her head. "What was the bird? With the rope? What the hell is in your head?"

I groaned. "That's a long story."

"Alpha secrets?"

"Sort of."

"Fine, we'll talk later."

Trista watched us closely. She finally pushed her plate away. "I need to get to school. My classes start up sooner than yours. I'll see you later."

She stalked out, shaking her head.

Conner snickered from further down the counter from where Trista had been sitting. "This pack is fun." He tipped his head back, drinking his coffee. "I'm liking this better and better."

His enthusiasm made me chuckle. "Just remember, an epsilon needs extra calories."

"On it. Eat more. My parents would be terrified of that direction, but I love it."

I smirked. "If you knew my family ... you can't scare me."

"Oh ... challenge accepted."

Norman chuckled. "I think that's our signal to leave."

Kelly shook her head, her face alight with amusement. "That and the time."

"Yes, that and the time."

Everyone stood to escort the parents out. The four of them packed into the car they drove up in, and Luna and Dayna said their final goodbyes.

A part of me was sad to see the last of the adults leaving, but a bigger part felt a sense of relief. There were fewer people for me to keep track of.

And then it was just my pack.

We headed back in, and my phone rang. I looked at the display. "It's my dad."

Dayna smiled. "We'll clean up the kitchen."

Waving thanks, I moved to the living room and sat on a couch. "Hi, Dad."

"Hiya, Applesauce. How are you?" It had only been a day, but I relaxed into his voice.

"Good. I just wanted to tell you about my latest premonition. It keeps coming when I think about you or Mom or Tennessee."

"Tell me."

I did.

"What happened before and after it was triggered."

With a sigh I gave him more of the story.

"Okay, we'll keep our eyes open, but don't forget, this premonition isn't figured out. You think you know what it is, but you have to stay open minded."

"I will. No putting the cart in front of the horse, and all that. Thanks, Dad."

There was a pause, then Mom said, "Tell me about the rest of it. How is Conner doing?"

"Did you know he's E, like Jade?"

I could almost feel the shock come down the line. "We always knew there could be more than one in the world, but Conner? My friend's son? That's ... do Tilly and Rory know?"

"Yeah, Conner called them that first night. He's been reading the book."

"Jade wrote a book?" Dad asked from a distance away.

"No, the book you gave Jade all those years ago. Though, I'm going to push her to actually do it. That, or demand weekly meetings until Conner feels secure. I'm not qualified to teach him. That said, I'm trying to help."

Mom and Dad chuckled. "I'm sure you're doing great, Applesauce."

We spent the next few minutes discussing what had happened since Mom left Wisconsin. Finally, Mom said, "Sweetie, why don't you have Conner talk with their subconscious. Maybe they're ready to be seen. You could have them run prior to the monthly meeting."

I wanted to slap my head. *Why hadn't I thought of that?*

"Thanks, Mom."

"I'm just glad I'm still useful to the great and mighty leader of the Wisconsin office."

I wanted to snarl but just huffed. "I love you, too."

Once I hung up, I found the other three in the kitchen. The house felt less oppressive with only three others in residence ... well, four, but Trista was out and about.

Conner wiped down a counter. "What did your Dad have to say?"

"I haven't told you, but I have premonitions. I wanted to talk with him about the one I'm having. Ever since this summer, it seems I've been too slow to figure them out on the first go, so I get recurring visions."

Conner paused, gazing up at the ceiling. "I think my Mom told me about that. She thought it was pretty cool that you saw things. You and your wolf are so connected." His face scrunched up. "We have a wolf in our pack that knew you when you were a baby, did you know that?"

The words felt like cold water dumped over my head. Slowly, I nodded. "Yeah. I did."

There wasn't a lot about my childhood I remembered. To be honest, I didn't work at remembering the years before living with the Stones. When Owen and I would go out running, he'd tell me stories, but only when I'd ask. He explained that I'd been found on the side of the road, and that a lone wolf who my parents had turned had left me there. He'd hunted down my parents, not knowing about me. When he'd abandoned me to foster care, he thought *he* was a monster, and I was just a girl. After one of the pack, my pack, found him, he joined the Floridian pack, learning what it was to be a wolf, much like I did here in Wisconsin.

He'd been a business partner of my parents, and though I could've learned about my past, I was happy with my past staying vague and undisturbed ... in the past.

"I could call him if you wanted to talk with him ... ask him questions. He's really nice."

"Maybe later. I have a lot of things going on right now."

His brow knit, then he nodded. "Yeah, okay. Just let me know when."

Luna stared at me with an odd expression. I didn't want to try to decipher it. Dayna shut the dishwasher. "Anything else from Tennessee? Or are we free to do ... something? What's today's plan?"

All three watched me, waiting for me to guide them. *Is this what it feels like to be a teacher? Everyone expecting you to tell them everything?*

"Well, I know you and Luna are excited about becoming wolves. And since we have an epsilon—"

Dayna's eyes widened. "He can bring our wolves out?"

Conner blanched.

"No!" My hands shot up. "Not even a little." Imagining Jade's years of having a ghost of a wolf in her head from helping her alpha bring out a wolf gave me the willies. I wouldn't wish that on my worst enemy. I cut my eyes to Luna ... *no, not even her.* "But if he can speak to your wolves and find out if they're ready to come out and play, *I* can pull them out. It's an alpha ability."

Luna and Dayna gaped at each other, Luna's face draining of color. They weren't part of the pack yet, so I couldn't get the full nuance of what they felt. The sweet, ginger smell filling the kitchen meant fear and shock. I could use scent, but going around sniffing everyone seemed weird, and only strong emotions emitted strong scents.

A smile stretched across Dayna's face; she wasn't hard to read. "I want to run ... as a wolf. Gods above, that would be amazing."

"Okay, we all just ate, so that should be good. Conner, are you up to trying your tricks again? I'm going to make you a peanut butter and jelly sandwich if you are. I don't want to see you pass out again."

Luna's lip twitched. "He just ate a full breakfast. That has to be enough ... even for this. It's just a quick check, right?"

I shook my head. "Not at all. A quick workout with a new ability, and then a run. I'd rather he eat too much than not enough."

She rolled her eyes. "Whatever."

I wonder if I can break her of that habit. Maybe I can speak with Dayna about it.

Conner watched, amusement rolling off him. "I'm game. Do we need to sit on the couches, or can I just try doing it in here?"

"That's up to you."

As I made the food, Conner reached out to first Dayna and then Luna. Each contact took a few minutes. I was so used to Jade, I forgot she'd been doing this almost half her life. Finally, he shivered and stepped back. "That is just so ... trippy. Their wolves are so talkative and excited."

Both Dayna and Luna looked confused, but I was used to this kind of description. "So, are they ready?"

"My wolf talks?" Luna's hands hit the counter. "Wolves don't talk."

Conner's mouth opened and shut a few times, then he shrugged. I could feel his befuddlement. *Maybe he thought Luna was aware of the conversation?*

I pushed the sandwich to Conner. "Luna, you're not helping. People also don't turn into animals, yet here we are. We have to start to shake off our doubts. Epsilon wolves are different. They can *do* things. One of those things is speak to our animals when they're mentally connected to us. Since our wolves are just an extension of us, it isn't *that* hard to believe, is it?" *Except when we can't communicate with our own wolves,* I wanted to scream.

She grunted. I looked over and the sandwich was eaten. Conner smiled. "Yes, both wolves were happy to come out and run today."

Dayna squealed, and we all headed out towards the backyard.

My phone dinged, and the display showed a text from Hollis. *Roller skating tonight. Fern is here and we have to get out of the house.*

I thought about it and decided by this afternoon we could all use a break from each other and a bit of normalcy. *What time?*

The reply came fast. *Three, we skate, then dinner. Then fun fun fun!*

I laughed as I shut the door to the backyard. All three stared at me questioningly. I shook my head. "Okay, Luna, you first."

"Why?" *Why did she have to question everything?*

"Because Dayna knows what to expect and watching you shift won't freak her out. I think giving you time to think about this won't make it easier. So, the two of us can go into the yard. You'll need to strip, hands and knees is best, and I'll pull out your wolf, or we can go behind the privacy fence."

Her gaze swept the backyard. "I don't care where, I just think I can do this myself."

Of course you can. New wolf, first time with two animals, and it isn't the full moon. Go for it.

She glared at me, as if she heard my words, then marched to the center of the yard and began to prepare. I took a moment to center myself. "Conner, stay here. Your epsilon calm will only mess things up."

"Got it," he said. "And you're ready for ..."

"I am." I followed Luna out. All her muscles tensed. "Try thinking about shifting one body part, like your hand. Make your hand shift to a wolf's paw."

Her eyes bored into mine, but then she gave a curt nod and continued.

It was cold outside, just below freezing. Though the yard was surrounded by trees, the wind cut through like ice knives. After a few more minutes of watching her, not shift, I knelt in the snow. "Can I help, please?"

With a huff of annoyance, Luna nodded. "Fine."

"I need you to look into my eyes. It may be uncomfortable, but it's part of the process." She did, fire and frustration burning into me. After placing my hand on her head, I looked beyond to stormy blue, deep, until I could feel the wolf and her desire. My wolf connected with her, bringing her into the pack. "Lucinda Millicent Zweck, shift."

Luna's eyes widened as I used her full name. It was part of the pack bond. It was always interesting to me too, learning full names, but Luna's shock quickly morphed into something new as her body was taken over with the shift.

It took time, as all new wolves did. When her red wolf stood in front of me, beautiful, tall and proud, with her black paws digging into the snow, and the touch of white on her nose, I saw death in her eyes. All new wolves shifted fully wolf. It took a few moments to remember they were part human. In that time, they attacked.

I braced myself as Luna launched herself at me. I wrapped my hands around her snapping muzzle. Once her teeth couldn't do damage, I rolled so that she lay on her back, pinning her down. She fought, twisting and snarling. I'd practiced holding a wild wolf down with Tanner. I could do this long enough for Luna to come to her senses ... I hoped. Luna wasn't trained in this shape, not yet, but once she was, she'd be powerful.

The struggles stopped and I slowly backed away. The anger and need to rend shifted to confusion. "It's okay Luna, all new wolves attack after their first shift."

Once she got back to her paws, she looked up at me. Her eyes, still a striking blue, just not as stormy, gazed into mine for several seconds before dropping. *Oh, yeah, she'll be powerful once she fully comes into her own.* "You did great, Luna. Let me get Dayna shifted, then we can run."

Conner cleared his throat. "Can I shift too, maybe behind the privacy fence? I didn't try to attack on my first shift. I think I should be safe."

I blew out a big breath of air. "I'd prefer you wait, just in case. You may not have attacked because it was your family. We're new to you."

"Okay, that makes sense."

Dayna got into position quickly; she knew the drill. When I gazed into her eyes, her bear snarled at me. I dropped part of my mantle and growled back. It took almost a minute for the bear to snuffle and back down and for me to see the wolf. "Dayna Ursa Briggs, shift."

Once her shift began, I slipped away and watched. Luna sat close, watching as well, but not too close. Dayna attacked, but her fight ended fast. She wouldn't be as high ranking as Luna.

Finally, Conner shifted. As he predicted, he didn't attack, just lolled his tongue out in a wolf laugh. Then it was my turn.

Shaking myself out, I separated the three of them in my head, then took off towards the woods.

We started the run on a well-worn path. The cool wind brushed through my fur, and I let the stress of the new year sluff off me as I ran. The wolf didn't feel the pressures that the human half did. Eventually, I veered to the right, snaking into rougher terrain. There was a fallen tree, about two feet tall, that I leapt over, glorifying in the power of my body as it soared through the air.

Hearing scraping, I stopped and turned.

Next to me, Dayna did the same. We watched as Conner managed to crawl over the log. Once over, he turned and we all waited as Luna attempted to make it over, then turned and tried again. On the second attempt, her paw caught. I felt her frustration as well as the pain as her paw slammed hard into the fallen tree.

There was a point, just in front of the tree, where she needed to launch. I tried to send her an image of the point and her leaping from there, muscles tight. I wasn't sure how our connection worked, but she'd sent me images before. Then I tried to send a set of ideas, like a still life action movie of the approach, the jump, and then her clearing the tree. All told, maybe a half-dozen ideas.

I realized my eyes had been closed. When I opened them, Luna stood, frozen. Then she shook her head, eyes narrowed. She took a few steps back before executing the movements much like the path I'd sent her. She flew over the log and landed with a grunt.

Dayna yipped in encouragement, dancing in a circle. Conner rocked from paw to paw, excitement pouring from him.

Luna's leap had her running into me. Words tumbled into my head. *Talk later us.*

Internally, I sighed. No good deed goes unpunished, indeed.

We ran, and I found the scent and then the trail of a rabbit. I signaled the others to stop and watch. It took a moment to get them to understand the signals, but finally they waited. I realized that wolf communication needed to be at the top of the list of lessons. We'd had a brief discussion before we ran, but I wasn't sure they remembered everything we'd discussed.

Moving silently, I stalked the bunny. Once I found my target, I pounced, dispatching the creature swiftly. I made sure everyone got a bite. Both Dayna and Conner were quick to dive in. Luna hesitated. I felt her internal battle in my head. She finally sniffed and edged forward, revulsion scenting the air.

A tremor traveled down her body, then all her muscles tensed. Mechanically, she dipped her head and took a small bite.

Her shock stabbed through my mind, and my tongue lolled out. I remembered my first real hunt, and I knew the battle she fought, the human versus the wolf.

She took a second, then a third bite, then snarled, backing up.

Dayna moved in, finished off the rabbit.

I led the group to the river, and we all drank deeply. Next, we ran fast towards a wild turkey ... at least they weren't cute.

Conner found a chipmunk along the way. We all waited while he tried to stalk and hunt the creature. His noisy approach was a complete failure.

Luna was the next to try ... then Dayna. By the time we got to the wild turkeys, they'd each found a few animals to follow. Dayna had been the only one successful with a fat squirrel.

Luna's anger at her failure pulsed in my head. When she saw the first turkey, she growled low, warning us all she was the first to go in. Her approach was quiet. In stealth mode, Luna got within a couple of feet of the bird, then struck. The flock scattered, but she had one of the beasts in her jaw, and with a jerk of her head, I heard a snap.

She was about to dig in, when some instinct had her pause and look at me. I stepped forward and took a couple of bites. I radiated my approval, pleasure, and joy of the day. Once done, I stepped away and let Luna eat, followed by Dayna and Conner.

As a group, we ran back to the river, the cool snow crunching under our paws, the wind raking through our fur. I reveled in the delight from the other three. My feet seemed to fly through the woods.

Once we drank deeply, the path home was quick. We each shifted and dressed. Having given my wolf such a long run, and it being our third run in as many days, she didn't fight me as much when I requested the human form back.

I was the first on two feet, so I headed inside and decided I didn't want to cook. I looked through the kitchen junk drawer and found coupons for a local pizza shop. Once everyone was in the kitchen, I asked what they wanted, and ordered three large pizzas.

For the first time, there were no arguments as we sat and waited for delivery.

Chapter 17 – Social Club

As we sat eating pizza, Dayna sighed in contentment. "That was as fun as I'd hoped." Her eyes almost glowed. "It was like ... everything I dreamed it would be when I drew those pictures as a kid."

Luna tilted her head and considered her cousin. "Is it that much different than running as a bear? Four paws, fur, lumbering around the woods?"

Dayna laughed. "It is *so* much different. I felt lithe and free. And the hunting ... that was exciting. And I can't wait to howl to the moon. I mean, I love my bear, she's majestic and powerful ... but now I can be a wolf, too. It's a dream come true."

Conner nodded. "It's also different running here from what I did in Florida. I know I only shifted once there, but everything was just so ... I don't know, it's hard to explain."

"I get it," I said. "I ran with my family in California. The smells, the sounds, even the ground under your paws ... though that changes by season, which is also a big difference here. It's all so different." I got up to grab a soda. "Anyone else want something to drink?" As I gathered what everyone requested, I continued. "Even how you smell with your epsilon calm is different than Jade's because you come from somewhere else. I know you can't really sense it, or I assume you can't since Jade can't, but when you meet the rest of the pack, they'll notice."

Dayna leaned forward, brows knit in confusion. "How is it different?"

"What do you smell?" I sat, handing out everyone's drinks.

Dayna sniffed. "You know, my sense of smell *is* more acute." She shook her head, and she focused on Conner. "Your scent is a combination of eucalyptus and citrus. Though, I think I also smell the chamomile tea."

Conner lifted his hand and sniffed the back. "I don't smell any of that."

Luna shrugged. "I do. It wasn't very obvious before, but now it is."

"Are those common scents around where you grew up?"

He nodded.

"Well, Jade smells like our woods. The pine trees and a stream. But like you, she has a bit of a chamomile tea essence as well."

Conner's gaze bounced amongst us. "That's ... I don't know *what* that is."

My phone rang, checking the display I saw it was Tanner. "Hi—"

"Get somewhere you can't be overheard."

When I stood, everyone in the room watched me as I walked out. There was no way they hadn't all heard Tanner's words. I headed up to the office and made sure to secure the door behind me. "Okay, I'm alone. I'm in the office, door shut."

"There's another body. It was obviously attacked by a dog, this time the person didn't try to hide what they did. The drop was near the zoo. Allison found it and called Easton."

My mouth went dry. *You are not alone. Use your pack.* "Have ..." The word stumbled out, mostly inaudible. I swallowed a couple of times and tried again. "Have the cops been officially contacted? Are you there?"

"No and yes."

I sat heavily on the office chair, trying not to think of it as Dad's. "It's not the same person, because he attacked you to keep you from questioning him."

"Right. But there's a similar scent. I don't think the perpetrator is family, but maybe from the same group. They share a stink."

"Are we under attack?" Somehow my voice sounded calm.

Tanner sighed. "Don't overreact, Pebble. This is just me informing the CEO. For all we know, it could be that other dog's partner is mad that we took him out. We don't know."

I leaned back, reeling in my racing thoughts. "Right, okay. So, we should just monitor for now."

"Sounds good. I'll keep you informed."

"Oh, Tanner, what's happening with the body?"

"Your call, boss." His voice was tight.

"Got it. Is there any reason to not call this in? The person has a family."

"No. I'll tell Allison to call the police and Easton to leave the scene."

"Okay, I'll add this to Sunday's agenda. Even if we're just monitoring, the others should know another dog is in town. The company should know that this is happening. Gods, there is so much to talk about."

"More than just Jade? And the new additions?" Tanner finally didn't sound angry.

"So much more."

He grunted. "Can we meet Friday morning with Clare to go over the company logistics and books? Friday morning is the best time for Clare. I know in a couple of weeks you'll be back at school, and we'll have to rearrange things, but right now, our standing schedule should work."

I nodded, thinking about the week. "Yeah, that would be good. Should I have Luna join since apparently, according to my inner soul, she's all that and a bag of chips?"

Tanner snorted. "Up to you."

"Right, okay. Talk to you Friday."

"Friday it is."

Since I was in the office, I decided to log into the computer. I hadn't checked the pack email since I sent out the notice about the meeting. I needed to get the account synced with my phone. Tyler, my Dad's right-hand man at work, should be able to help me on Sunday. The pack's security has extra layers of protections Dad hadn't had time to show me.

Looking over the messages, nothing appeared urgent. Everyone would be at the meeting, though there were a few grumbles about another meeting a week after the last one. Once they got all the information, they'd stop griping.

I got up and headed back down to the kitchen. I had about half an hour before I needed to head out to meet Hollis and Fern. "So, we've had a long day, and a lot of things were accomplished. I think we should take the rest of the day off and meet up again tomorrow."

Luna's eyes narrowed. "You have plans. What are they?"

For a moment, I just stared at her. *Why is my life like this?*

"I don't know that my plans are your business. The four of us are spending a lot of time together and will continue to do that. Spending time apart is probably good for all our sanity."

She shook her head. "Why are you being sketchy, Pebble?"

I sighed. "I'm going roller skating with Hollis and Fern, are you happy?"

"I want to go with," Luna demanded, her tone haughty.

Dayna leaned forward. "Oh, so do I."

Conner rubbed the back of his neck. "If it comes down to it, I'd like to go, too. I haven't roller skated in years, and that sounds great."

I opened my mouth to protest, but Luna smirked. "Didn't you say that once we got our wolves, we would need to practice being in situations with more people? Wouldn't this be exactly the type of thing we need?"

I know she pays attention to training, but why does she have to use what she's learning against me? It's like she's only paying attention to figure out how to use the information for evil.

With a low growl, I sat in one of the island seats. "Don't you think we should spend time apart? You make it obvious that spending too much time with me annoys you. Why do you want to spend social time together? There's a whole city available."

Luna shrugged. "I don't know, I just do. Roller skating sounds fun. Are you that opposed to me joining you?" An apple scent of curiosity wafted from her.

A huff of air left me like a deflating balloon. "No. I actually like being with pack, it's always calmed me. Now you *are* pack. Even when you're being ... you," I shrugged, "you're still pack. If you close your eyes and think about it, you can feel where I am. So can Dayna. It's a pack member alpha thing. It isn't a super strong connection, but it's there."

Luna closed her eyes, then grunted. "Is that why you knew my full name?"

"Yeah, that's part of it."

Conner leaned on his elbows. "If you like spending time with us, then what's the hold up?"

"Nothing huge, I just need to figure out what I'm going to tell my friends. You're easy, they don't know you and they know I have guests in town. As to why Dayna and Luna are guests ... that's going to be harder. First off, why would they be here? Second, why didn't I tell them a week ago?"

Luna shrugged. "That sounds like a you problem. Let's go. You don't want to be late."

Her spike of joy at my complication belied the reason she was pushing for us to leave quickly. My hope was the skating rink would be big enough that everyone could roll in their own area.

It took a few minutes for everyone to change and get into the car. The drive was quick, and the whole way Dayna and Luna discussed the last time they'd gone skating.

I hoped we'd get there before Hollis and Fern. Maybe we could be out on the floor and when they arrived, they wouldn't even notice Luna was there.

There was a line to get in and a line to get skates. Somewhere between the two lines, Hollis and Fern found us.

"Pebble!" Fern engulfed me in a hug. "Happy New Year!"

Warmth and calm filled me about the situation for the first time since Luna asked to crash the party. As before they wore a woodsy perfume, way nicer to smell than anything else at the skating rink.

I should be using touch more with my pack. Why am I forgetting werewolf basics?

Fern pulled away. "I'm so excited to be here. At first, when I got home, my Dad said there was no way I'd be able to return for a visit, but then he changed his mind. It was amazing, right Hollis?"

We both turned and saw Hollis ignoring us. Her focus was behind me.

Slowly, Fern turned, and I knew the moment they recognized who I came with. Their whole body tensed. "Hi, Luna, Dayna. What are you doing here?"

Any scent I could read from the situation was swallowed by the overwhelming odors of the rink. Sweat, bodies, food, and the spray used to disinfect the inventory. Despite that, the pleasure from Luna spiked in my head.

She smirked and moved her gaze from Hollis to Fern. "You are such good friends of Pebble, and she didn't tell you that Dayna and I are staying with her? I'm shocked. I wonder what that's about?"

She pushed past me, got her skates, and sauntered off.

Anger surged in me and the buzz of the rest of the pack began swarming my head. For a moment I didn't think I could get everything back in place. *Why did she agree to all of this when her daily ... hourly goal is to sabotage me?*

Dayna sighed but rubbed my arm, helping my control. "Sorry about that. I'll, I don't know what I'll do. But talk to you later."

She got skates and followed Luna.

Hollis and Fern's gazes followed them, expressions hard.

Conner placed a hand on my shoulder, and more tension eased from me. I moved forward and got skates so we wouldn't be holding up the line, as did Conner. Then the four of us headed to a bench. "Look, it turns out Dayna's parents and mine go way back. Since my parents have to be out of town, Mom asked if Dayna could stay with me, so I wasn't alone. Luna was staying in Chicago and tagged along. This all just happened. I figured I'd tell you about it today. As for him," I pointed to Conner, "he's who I was talking about the other night. He's from Florida and is transferring to UW-Madison."

Hollis's face relaxed. "That sucks. You're stuck with Luna over winter break?"

I smiled. She had no idea. "In a word, yes." Eventually I'd have to figure out a better story, but this was a start.

"How can we help?" My friend looked around, trying to spot the other two. "Can you stay with me a few nights? Hang out with us more?"

"No, I can't have people—guests—at my house and not be there ... it would be awkward. But maybe Saturday we can go to lunch, just the three of us."

"Saturday?" she screeched. With the music and the skaters, her reaction could barely be heard. "Why not tomorrow and Friday?"

Fern placed a hand on Hollis's knee. "She can't abandon people staying at her house. Not to mention, Conner shouldn't be left to fend for himself. Saturday is good."

Conner's face lit up. "I'll play interference next time, make sure they don't invite themselves along." He ducked his head. "I just really wanted to roller skate."

A wide smile blossomed on Hollis's face. "It's fine, this place is big enough for all of us. And if you want to skate, there's only one thing to do ... skate!"

Conner and I got a locker for our shoes, then the four of us shot down the ramp to the rink. Conner didn't try to stay with the three of us. He seemed to have fun just dashing around, avoiding the younger kids, and moving to the music. Hollis and I goofed around. Fern didn't seem to have much experience, so we helped them not to bowl half the other skaters down.

After what felt like hours of dancing, grooving, and laughing, we headed off the rink to get soda and nachos.

Hollis snorted. "Fern, why didn't you tell us you didn't know how to skate?"

Drinking heavily from their cup, Fern held up a finger. "One, I didn't know you two were so good. I thought this was just stand and roll. You two, you were going backwards as much as forwards ... what is that?"

"It's fun, is what it is." Hollis snorted.

"We've been coming here for years," I added. "It's close to home and a place to expend energy, even in winter. I think it's how our parents figured they could wear us down when we got too rambunctious."

"Do you ever skate out in the big bad world?" Fern started in on the nachos.

Hollis nodded vigorously. "Speaking of. Why didn't you bring your in-lines Pebble? Why use their skates? They're awful!"

I shook my head. "I left them in the dorms."

"Idiot," Hollis berated. "I bet those suck."

"Oh, they do. Teach me to never chance not having my own with me."

In the back of my head I could feel a spike coming from both Luna and Dayna. It had been building, but they'd managed up until then. My heart started to beat faster. "I know this sounds awful, but I'll be right back. I'm going to go check on the others, make sure they're okay."

Hollis sneered. "Why? They tagged along. They can leave when *we* want to leave."

Fern placed a hand on Hollis's arm. "She's trying to be responsible." They looked at me. "Five minutes?"

"Yeah, that should do it." I got up and, as quickly as I could, got back onto the skating rink. I found the two of them against the wall, along the curve. Without slowing down, I slid my body between theirs, twisting at the last moment so my back was against the wall.

They both gaped at me, but I grabbed their hands before they could move away. "Hi, how's it going?"

Luna's face started off scrunched up, and I could feel her need to snap at me. Then she lifted our joined hands as the tension began to drain and her breathing evened out.

"Okay." I looked at each of them as they focused on the chaos of the skaters. "I need you to imagine you're a princess, or queen, or maybe a goose on a cloud," I squeezed Luna's hand with that word, "in your mind. Build up a castle, with thick walls. Don't let any of this noise, or scents, or emotions in. It's hard to hold it all back."

Before I got too far, Conner slid in next to Dayna. His breathing was choppy, and he took her hand. Dayna relaxed more—the power of epsilon. I could sense his release of stress with the touch as well.

I continued. "Now, when something gets through your defenses, think about boxing it up. If you think you'll need to examine it later, fine, put it in a different headspace."

Luna grunted. "Like that thing with Trista we need to discuss?"

There were probably a lot of things I needed to discuss with Luna, but Trista wasn't high on my list. "Right, yes, like that. However," I didn't want the others thinking too hard about what Luna and I may need to discuss, "there are a lot of things that you never need to face again. I usually think of a big incinerator in the back of my mind and let those boxes burn."

Conner muttered, "Burn, baby, burn."

"Touch is also helpful. It doesn't have to be me. Holding hands is good. Conner may be the best since he's an epsilon and has that extra layer of calm, even when he's not releasing any of his power."

Dayna sighed. "No, you're just as good as him, alpha. You both add a great layer of protection. You're like uber moats around the castle."

A laugh bubbled out of me. "Okay, well, I need to go before my friends look for me and are really confused about why I'm holding hands with the two of you."

Luna scoffed. "Tell them we went from enemies to lovers."

I cut my gaze to her. "While I'll admit we aren't enemies anymore, that latter is a bit of a stretch." I winked at her. "Though, remind me to tell you of the wedding prediction."

I dropped their hands and skated off before she could react to my comment.

Hollis and Fern were exactly where I'd left them. They even left a few chips for me to eat. Once done, we spent another hour skating. Then the rink was too crowded to do anything but slowly skate in an oval.

It was time to leave.

Outside the rink I gave Hollis and Fern hugs while the rest of my group piled into the car. As I turned to leave, Luna said from behind me, "Don't let her fool you, ask her about her real intentions towards me the next time you get together."

With that, Luna sashayed to the car, leaving Hollis and Fern slack jawed behind her.

Chapter 18 – Welcome To The Train Station

My head buzzed when I woke up. I wasn't sure if my guard was low, or if the pack was a titter with something, but I needed to move to try to quiet all the voices, or emotions, or whatever it was that had the pack excited.

I checked my phone and saw I had a text from Trista from the middle of the night. *Having a hard time. Maybe we can talk later. See you when I head off to classes in the morning.*

Closing my eyes, I tried to find her in the maelstrom of emotions, but she was asleep. Nothing there.

Pushing myself up, I changed into exercise clothes and headed to the barn. On the way, I filled a bottle with water. With the emotions of the pack swirling in my head, I couldn't run from my issues, but the movement seemed to help. My plan was a fifteen-minute run, followed by a full upper body torture day. Dad would be proud.

A few minutes into my run, I heard footsteps on the stairs. I grumbled at the interruption. It turned to a snarl when Luna showed up.

I just can't with her negativity right now.

It took only a minute for her to catch up with me. With a huff, I shook my head. "There is a lot of track. Is there a reason you want to specifically run next to me?"

"I figure this is as private as the office if no one else is around."

She had a point. We were far from the house and the likelihood was that Dayna and Conner were still asleep. "Okay, what do you want to talk about?"

"What was that image you sent me? That vision?"

I wanted to scream at my wolf: why her? Why this person of all the people in the world? Then again, she smelled and sounded sincere. Maybe she was finally ready to embrace this side of things. Either way, I was alpha and, until she decided to step up, *her* alpha. As her trainer, I needed to answer her questions. "The run or the other one? Because only one was done on purpose."

There was a pause where I thought she debated snarling, but then she just sighed. "In the kitchen. Though, we should discuss all of it."

"It wasn't a vision. I get premonitions. You saw part of it. Somehow, some of what I saw leaked over to you. I don't always know what they mean. I've been working with my Dad to try to figure them out."

For almost a full lap, the only sound was the slap of our feet on the floor. "How many premonitions do you get?"

"I don't know. Sometimes not many, sometimes a lot."

"And you never know what they mean?"

I grunted—it was easier than a sigh. "They vary. Sometimes they make sense to me. Other times they don't. In hindsight, they usually seem clear enough."

"How so?"

"Well, all last semester I had one of a person in a dorm room reaching out to me, a phantom really. It started out vague. Then, after meeting you, the person started demanding that I find them. After about a month, I thought I heard traffic outside the window."

"Traffic?"

"Well, I heard a honking sound."

Luna laughed, the sound light and almost joyous. "Oh, I can see how it's obvious now, but if you didn't know about geese shifters it wouldn't be so clear."

"Yeah. My wolf can be clear as mud."

"Are premonitions common in wolf shifters?"

"Werewolves, and no."

"Then why you? I mean, I don't want to sound rude, believe it or not, I'm just curious."

For a moment, I debated how much to tell her, then decided if I wanted her to be part of the pack, she had to feel welcome. My story wasn't top secret so there was no reason to hide it. "I was bitten when I was five. Most kids don't survive the change that young. Actually, from what I've been told, no one has heard of any before me. Then my parents were killed, and I was put into the foster system. Most of this I only remember from stories told to me. I do remember my parents, my adoptive parents, finding me and bringing me home ... here." I chuckled. "That first impression of the pack den ... it's memorable. Anyway, my family did everything they could to raise me so the wolf wouldn't take over too soon and destroy my youthful innocence."

"You were five?" A mixture of horror and wonder colored Luna's voice.

"Yep. I don't remember a time when I didn't have a wolf soul in me. I am so intertwined with my wolf that our connection runs deeper than most. I think *that's* why I get the premonitions."

"Can you tell me about the one I saw?"

"Sure, though it's really been a series of them." As we continued to run, I told her about the different premonitions I'd had.

She nodded. "Okay, those are what you saw. How about when you had them?"

"You saw the first. It was during the pack meeting, and of course the third in the kitchen. The middle one was when I was out to dinner with Trista."

"I bet it's Trista. She's bad news."

"Is that because you didn't like her for the two minutes you met her?" I wanted to scream. What was it with some people? As I spoke, I could hear the growl in my voice. "Every time one of the premonitions came, I was thinking about my parents and the Tennessee pack."

Luna shook her head. "We will have to agree to disagree about that. You focus on Tennessee, I'll watch her."

"Does that mean you've decided to stay and help run this pack?"

Luna's steps faltered. "No."

My disappointment surprised me. Our run and discussion felt right somehow, but one successful interaction didn't make a team ... I guess.

She shook her head. "Deciding to help run the pack is a big decision. I've been a wolf for less than a full day. I don't want to make such a big decision on a whim. But I'm here for winter break, and I don't trust her."

There was some logic to that. "As long as you are being so open and honest, why did you mess with me and my friends yesterday?"

She chuckled. "I did that because it was fun."

I slowed to a walk. My run time was over, and I decided I'd had enough bonding time with Luna. I checked my book to see what upper body exercises I should do. She followed, matching me set for set.

As I started the second set, I flinched.

"What was that?" Luna's eyes narrowed at me.

"As alpha, I have all of the pack members attached to me. The emotions today are running high. It's ... intense."

"So, you're saying you're bad at your job."

My teeth bit into the inside of my cheek before I snapped. *Just when I thought things were going well. Why did I think we could work amiably together?*

I took a slow breath in. "No, I'm saying I'm new at my job. It's been a week since all this started. And even Mom didn't have as many wolves in her head as I do now, especially with you, Dayna, and Conner added to the mix. She also didn't have someone telling her what a bad job she was doing at every turn."

Luna tilted her head. "Oh. If I stepped up, I would get like half the pack and be suffering like you?"

I squeezed my eyes tight. "No, you'd probably get like three or four of the pack." Gods, why was I bothering? My jaw tightened, but then I decided that at least she was getting this information despite not wanting the training. "There's always a main alpha for the head space and a secondary with a few. It helps with the organization. Also, if you decide to step up as alpha, with your mantle, you'd slip from my headspace since as an alpha pair, we don't need that extra connection to be pack."

She rolled her eyes. "Sounds like a lot of benefits for you and none for me." Standing, she headed out of the barn.

After finishing up my last set, I took a moment to enjoy the silence before returning to the main house. Someone had made coffee. I poured a mug and went to shower. Back in my room, I slipped on comfortable pants and a long sleeve shirt that said, *Chubby Unicorn* and had an image of a rhinoceros on it.

Before leaving my room, I checked my texts. Tanner had sent one while I'd been in the washroom. *Give me a call when you can.*

Sitting on my bed, I closed my eyes and relaxed. *Please let this be a restaurant for our Friday meet-up. He wants to have brunch instead of meeting here. Maybe take me out for ice cream to celebrate how good of a job I've done.*

The myriad of realistic reasons cascaded through my mind. Since none of my mental connections were loud, at least I knew no one was hurt. Finally, I navigated to the phone app and called.

"Hi, Pebble. We have another body. This one was in the park where we found the first one." All my muscles stiffened. Though it had been on the list, I'd hoped it wasn't the reason for the call.

"Near Willy Street?" My voice was steady, calmer than my insides.

"Yeah, that's the one."

"Was the person a college student? A local?" My body shook with apprehension. "Did you get any scents?"

"We still don't have a lot of that information. I can tell you the attacker was different from the one by the zoo."

A chill ran down my spine. "Who found the body?"

"Someone out for a morning run. Easton got there, but we weren't the first on the scene."

Another punch to the gut. "Does it look like an animal attack?"

"Yes."

"And it's another dump job?"

"Yes."

With effort, I held back a scream. "What are the police saying?"

"They think there was some sort of body dump to hide their location."

My jaw clamped for a moment, then I forced myself to relax.

"Should I move the meeting up to Saturday?" I really didn't want to do this. It would upset everyone, including me and my own plans, but this was so much bigger.

"No, everyone is already planning on being there Sunday, including Jade. One day shouldn't make that much of a difference."

"Is it still too soon to send a warning out to the pack?" Last time I had suggested this, my parents and Tanner shot the idea down. But that time there'd been only one attack.

"Yes and no. I think we should warn everyone, but again, Sunday should be soon enough. We'll talk with Clare tomorrow. If she thinks we should send out the warning right away, we'll move up the timeline."

I rubbed my face. "Can we get patrols monitoring the neighborhood? Since college isn't in session, this is where everyone is."

"Good idea. I'll set up a rotation." My mind wanted to fracture, horrified at the situation, yet thrilled with Tanner's approval. I'd finally gotten an answer right.

"Thanks, Tanner."

"It's what we do." He hung up, and I slumped.

Blowing out a huge breath, I tried to clear my mind before joining the others. I didn't want to bring any of my stress to them, and knowing Luna, she'd pick something up, and I really didn't want that. Unless she changed her mind about being alpha, she didn't get any early information, especially since she'd probably find a way to blame me. As for the others, they didn't need to know about this until the rest of the pack found out on Sunday.

The pressure in my head mounted. I wasn't sure if it was Easton or Tanner, or something to do with the text Trista sent, I just knew emotions were high and my head hurt. When I got to the kitchen, I made a bagel and sat at the table with coffee.

I ate slowly, trying to decide if it was the food or my head that made me nauseous.

Luna was the next to arrive. I held up my hand before she could say anything. "Can we call a truce for the rest of the morning?"

Luna scoffed. "Still struggling to master the basics of your duties?"

I should've known that wouldn't work. Instead of engaging, I ignored her and focused on my meal. I held the mug up to my nose, letting the scent infuse my senses.

Conner came in and began to prepare something to eat, his mood as chipper as always.

Trista walked in and headed to the refrigerator to grab a soda and a banana. "Hey Pebble. Did you get my text?"

"I did. You're off to classes, right?"

She nodded. "Yeah, I have to go. Can we talk later this afternoon?"

Behind her, Luna rolled her eyes.

I smiled. "Of course. I should be here."

Trista beamed. "Great, see you then." Spinning on her heel, she retreated and left the den.

Luna dropped into a seat across from me. "Couldn't you tell she was trying to hide something from you?" Her voice mocked me.

"What are you talking about?" I finally sipped my coffee and put the mug down. The rich flavor soothed me.

"Her scent. She had a garlicy, bitter smell. It was awful. You told us from the start to use our nose, and there you were with your coffee covering your face. What does a garlic and bitter scent mean? Isn't it that she feels guilty and she's hiding something?"

My jaw dropped. "You've been paying attention to the lessons?"

"What else would I do while sitting around this house? You don't have a pool."

I counted slowly in my head, so I didn't snap at her. "Yes, that is what those scents mean. Are you sure that's what you smelled?"

"Yes, and if you were better at being alpha, you'd have smelled it too."

Heat infused my body, and I debated tossing her out. Why would I spend time sniff testing every pack member? They were pack. *But what if she's right?*

"Wait," Conner's voice cut through my misgivings, "I got this one. I swear my parents repeated this more times than I can count ... and I'm going into engineering, I can count pretty high." He snorted at his own joke.

Crossing her arms, Luna shifted her skeptical gaze to him.

Despite her obvious doubt, he brightened. "Being new to having wolves, all our senses are intense. We see, hear, feel, experience everything in techno ... well, everything. What we need to do, by going to the roller rink, or a movie, or even the mall, is learn how to make everything white noise. Sure, there are scents that tell us a lot, but we can't be analyzing everything."

One of Luna's eyebrows rose as if to counter his statement. I wanted to say more, but I sipped my coffee, giving Conner time to finish his point.

His eyes darted to me before he continued his lesson for Luna. "Think about when you drive. You don't focus on every car in every lane, or every house, or every billboard. When you eat at a restaurant, there are people having conversations at other tables, yet we all learn to tune them out ... make them white noise. As wolves, we need to do that too."

"But this time it was dangerous. Trista is hiding something. What if it's important?" Luna snarled out, low and menacingly.

Again, I started to respond, but Connor gave a small shake of his head before speaking. This time he didn't drop Luna's gaze. "First of all, we are in the kitchen at pack house. This should be, and is, the safest place to be. If there is anywhere Pebble can relax, it is in the heart of the pack den." Luna opened her mouth, but Conner's hand flew up. "Moreover, she wasn't alone. The point of pack is to protect each other. That's why we call each other a pack, a group. Today, you helped her. Another time, she'll help you ... she has been, actually, all week. That's what pack does. It's one of the lessons you've been ignoring."

Luna's head snapped around so she could glare at me. "And what if I don't want any of this?"

Hands trembling, I stood. "Then make a decision and act on it." Then I walked to my room to get away from her before I said or did something I regretted. My head hurt and my stomach roiled for more food and coffee, but I'd get that later.

It was early, but not that early. After a few calming breaths, I pulled out my phone and texted José. *When you get this, please give me a call.*

Navigating to my book app, I started to read. It was hard to focus, but it was a book I'd read before. I just needed the escape.

Before I got to the second page, my phone rang.

"José? You're awake?"

"I am for you. What's up?"

"I'm feeling sick. My head is pounding. It's so much." I could hear the frustration and tears in my voice. I didn't know who else to go to.

"Oh, Pebble. First off, breathe." I did. "Good. Now, I know you have a huge number of members in your head. I'm guessing there are big emotions right now."

I took another shaky breath. "Yeah, they're stabbing into me. What used to be a swarm of bees has turned into juggling knives, and the performers sucks."

José laughed. "Close your eyes and imagine the group. You have them behind a fence, right?"

"Yeah."

"Okay. Can you sort them into low and high emotions?"

"I can do that. The high emotions are the ones with their *nails* out ... those are the knives."

He hummed. "That makes sense. How many are digging in?"

My body trembled as I tried to focus. "Um, five of them. Easton, Tanner, Luna, Trista, and Julez." My throat was dry. I tried to swallow. "I think I know why each of them is upset. Well, not Julez, but all the others."

"Okay, here is the big question, Ms. Leader. Is there anything you can do to help them, right here, right now?"

My head started to shake. "No. I mean, maybe Luna, but she's a piece of work. We're having problems here, José, like what you faced there. I think I'm in over my head. I don't know if Tanner thinks I'm doing everything wrong. Luna absolutely thinks I'm a hack. But I'm not sure what else I *can* do."

"Tell me, if you think it'll help."

I started talking, and before long, I'd laid the whole story out to him. "I'm sorry. You have your own group to lead, and kids, and everything. You don't need all my stuff, too."

"Pebble, like the very smart Conner said, you're not an island. More than that, to me, to us, you're family. I'm glad you reached out to me for help. Even if it's just to hear that you're doing fine. You have Tanner and Easton doing what they do best. You're working on training the new recruits. Take comfort that you've done what you should do. As for Luna, she's just trying to get under your skin. Pretty soon you're going to have to tell her with more finality to make a decision. Be a team player or leave. Undermining you is *not* an option."

His take on the situation brought a level of ease, though I still had Luna's voice badgering me in the background. "Thank you, José."

"Of course. Now, just like with the extra sensations we get every day, if what you're getting from behind that fence isn't anything you need to rush out to deal with today, pack it up. Don't let it overtake your mind."

Having the words I gave Dayna, Luna, and Conner echoed back to me reinforced that I had to slow down and think. I knew this. I *could* do it. "You're the best, you know that, right?"

"As are you. Talk to you soon. And just think, in two days you'll have Jade to talk to as well." He chuckled. "Two Es in one place. My mind boggles."

"As does mine."

Feeling better, I spent a few minutes getting my head in order. Once my hands stopped trembling, I went to get more food and coffee. I was braced to face Luna but found Dayna instead. She smiled wide when she saw me. "Morning, Pebble. I heard you on the phone this morning. Did I hear something about a death?"

I sighed. "You know, you and your two animals are going to be a nuisance. That extra level of hearing will not be my friend."

She chuckled as I made a second bagel and poured coffee. "So, there *has* been a death?"

"Two, actually. Tanner and Easton, his son, are monitoring the situation. I'll be bringing it all up at the pack meeting on Sunday." I sat and started eating. This time I didn't feel nauseous. "Could I convince you to forget you heard anything and wait until then?"

"Or," she said with a wide smile, "I could give you some friendly advice?"

Her words hit me as less helpful than she probably intended, but I shrugged. "You could."

"Why aren't you bringing any of this up to Luna?"

With a sigh, I shut my eyes, then focused on her. "For a few reasons." Dayna just watched me, waiting for me to continue. "Well, she told me this morning she wasn't sure she would be staying with the pack. If she's going to leave, she's really not my partner or co-alpha."

Dayna's mouth dropped open a bit. Then she snapped it shut. "Okay, is that your only reason?"

"No. I also am tired of her constantly critiquing me and finding me lacking. I'm sure if she heard about the killings, she'd find a way to make it my fault. I decided I'd put that off for a day or two. You know, spread out the mockery."

Dayna's face hardened. "Right. She just needs to realize there's more in this world than Luna Zweck."

Chapter 19 – A Lesson For Everyone

After breakfast, the rest of the morning went smoothly. Conner and Luna joined Dayna and me in the kitchen, and we all continued with the training.

Whenever Luna started to get her attitude, Dayna shot it down. At one point, the laid-back Dayna lost it, something I didn't think was possible.

"Luna, what is the point of making these sessions horrible? We're all here for a purpose. Conner is excited about the move, I'm thrilled to have finally made the shift from bear to wolf, Pebble is giving up her winter break to teach us, and here you are acting like a jerk, making everyone miserable. You know, you *could* just go back to Maine. It's always an option."

Luna's mouth hung open. "What have I done?" She smelled genuinely confused. "I came here. I let her bite me. I'm now a wolf. I've been sitting here acting nothing but pleasant while she drones on."

I bit the inside of my cheek to keep a blank face.

Dayna barked out a laugh. "You have done everything *but* be pleasant. You've put Pebble down at every chance you've had. You know what, there are five other werewolf packs in The US, why not go to one of them? Though, if I were you, I wouldn't select California, it's made up of her family. That leaves ..." Dayna faltered.

Conner picked up her sentence, though he spoke conversationally. "Florida, Tennessee, Colorado, and Massachusetts." His smile widened. "But since Pebble's parents are leading Tennessee, I'd avoid going there, too. Then again, you're alpha level. You could take over there and they could return here."

Dayna waved a hand at him. "There you go, options. If you go out East, you'll even be close to the other geese gaggles."

Luna rolled her eyes. "You're forgetting, I could also go off on my own and not be under the rule of some alpha.

Become a—" she snapped her fingers, brow furrowed, "—lone wolf."

I nodded. "You could. That tends to be hard because other lone wolves can sense you and some of them are unstable. Attack first, question never."

She rolled her eyes. "Whatever. Scare tactic much?"

"Not really, but you'll learn about lone wolves if you stick around." I blinked slowly to avoid showing my frustration at her. "That said, we're getting off topic. Before any decisions are made, you need to know as much as I can tell you. You can make your final decision after the first run. That's usually when you and your wolf know what you really want."

"So, you want us to stay until Tuesday," Luna said snidely.

"Wednesday. The run is at night, and we won't get done until technically Wednesday morning. As for what I *want*, I want to spend winter break with less stress. Since that is obviously a lost cause, what is best is for you to learn what you can so that you're informed for whatever choice you make ... kind of like your mom mentioned."

Everyone took that in, then I said, "Can we move on?"

Luna rolled her eyes—again—but didn't make a snarky remark.

At two in the afternoon, Trista returned, the red glow around her apparent. I'd gotten used to everyone else's to the point I'd forgotten they were there.

I decided to call it quits for the day. Dayna pulled me aside. "I heard you telling your friends you'd have lunch with them on Saturday. Is there any reason to not go out with them tonight? I think getting away may be the best thing for everyone." Her eyes cut to Luna. "You two need some time apart."

Conner came up behind Dayna, nodding. "Sorry to be listening in, but I agree. Luna needs some time to let things sink in. She's had a lot of changes in her life. She's taking all her stress out on you. If you weren't here, she'd have to find a different outlet for everything she's feeling. She may even have to process something."

I bit back a smile. "Are you sure?"

They both just looked at me. "Okay, yeah. I'll send them a text making sure they're available. If they are, after I talk with Trista, I'm out." I gave them each a hug and instantly felt better from the pack touch. "Thank you."

Conner smiled. "As I said earlier, it's what pack does."

That settled, I sent a text to Hollis, then led Trista to the office. I figured she'd want privacy. She sat in the seat across from me with a tight smile. She wore a cheap perfume that had to be mostly chemicals. I tried to breathe from my mouth to avoid a headache. "So, you had a rough night? Did something happen with your family? Is your grandfather okay?"

She leaned back and rubbed her hands on her thighs. "My family? Oh, yeah. He's doing okay. I mean, I think so. They haven't contacted me since we spoke ... my family isn't great with communication." I could hear the frustration in her voice about that and knew that was truth. "As for what I wanted to talk about ... I don't even know where to start. After classes, I went out with a friend. He said we'd have a great time. We went to this restaurant and bar on Willy Street ... you know where that is, right?"

"Willy Street?" I nodded, though dread tickled down my spine. It was a pretty well-known street on the near east side. It was also where two of the bodies had been dumped. "Be careful around there. It's not the safest area. Actually, if you plan on going to Willy Street again, I'm going to ask that you don't go alone."

"So, you want me to call you?" She didn't sound angry, just inquisitive.

"Or someone else from the pack. There's safety in numbers."

"I was with my friend," she shot back, then shook her head. I tried to hear if she spoke the truth or in half-truths like at other times, because I couldn't easily use scent. She was still adjusting to being a wolf and our way of speaking truths. With Trista, it was hard to tell. She sounded like *she* wasn't sure.

I'm failing as her alpha, as Luna keeps telling me. I need to do better!

Her head tilted as if she could hear me, though I knew she couldn't. Then she continued. "Sorry, I'm just used to being independent." That was a lie, but not worth calling her out on. I got that being in college and on your own for the first time was exciting. "I know you just want what's best for me. I can make sure I'm not alone if I'm ever down there again. Being with a school friend, is that good enough?"

"That should be good. As long as you aren't by yourself. And thanks." Relief flooded me that she was so understanding. "And, yes, as long as you two were together the whole time, that should be fine. No walking alone."

I sneezed and realized whatever she was wearing ... this couldn't happen again. "Are you wearing perfume?" Despite not breathing deeply, the smell made my head pound.

"Oh, sorry. Someone at school got something new at Macy's and sprayed everyone in class. She got me before I could stop her." Trista looked up at me with wide eyes. "I was going to shower when I got home, but it reminded me of my mom."

As always, her emotions were in turmoil. I rubbed my face. "Yeah, okay." I could tell she was still speaking in half-truths, but breathing in deeply wasn't an option.

A fox tangled in a web isn't a spider.

With the scent knifing through my brain, I didn't need riddles from my wolf as well. *Not helping!*

Trista smiled wide. "Is this what being alpha is? Keeping everyone safe?" She sounded so curious.

"When it comes to my wolves, yes. Just so you know, this rule about not being on Willy Street alone isn't something I'm implementing forever, just for a few days, maybe a week."

She narrowed her eyes. "Are you testing out your new power?" There was a teasing note in her voice, and she smirked at me.

I chuckled, trying to relax. "No. There have been some reports of dangerous things around. I'd rather wait until I know more before I talk about it. I'll be giving more information at the full pack meeting on Sunday."

Her face scrunched up, then she nodded. "You know you can trust me, right?"

All my muscles tightened, masking any response from showing. I wanted to say 'yes, you're pack, of course I trust you,' but the words stuck in my throat. There was too much confusion surrounding her ... too many questions. My head tilted. "Sure, as much as anyone ... you know."

Her smile was wide and genuine. "Because you're like my best friend in this city. I'd do anything to help you. I'm also a lot more powerful than I seem. If you need help, like a partner, you know I'm always available."

My gut twisted at the thought, and I felt phantom claws digging in.

"Are you talking about aiding with the pack?"

She shrugged. "Maybe. This is all new to me, but I know you've been under a lot of pressure. If you need support, I'm here. We're friends. I don't judge you. I never will."

I paused before answering. There was an underlying *like others judge you* that she didn't need to say. Despite that, I agreed with my wolf's visceral reaction. "Thanks, Trista. I'll keep that in mind. It'd be amazing to have the help. Let's talk after the next full moon run. Right now, I'm just trying to prepare for my sister's visit and the upcoming meeting."

Her face lit up. "Great! I've really felt a connection to you since we met. I'd even be willing to explore that connection more, you know?"

I didn't know and I needed to change the subject. This wasn't what I thought we were here to discuss. "So, what happened between you and this friend on Willy Street last night?"

Trista slumped. "He was awful. We had dinner, then we took a walk. But he killed the mood by the end, you know what I mean. I was so ... I don't know."

Her wording, though perfectly acceptable, sent chills down my spine. Death and Willy Street in any combination, made me wary. "Are you going to see him in classes again? Hang out?"

She shook her head. "No, I don't think so. We shared a class last semester. Now we just study together now and then. After last night, I think I'm done with him. Dead and buried, so to speak." She slapped her hands to emphasize her words, then rubbed them as if they were cold. "I just needed to get that off my chest. Officially say I am done, and he is released from my consciousness." Her arms stretched out and she looked up at the ceiling.

Like Trista with this guy, I felt like I was done with this conversation. Everything from the scent to her descriptions made me uncomfortable. "So, do you feel better?"

She dropped her hands back to her lap and gazed at me. "Yeah, I do. Thanks for listening to my confession ... of sorts."

One of my eyebrows rose. This was getting too weird. "Confession?"

A laugh burst from her. "Your face! Sorry, that's what my dad would always say." Her smile morphed into a sadder expression at the mention of him, the spicy and earthy scent of her anger and sadness cutting through even the perfume. She shook her head and huffed out a breath. "He'd always say, 'confess what you've done, Trista,' and I would."

I tried to smile, though I wasn't sure how successful I was. "Thanks for sharing that with me. I know it's hard to remember your parents, but thinking about the happy times is always good." For a moment, I thought anger crossed her face, but it was gone too quickly for me to be sure. "Anyway, I'm glad I was here for you, though I'm going to introduce you to the submissive wolves on Sunday. They're really good at helping with emotional things too. Probably better than me."

Trista's nose scrunched up. "I guess, but I like talking with you."

"When I'm around, sure. But I'll be in classes soon as well."

She squinted past my shoulder, as if trying to figure something out. "Right. I'll talk to you soon."

"Talk to you soon." I leaned back as she walked to the door.

Once it was shut, I pulled out my phone. Hollis had texted back that she was thrilled at the idea of dinner. She knew exactly where we should go. *Be here by five. Fern and I are ready to blow this joint (up!)*

I checked my watch. It was just after four. In my room I changed, then I found the others in the living room. "Okay, I'm off for the night. I'll see you in the morning. I have a brunch meeting with a few of the pack members at nine in the office so tomorrow will be a late start."

Luna's face scrunched up, but Dayna glared at her and she shrugged.

Dayna smiled. "Have fun and don't worry about us. We're thinking of taking Conner on a driving tour of campus ... if we can take one of the pack cars."

"Assuming you can drive and you're willing to fix any damages, sure, go for it. Have some fun." I headed out before anyone could say anything else.

Chapter 20 – Dinner And
A Dance

It didn't take long to get to Hollis's house. She and Fern weren't waiting outside; it was too cold.

Hollis lived on a quiet street with two story homes on both sides. Her small, light blue house had a two-car garage, white trim, and a small porch that her parents left chairs and a table on year-round. Currently, the set was covered with frozen leaves and a dusting of snow.

The driveway had two cars in it, and I knew there was at least one more in the garage. After parking on the street, I made my way to the door and rang the bell.

Mr. Panto answered. "Pebble! It's been a while since I've seen you. How did your first semester go?"

"It went well ... I survived. Thank you."

He waved me in. The front door opened to a wide living room with a couch, two recliner chairs, a small table full of mail, books, and other items, and at the far end, a TV that was paused.

Beyond the living room, Hollis's mom stood in the kitchen. "Evening, Pebble. Hollis and Fern are in Hollis's room. Why don't you go hurry them up?" She waved down the hall to my left.

I didn't make it two steps down the hallway, with its outdated, flowered wallpaper in blues and greens, before my friends came out of the room, both smiling.

Hollis leaned in, trying to speak quietly. "Dad wants me to drive my car. He said I haven't been using it enough and the thingy will get somethinged."

"It's true. And you need to learn more about cars, Hollis." I winked at her.

Fern snorted before giving me a hug. Their woodsy perfume calmed me. After the day I'd had, I could bathe in that scent. "Gas and oil will get old," they said to Hollis.

"See! Your friend gets it." Mr. Panto sounded proud of Fern.

I shrugged, stepped back, and held out my hand, knowing the answer to the next question before I asked. "Do you still want me to drive?"

"Please. I hate driving." Hollis tossed me the keys.

We all headed out of the house, Hollis and Fern collecting coats on the way.

Outside, I realized some of the color from the hallway followed my friends. Hollis had a bit of a green glow to her and Fern a blue. *Is this connected to Luna? If I get rid of her, will it go away, too? Nope, not thinking about anything outside of normal teen drama from here on out.*

In the car, I asked Hollis, "Where are we going?"

"That great Thai place on Willy Street." She clicked her belt on, her excitement evident.

"Really?" The street was becoming an epidemic in my mind. "Why there?"

Hollis's mouth dropped open. "Besides being your favorite?" She reached over to touch my forehead. "Are you sick, by the way? I can't believe you're questioning my brilliance. If you've forgotten, Fern's never had it."

There was no way I could explain why this was a horrible idea. And the thought of the restaurant made my stomach rumble its agreement. Then again, there were three of us; safety in numbers.

Feeling a whole new stress, I took a deep breath, and Fern's perfume instantly relaxed me. In a better mood, I started the car and headed towards the restaurant.

Parking in that area was awful. We ended up finding a spot a block away on a residential cross street. As we passed a small artist's shop on the way to the restaurant, I paused. "Oh, my gods, I totally forgot!"

"What?" Hollis asked, coming up beside me.

"I bought a birthday gift for Owen, and they emailed me when I was on the school trip that it's ready." I looked at the door and saw they were open until nine. "Remind me after dinner to stop in and grab it."

Fern searched the display. "What did you get?"

"My brother loves exercise and creating programs for people to follow. He works as a trainer. I had vintage gym posters created. A half dozen of them. Since my sister is coming on Saturday, she can bring the gift back. I don't even have to mail everything and worry about what will happen in transit."

"That sounds cool." Fern studied all the fascinating items in the window display. "I bet he'll love it."

When we got inside the restaurant, the wait wasn't too bad. Fern was the only one who didn't know the menu, and it took them time to decide. Once we ordered, Hollis leaned forward. "What did Luna mean when she said that thing about real intentions?"

I slumped, then sipped my Thai coffee. The gods knew I needed it. "She was being Luna, that's what she meant. She's been a pill ever since she arrived, and I'm ready to send her home."

"Then why don't you?" Hollis insisted.

I sighed. "It's a long story, and I've been living the Luna drama for several days. Can we please talk about literally anything else?" I gave my best puppy dog eyes. "I want to hear how Fern convinced their parents to let them come visit. And how long do you get to stay?"

Fern smiled wide. "Now, that's a fun story."

Hollis harrumphed but winked. "It *is* fun. Fine."

"Okay, so, my dad really didn't want me to spend any extra time here. I wasn't sure why, but he didn't. After Christmas, he was set on my staying home until the Saturday before classes start ... like *that* dead set on me not coming here."

"Huh, interesting." The server brought our appetizer, and we started munching on chicken satay.

"I know, right? But let me back my story up ... like a lot. I told you my mom went to college here. Dad went to school in Georgia at the same time. They both graduated like thirty-some-odd years ago."

I chuckled. "They're about the same age as my parents. They graduated from Florida State like," I thought about it, "thirty-two? Years ago. I'm pretty sure that's it. They don't talk about it a lot, but every once in a while it comes up."

Fern's eyes narrowed. "Yeah, that sounds about right for my parents. Mom transferred to Georgia for graduate school and that's where they met. Anyway, Dad had a great job, but then after mom graduated, she wanted to move closer to her family. So, they moved north. Well, about ten years ago, Dad transferred to a different branch of his business. We ended up in Kentucky, not near any family. It was a bit hard for us to adjust, but now it's home."

I shook my head. "Okay, this was a fun walk down memory lane, but it doesn't explain why you're here now."

"Maybe I just wanted to share my past."

I lifted an eyebrow.

"Or," Fern said, "it's all connected. Dad's work near Mom's family, their CEO left. Dad got a call a couple of days ago. It really upset him. When he left, he made it clear he was leaving because of the people as much as anything. The idea of going back to that location, even as CEO, upsets him. But I guess there's a lot of pressure."

Our food came and we all dug in. After we made some headway, Fern sighed happily, then continued. "Anyway, Dad was storming around the house, not being pleasant. When Hollis reached out yet again, my parents decided my not being around would make their negotiations easier."

"Are you saying that your family has shipped you off so they can move? Will they at least let you know where they're moving to?" I teased.

Hollis snorted. "I wondered the same thing."

"Mom said she thought she remembered some of her friends who lived here. She may try to contact them to contact me, but it isn't a high priority since she's dealing with Dad's issues, and she knows I'm happy with everything. She said if *things change* to let her know."

"What type of things?"

Fern shrugged. "No idea. I plan on hanging out with the two of you and enjoying my winter break."

It felt like Fern was leaving something out, but then again, weren't we all? It sounded like their Dad had his hands full with work.

I leaned back as we finished our meals. "So, should we go back to your place and have ice cream sundaes and watch an old movie?"

Hollis's eyes widened. "Yes, it's been too long."

Fern leaned back. "What movie?"

Joy filled me. "Hollis, you choose." I knew what she'd say.

"As you wish!"

Fern laughed. "I love that movie! I haven't seen The Princess Bride in ... gods, like forever."

When the server came around, we paid and left.

The shop with Owen's gift was just over a block from the car. The rule was no one should be alone, but the air was cool and clear, and no one was around. I could slip into the store and be back to the car in no time. If I were to guess, whatever wolf had come to my pack's territory wasn't trained like I was. I could just get the gift and be on my way.

I handed Hollis the keys. "Go warm up the car, I'll be right behind you."

"You sure? We could all go in."

Guilt gnawed at me. This was exactly the opposite of what I'd told Trista earlier. But, again, I knew how to fight. I shook my head. "The store is small. This will only take a second."

Hollis smirked. "Great, we can make out in the backseat of the car and really steam it up."

I groaned and reached for the keys, but Hollis backed up, laughing.

Shaking my head, I entered the store. There weren't any other customers, and the artist glowed as I picked up the artwork I'd already paid for. She even had everything bagged and ready to go. I was in and out in probably less than a minute.

Hopefully I could catch up to my friends before Hollis made true on her threat.

As I turned the corner, I heard a scream and a grunt.

No! It can't be. I was only away for a second.

Another yelp and I recognized Hollis's voice.

My blood ran cold, and my feet ran before my mind could process. I'd left my friends alone when I knew—*I knew!*—there were dangerous wolves around.

"I got this one. Leave her, she's a nobody." The gruff voice spurred me on faster.

There was a small alleyway behind the artist's building. A man stood just inside the alley with a knife to Fern's throat. One sniff told me he was a wolf. I dropped my bag, but Fern shook their head. "Get away, Pebble, it's not safe."

Another scent and whimpering had me turning. A second wolf, in animal form, was gnawing on Hollis's leg.

"Pebble, run!" Fern yelled. They didn't sound freaked out, more like they wanted to protect me.

Run? As if.

With a snarl, I released the full force of my alpha mantle, blanketing the area. I'd never let it all out before, knowing that much power could shock some wolves painfully, if they weren't ready.

The wolf holding Fern dropped to his knees and started to whimper. I pulled out my phone and unlocked it, handing it to Fern. "Call Tanner. Tell him where we are and what you see."

Fern nodded.

I darted towards the wolf, whose mouth was still on Hollis, but it wasn't moving. I tackled it. It tried to fight back, but I easily overpowered it. I held it pinned as Hollis crawled away.

"Hollis, did it puncture your leg? Are you bleeding?"

She patted herself down.

"I ... I ... what are you doing? How are you holding that thing? Should I call the cops? Animal control?"

I shook my head. "Fern is calling someone." I gazed down the alley. "Fern! Did you make the call?"

They nodded "He said he was on his way. He said Easton was closer and would be here in a minute." There was an intensity to Fern's gaze as they watched me. "Pebble, you're not scared of the wolf, are you?" There was a matter-of-fact-ness to their voice.

I heard footsteps approaching and pulled back the mantle. Immediately, the wolf struggled more.

"Pebble, it's me." I'd never been so happy to hear Easton in my life.

"Easton, the man over there is one of them, and I have one pinned. My two friends are with me."

His head popped around the corner. With no lights in the dark night, he was like a shadow. As soon as I'd pulled my mantle back, the other man stood, but Easton grabbed him. "What should I do with him?"

"We need to know what they want."

Fern shook their head. "They wanted me."

Chapter 21 – The Secret Is Out

The wolf I held started to fight in earnest, attacking, biting, and scratching.

"Easton, do you have that one secure?"

"Sure do, boss."

I sighed. With a jerk of my arm, I snapped the neck of the wolf, the sound echoing in the silence of the night. Everyone in the alley froze, gaping at me. Easton was the least surprised; it looked like he just reacted to the sudden sound.

Fern opened their mouth, then shut it with a snap. Hollis trembled. Looking her up and down, I didn't see any blood. I knew I needed to do a better check on her, but there were bigger issues first.

Easton put plastic restraints on the man. "I'm taking him to ... you know. I'll be there when you're ready. Do you want me to wait to question him?"

I pushed myself up to standing.

The man dropped to the ground, white froth coming from his mouth.

Easton swore, then knelt. "He had a pill in his mouth. It never occurred to me the lengths they'd go to avoid talking with us."

I bit back a snarl. "After the last one, we should've planned better." In the back of my mind, I wasn't sure how I could've predicted in all the ways this group would try to take themselves out, or even why. Maybe I should've demanded the meeting with Tanner and Clare sooner.

Tanner appeared behind Easton. He took in the scene at a glance. "This group is doing our job for us ... but they're also a pain." His gaze fell on Hollis and Fern and his face tightened. "Well, this puts a wrinkle in things."

"My friend here thinks they were the target." My jaw hurt from how tightly I clamped it shut.

Tanner stepped forward. "And why's that?"

Fern gazed at Tanner, then Easton, then me. "None of you are surprised by any of this."

Hollis practically squealed her frustration. "I am. What is going on? Why did a man throw me at a wolf? Why is there a wolf in the middle of town? And why is everyone so damn calm about it?"

Her arm shot down to point at the wolf. As it did we all looked to where the wolf slowly began to morph back to his human shape. I shut my eyes and sighed. "Tanner. Can you deal with this? I need to take these two somewhere and have a long talk with them."

Tanner shook his head. "Who is your friend?"

Fern watched the man, then huffed out a laugh. "Are you all wolves, then?"

I clamped my mouth shut tighter to stop myself from gaping.

Hollis trembled, shaking her head back and forth. "What do you mean by that question, Fern? What is going on? What is happening to that wolf?"

Tanner nodded. "Fern? Fern what? Who is your family?"

"I'm Fern Meadows, my Dad is—"

"Ronny. Ronny Meadows." He emphasized the last name with a snarl, biting it off as if it answered a question he'd been trying to answer for a while. "Your mom is Amy." Tanner's low voice cut through the night. "Well, hell, it's a small world, isn't it."

"Tanner," I said, low and calm. At least I tried to be calm. "Who are Fern's parents?"

"Fern's Dad is the one your parents are looking for. He would've taken over in Tennessee, if that bunch of mutts weren't so disrespectful. He left at the same time Maddy's family left to join up in California, only Ronny didn't want to live under another leader's rule."

"No," Fern said. "It was his job. I mean, part of it was not wanting to start over in a new," their face scrunched up, then they continued, "start over with a new group, but part of it was the only other location of his job was Kentucky. Mom and Dad decided they were powerful enough to be alone in a state without others."

Tanner nodded. "Will he go back and take over?"

Fern shrugged. "I don't know. He really didn't like how they treated me. I wouldn't go back there, but ... I don't know."

I put up my hands. "This is fun and all, but can we put this discussion off until we're not in an alley where people can come across us and two dead bodies?"

Tanner nodded. "Right. Fine. Bring Fern to the meeting tomorrow."

"Easton," I called out. "Will you help your dad with clean-up while I get these two home?"

"On it."

A rock had settled in my gut. I still didn't know if Hollis had been bitten badly enough to be a wolf, but that would be a problem for another day. For now I had a lot of explaining to do. How would I explain the werewolves to her, much less that most weren't dangerous ... or that I'd just killed one?

The enormity of it all hit me, and I tried to stay calm as I unlocked the car.

We got into the car, and I drove to the lake. The tension was thick and uncomfortable. Once I parked, I turned to look at my best friend. "Okay, so I've had a secret I've kept from you for ... a few years."

"A few years!" she screamed. I didn't cover my ears, though the pitch of her voice hurt. She was angry and I knew I deserved her anger. Even if I had no other choice, she was my friend and she was hurt. "My God, Pebble, what the hell was all that?"

"There are werewolves in the world. It's a tightly held secret. We don't tell anyone."

Her face hardened with each word. The spicy scent of her anger filled the car more and more as I spoke. It took an effort not to sneeze.

I licked my lips. "Though I wanted to tell you for years, it's a pack law that I couldn't."

"Why did that guy call you 'boss'?"

"My parents were the alphas of the pack. When they had to leave for their emergency, I took over until they get back."

Hollis's eyes widened. "You're acting alpha of a werewolf pack?"

Fern coughed lightly. "Well, that explains a few things."

Hollis glared at them. "I'm going to get to you next." Her head whipped back to me. "Wait, is there even a 'great aunt'? Or was that a lie, too?"

My mouth opened and shut a few times before I blew out air. "I had to tell you a reason they left. I couldn't say another werewolf pack had been attacked, and my parents were needed because we have the strongest pack in the country ... and a third alpha who can step up."

"Would you have ever told me?" Hollis sounded hurt.

I lifted my shoulders to shrug. "I didn't want to keep this from you, Hollis, but I really didn't have a choice. Again, it isn't just my pack, it's a werewolf thing."

"So that's a 'no.'" Her scent kept shifting from spice to cinnamon to earthy to nutmeg. Angry, annoyed, irritated, sad, and on and on. She was as confused as I was as to where she'd land.

Despite that, there was more I had to tell her. "I'm going to ask that you now keep the secret. You can't tell anyone, not even your parents. No one."

Her face tightened, the spicy anger winning out. "So, something happened to me. I could've died. You're not taking me to the doctors. And now I can't tell anyone but the person who caused the issue. How magnanimous of you."

"I'm really sorry." My voice was small, but I didn't know what else to say.

"Why don't you just take me home?"

"Can we make one stop first?"

"Whatever."

I quickly texted Conner, then headed to the pack house. He met us in the driveway. Hollis's eyes widened when she saw him and a few pieces fell into place. "Wait, he's a werewolf, too?"

I slowly nodded. "He is a specific kind of wolf, very rare. He can do things no other wolf can do, including determine if the wolf that bit you left any of his saliva behind."

Hollis's eyes got huge. "Are you saying I could be a werewolf now?"

Blinking back tears, I hated everything that was happening. Now that Hollis knew, so much of my life would be easier, but at the same time, this wasn't how I wanted any of this to happen. It felt like that rogue wolf had ripped open my chest and shredded my insides.

With effort, I swallowed the lump in the back of my throat and nodded. "It isn't a guarantee. Conner can let you know. Or, if you want to wait until this weekend, Jade can do this. They are the only two people in the world that I know of who have this ability."

Fern gasped in the back seat, their voice low when they asked, "He's epsilon?"

Over their words, Hollis sneered, "Oh, how convenient." She crossed her arms. "Whatever."

Conner reached in and offered his hand. Hollis took it. Leaning on the car for support, Conner took a few minutes. I really missed Jade's ability to do this instantly. She would have to teach Conner how she did it.

Finally, Conner pulled back. "I'm pretty sure she's not going to be a werewolf."

Next to me, Fern cleared their throat. "Can you ... um. Can you check me? I wasn't bitten, but I've also never shifted. I have two werewolf parents and just ... I'd like to know."

Conner smiled wide. "Of course."

My hand shot up. "Have you eaten enough?" Just my luck he'd pass out and I'd have something else to explain to my friends.

His mouth quirked up to one side. "Yeah, I should be good. But thanks for watching out for me."

It went much faster this time. "It looks like you have a black wolf, like mine, with a white-tipped tail. Your wolf said they'd be ready to run in three moons. It was the weirdest thing. Now, if you'll excuse me, I need to go find more calories."

He swayed a bit as he walked back to the house.

I need to create a snack bag and make sure he always carries something.

Fern's hand trembled as they turned to me. "March. I'm going to be a wolf in March." The vanilla scent of joy blasted from them as they sat, smiling.

"That's all fine and good for you, but can I go home now? And maybe, if you're so happy about being a wolf, you should pack up and stay here. The house is plenty big enough to host you."

Fern paused and their face fell. "I'd rather stay with you, but if you need space ... I'll do what you'd rather."

Hollis grunted, but didn't say anything more.

I started the car and headed to Hollis's house. She was quiet for most of the ride. As I pulled into her driveway she sighed. "I need time. I think you should stay with Pebble, if she has room for you."

Fern gazed at me, their expression a mixture of hope and sadness.

I merely nodded.

Chapter 22 — Meeting Of The Minds

I slept in on Friday morning. After arriving home and getting a room set up for Fern, we talked about Hollis and if we thought she'd come around any time soon. Once Fern seemed to be calm, I went to bed.

Pushing myself from bed, I decided to skip exercising. I dressed and made my way to the kitchen. Fern and

Dayna sat with coffee and food. I poured an oversized mug of coffee and put a bagel in the toaster.

"Morning," I yawned. "Where are the others?"

Dayna took a bite of her cereal. "No idea. I just got here."

I nodded. "Sounds good." I checked my watch. "I have a meeting at nine. Tanner and Clare will probably be here in the next half hour."

Conner came up from the barn, body covered in sweat. He waved at the three of us. "Dayna, want to head back to campus and walk State Street?"

Dayna's eyes twinkled. "That would be great."

"Let me go shower." Conner headed for the hallway, the citrus scent of excitement coming from him and Dayna.

I waggled my eyebrows at her. "Well, that was easy. You two will have fun today. Don't get into trouble. I have enough on my plate." I sipped my coffee. "But do text if you need to."

Her cheeks colored a light pink. "I think so. He's so nice and always so positive. It'll be nice to show him around."

Smiling wide, I leaned in. "Don't forget cheese curds. He can't call himself a pack mate if he hasn't had cheese curds."

With a chuckle, Dayna nodded. "Gods above, yes. Maybe we should try a few different locations, compare them. With his epsilon thing and my two animals, we probably need an excuse to eat at more than one spot."

Approval washed through me. "Sounds like a plan."

Fern leaned back with a small smile. "Epsilon." Their voice held a hint of wonder.

"You've heard of them." It wasn't a question.

"Yes, when I was young. There was rumor of an epsilon wolf in another pack. My alphas were so jealous. They wondered if they could figure out a way to get her to join our pack. But then she went out to California ... oh, my God, that's your sister, Jade, isn't it? You said something about that last night."

"It is. You've been out of the loop for quite a few years."

"I have. For the first year or two I texted with Maddy, but then she got busy. She's older than me and had college and a new pack to worry about. Also, after her mom died she became distant."

"I remember hearing about that. Those idiot Dynasty wolves. All they had to do was stay in their city and not bother the California pack. But no, they kept coming back, wanting to prove they were so much better. Sneaking onto their territory, fighting, and even starting that final battle." By the end my voice was a snarl.

Fern's face fell. "I don't know much of what happened. We were kept from the story in Tennessee. The alphas liked that there was a place to send wolves who didn't quite fit in."

My jaw dropped. "What? Really?"

"Yeah. Again, that's why we moved. Dad always struggled with me, but he figured he could since I was his kid. Anyone else should just roll with it. He always called Maddy what she wanted to be called, name and pronouns. It was only that he was losing a son that was a bit hard on him. Beyond that, I'm his kid, and he loves and supports me."

"Wow. Enough to leave the pack and become a lone wolf?" It boggled my mind, but I knew my family would've done the same thing.

"Yep."

The door opened and a moment later Tanner, Clare, and Aunt Allison came in. I stood and gave each of them hugs. "I'm glad to see all of you." I gestured to Fern. "Aunt Allison, you know Fern, though, not their whole story. Tanner, you met them last night. Clare, this is Fern, one of my new friends."

Clare shook Fern's hand.

Conner, Dayna, and Luna came through the living room. Tanner narrowed his eyes at the group.

Seeing where Tanner's gaze landed, I asked, "Luna, are you going with the others downtown?"

Luna's lip twitched. "Do I have to check in?"

I sighed. "No, I was just asking."

Tanner shook his head. "I'd like Luna to be at our meeting, if it's all the same. Some of this business should involve her as well."

My gut clenched and I gazed up at him questioningly. He grunted. "Things are getting big. We need to look at the larger picture and decide on issues that affect the entire pack. Luna is here and until she has decided to not join the pack as alpha, and is off our territory, I'm going to treat her as your wolf does. In my eyes, she's one of the leaders."

She rolled her eyes. "Fine. Dayna, go have fun. I have to sit and be bored."

Clare's face tightened. Tanner's didn't visibly change, but I could tell he was ready to snap.

Aunt Allison walked over to Luna and placed a hand on her shoulder. "We are not your keepers, Ms. Zweck. You are welcome to go with your friends. To us, this is life and death, not a game. If you're going to throw our world in our face as if it's nothing more than trash, my vote would be for you to pack and leave. I'm sure your parents would love to have you back in Maine. But, being nothing more than a submissive and the heart of the pack, I can't enforce my vote, just state it."

She smiled, spun on her heel, and walked up the stairs, waving at Fern as she passed.

Tanner had a small twitch at the side of his mouth. *Was he laughing?* Clare just nodded. The two of them followed Aunt Allison towards the office.

I stood next to Fern. "What'll it be, Luna? You have to decide. The choice has always been yours. Meeting or State Street?"

"What did she mean, life or death? All of you are so dramatic. And what is Fern doing here? I thought this was all supposed to be hush-hush."

Fern opened their mouth, but I put a hand on their arm.

"Answers lie upstairs in the office. The choice is yours." I didn't wait for her response. Tugging Fern's hand, I followed the others up and sat behind the desk, the leader in this meeting of minds.

Before the door swung shut, Luna sauntered in. She closed the door and took the last seat. Once everyone was settled, I faced Tanner. "Did you fill Clare and Aunt Allison in about everything that's happened this week?"

He shook his head. "Nope. I thought I'd let you have the privilege ... boss." He smirked after he used the word Easton had in the alley and Owen's favorite term.

Thinking of family, something in me loosened, and I smiled wide at his choice of words. It took several minutes to catch everyone up on what had happened. Between the two deaths and Fern's family history, the news was longer than I'd realized.

When I finished, Clare's face was hard. "So, the group of lone wolves that has come up here has lost three. Do we have any idea why they are here or how many there are?"

"They could be here because they heard Mom and Dad left and think we're easy pickings." The thought left me cold inside. "All I know is they are hiding something big enough that they are willing to die to keep their secret."

Luna opened her mouth and dread at what she'd say slammed into me. I held up a hand. Since she was new to the pack, I'd given Luna some freedom, but we were in a meeting and things were different. "Before you speak—and this will be the only warning I'm giving you—if the words that come out of your mouth are meant to mock or critique me in any way, I'll have Tanner throw you out a window."

Tanner's eyes glowed and the vanilla scent of pleasure wafted from him as he mumbled, "Or off the roof."

Her eyes narrowed. "You wouldn't."

"Actually, I would. This is a werewolf pack, and dissension in the ranks is not tolerated. I put up with it for a few days because you're new, but I'm done. People are being attacked, people are dying, and we have to work together, as a team, to figure this out. When a group attacked the California pack, it took them almost two years and a lot of deaths to clean out their city. I don't want that to happen here. And no, I'm not trying to compete with that pack, it's a desire to avoid death at the hands of people who probably shouldn't be wolves."

I gazed into the eyes of each person in the room. "Yes, I *am* new to being alpha and I *am* young, but I have been a wolf a long time and have a connection to my wolf unlike anyone I know. The Wisconsin pack has some of the most powerful wolves in the country. This group of riff-raff doesn't stand a chance ... as long as I'm not dealing with middle school antics."

Luna glared at me, then nodded. "I was *going* to say, maybe they are hiding the fact that they know someone in the pack. Have an inside line. How else did they know where you would be last night?"

I tilted my head worried she was thinking about one person. That said, a tension within me relaxed that she was taking this seriously. "No one knew where I'd be last night. We didn't decide until I picked up Hollis and Fern. Could there be a tracker on my car?"

Fern shook their head. "We took Hollis's car, remember? Maybe your phone? Or in your purse?"

Tanner snarled. "Easton and I will go over the house and car before the end of the day."

Sitting stiffly, Luna clasped her hands in her lap. "I agree that that's a good start. However, I think we should also think about checking out the people around us. What about your premonitions? You've had at least two—one during the pack meeting and one in the kitchen."

Everyone turned to me. "You have a valid point." I told them about my premonitions. "Though," I continued after relaying the three images I'd seen, "I still think it has to do with Tennessee. I know I shouldn't force my premonitions in a specific direction, but I was thinking about Mom, Dad, or Tennessee every time."

Fern narrowed their eyes on me. "You really have premonitions? You said something about it in the elevator but were vague. And your nightmares? And—"

My hands flew up. "Yes. Guilty."

They rubbed their face. "I agree with Luna. We shouldn't close down any avenue of investigation until we have answers."

Clare nodded. "Agreed. It'll be tricky, since half the new people are sitting in the room right now." One of her brows rose as she looked between Fern and Luna.

"I'll ask everyone at the meeting on Sunday to be mindful of people in their life who may be new or overly curious." I pursed my lips, then sighed. "One more thing. Until the pack meeting, we need to keep all this amongst us. Well, us and Easton. He knows what's going on. But we can't tell anyone else. If no one else knows, that will help us narrow down leaks."

Tanner smiled. "I agree. We're already a big group, but of the people in this room I know, no one will talk."

Aunt Allison smiled. "Was there anything else? I'd like to head back to my cats." Fern got a far-off look on their face. Aunt Allison patted them on the shoulder. "I would invite you, but you need to adjust to life here first. Maybe next week."

"That would be amazing."

Tanner grunted. "Maybe, maybe not. If we can get things locked down here, I wanted to speak with you about going home to speak with your dad. I could go with you."

Fern gaped at him. "Could Pebble join me? Kentucky isn't *that* far."

Closing my eyes for a moment, I thought. "Only if we get things figured out here or," my focus shot to Luna for a moment, "other things get figured out." I looked at Tanner. "This can be discussed after the full moon run, right?"

He nodded slowly. "Right. You'll have over a week before classes start, so a couple of days to get there and back should be doable."

"Well, let's get past my first full moon as an alpha and *then* make larger plans."

Everyone stood to leave. Aunt Allison waved. "I'm going to check in at the zoo. I'll be back at three for the next meeting."

"Sounds good." My shoulders dropped. One more obstacle out of the way.

Tanner and Clare stared at me, but I shooed them off. I turned to Luna. "We have until three. I'm going to spend some time talking with Fern about what happened last night. You are free to do whatever."

She shrugged. "Maybe I'll take to the skies. It's been a few days. I need to stretch my wings."

For a moment, the idea of flying sounded glorious, and I was jealous. "Sounds great."

Chapter 23 – Home Sweet Home

We ended up in the barn, walking the track. I had started off giving Fern a full tour of the house. It had been too late the night before. The last stop was the barn, and since it was too cold outside to walk the running path, and we both wanted to move, it was the perfect place to talk.

"I'm sorry you're not at Hollis's place anymore." I scrunched up my face. It wasn't really what I was sorry about, but it was a place to start. "I mean, I'm sorry about everything. I know you think those jerks were after you, but this has been going on for a few months. I don't know that they knew who you were."

Fern's shoulders lifted slightly before they dropped. "Yeah, I guess. It could be they only wanted one of us. But he seemed focused on me. It felt more personal, like maybe they wanted to find my dad."

I thought about that for a few seconds. "If they were the group that took out the Tennessee alphas, then yeah, that would make sense. They wouldn't want anyone taking over there. I wonder what that pack did to them that has made them so angry."

"Are you sure it's that pack?"

"Well, I mean, that's where they first attacked, right? Where else?" There was a huge puzzle in front of me with hundreds of pieces, but the images were covered up. Somehow, I had to figure out how to piece it together without knowing what the picture was supposed to look like.

"Here. They've attacked here three times. Four, if you count last night." Fern crossed their arms. "If that snake premonition has to do with them and it's about here and not Tennessee, then there may be a fifth attack or intrusion that we've, or you've, not seen." They stopped walking and turned to me. "Can I stay here? You know, because I'm not a wolf yet."

Warmth infused me. Finally, something I could easily answer. "Of course. Not only have you been part of a pack, you're a future wolf. I'd love to have you part of *my* pack, any day, any time. That room, it's yours. It used to be my sister's, but she left years ago. She'll be surprised when she comes back tomorrow that I'm foisting her down into the basement, but that's okay. She isn't moving back."

Fern's jaw dropped. "You're giving me your sister's room?"

"Yeah. I liked the idea of you being across the hall from me, at least for now. It's comforting."

Without warning, Fern sprang forward and engulfed me in a huge hug. I squeezed them back, a sense of calm and rightness coming over me as the woodsy perfume they used surrounded me.

They backed up, smiling. "Thank you. I know it's only been a few hours, but I grew up in a pack house. As soon as I walked in I felt ... I don't know."

I waited a beat, then reached out to take their hand. "I get it. There's a feeling of belonging and home I get every time I return from a couple of weeks at the dorms. I love being at college, having time to hang out with Hollis, meeting new people," I tightened my hold on Fern's hand, "and everything. But being here settles something deep within me."

Fern closed their eyes for a moment. "Yeah, that's it. For the first time in probably years I felt like I was coming home. It's in the air, the foundation of a pack den. I love it."

"Well, Fern Meadows, welcome home."

A vanilla and citrus scent filled the air. Hope, excitement, joy.

We walked in silence for a few minutes. Then I asked, "Should we call your dad? Let him know what's happened?"

"Yes, but not yet. He'll be at work and busy. Let's call him after the three o'clock meeting."

"What about Hollis, do you think we should call or text her?" What I really wanted to do was drive over and sit on her porch and wait until she was willing to talk with me ... us, but I didn't know if that would be a good idea.

"No, probably not. She's scared and hurt. I texted her this morning, telling her again I was sorry I kept secrets from her, that I love her, and was here when she was ready to talk. Beyond that, I don't want to push things."

A cold lump filled my gut. I couldn't imagine losing a friend I'd had since fifth grade. "Okay, I'll text her at lunch ... something similar. That way she'll know we're both here. Then the part I'm bad at." I sighed dramatically. "Waiting."

Fern clapped their hands. "Okay, new topic. Can you explain to me how the whole Luna thing happened? I've been trying to piece it together for days and I've got nothing."

I threw my head back and laughed. As we circled the barn, I told Fern about Jade's wedding and my first premonitions. The dreams, and how they evolved.

"You thought the honking was cars? God—wait, I can go back to gods."

The idea that they'd been good amused me. "You've never said God, for the record. I was going to ask but then debated waiting until we had time to talk, just you and me."

"Wait." They blushed. "I didn't?"

Chuckling, I shook my head. "No, you've said 'gods' every single time. I figured since I said it too, I wouldn't ask until you did."

Fern snorted. "I did notice you saying it. When I first heard it, it brought me back home and I didn't want to question you because I thought you might stop. Then when you had a family 'thing' every full moon. I mean, the pieces were all there. I didn't put them together because I kept telling myself I just wanted it to be true so badly I was seeing wolves where there weren't any. Though, the trip to Chicago right before Thanksgiving, when you talked about Jade and Bevin wishing they could go to the concert. Growing up, I'd always heard of the infamous epsilon wolf Jade from Wisconsin. My Mom and Dad always said, 'it's a shame her brother Owen wasn't an epsilon, too.' I was too young to know much more than those two names. I did hear the alphas complaining about that darn epsilon going to California, so the Tennessee pack couldn't get her. So, then when you said Jade and Bevin from California .... I kept thinking, if your brother had been Owen, not Bevin."

"You thought Bev was my brother?" That got me laughing. "Well, I mean, you're not too far off. They all treat me like a little sister. But I've always had a special connection with Owen. That said, Owen didn't love that band as much as Bevin. And if you ever see Bevin and Jade together, you'll see why I link them in stories. They act like twins sometimes."

Fern smiled.

I sighed. "I guess I wasn't being as subtle as I should've been."

"Well, I didn't completely figure it out and I am the child of two wolves, so I think you're fine. But finish your story."

I continued to tell them about Dayna learning my secret at Thanksgiving, and then the biology trip to Colorado.

"Whoa, you were partnered up with Luna, and then the two of you were attacked? And *that's* how you learned about each other."

"Yeah, it was a wild and crazy trip."

Luna came into the barn, glared at us, then went into one of the private rooms and turned on a YouTube exercise video. It was loud enough that we knew she couldn't hear us talking.

"Okay," Fern eyed the room suspiciously, "I'm mostly caught up. I just don't understand how you two got here. She's so ... prickly. She doesn't seem to want to be here. Are you forcing the issue? Are her parents?"

I shook my head. "No, and the annoying thing is, if you watch her with Dayna or Conner, she can be nice. She's really pleasant with anyone she considers her own."

"Then why not send her away? Just make the decision and be done with it?"

"I've thought about it, but if she'd be good for the pack, I'll put up with almost anything. My wolf thinks she's who I need, and my wolf has never been wrong. The Wisconsin pack is amazing. We're strong and a tightly-woven community."

In the end, I can't be the one to be this pack's undoing. My parents left me with something amazing. I haven't even been in charge for two weeks and I worry I've already messed up so much. Despite knowing Fern would try to bolster my self-esteem, I felt like only Luna saw my mess-ups for what they were and told it to me like it was.

Yes, I was trying my best, but when it came to life and death, was my best good enough?

Fern clasped our hands again. "But, Pebble, pack isn't everything. What about you?"

"Right now, it has to be about pack. I'm young, I'm new to being an alpha, and we're in a sticky situation. I can't fail. As I said, my wolf believes Luna is the right match to keep our pack strong. She's never steered me wrong."

We continued in silence for a few seconds. "I guess, if you want to be philosophical, Luna possesses the essence of yugen. Her own mysterious beauty."

I squeezed my eyes shut for a moment. "Yugen?"

They laughed. "It's a Japanese concept." Fern waved their hand back and forth. "It's a hard to describe aesthetic. It's about finding the good in a difficult or deep experience or situation."

That made me snort. "Got it. So ... Luna."

Fern slid an arm around me. "Okay. I just want you to remember you are more than the Wisconsin pack. You deserve things, too. If I need to have a talk with your wolf to explain that to her, I will."

Amused at the thought of Fern wagging a finger at my wolf, totally unafraid, I imagined them in front of a line of wolves, feet wide, chiding them for their misdeeds. "Why do I have a feeling you've yelled at wolves in your past?"

They winked, a smile stretching across their face.

Chapter 24 – Dog Pile

Fern and I sat in the living room relaxing when Dayna and Conner returned. They sat together on the loveseat. Conner leaned forward. "That was great. I love that street, and I love the campus. I mean, it's cold, but I think this was the right move."

Dayna's eyes twinkled and she was all smiles. "We tried cheese curds at three different restaurants. They were all good, but we've decided we're going to set up a rating system and over the next few months have everyone in the pack participate. That way we can all judge the food, as well as each other's pallets."

A laugh bubbled out of me. "Gods, that's hilarious. I think the pack will get behind that. Friendly competition is always fun. Maybe we could add pizza, though we'd have to determine a specific topping to be consistent. I can ask at the meeting on Sunday what everyone thinks ... unless one of you wants to bring it up."

Dayna practically vibrated. "Oh, I could do that. It's the kind of impression I'd like to make as one of the newest members."

There was a crunch of wheels in the driveway. Noting the time on my watch, a quarter to three, I pulled my phone from my pocket and sent a text to Luna. *Our next meeting is at three. Please meet me in the living room.*

The front door opened, and a sense of peace enveloped me. Chris and Andy walked in, and I stood to give each of them a hug. Chris gave me a once over. "Well, you look like you've survived your first week as being our fearless leader." He spun his finger in the air. "Go ahead, turn."

I chuckled as I twirled. When I faced the pair again, Andy had his hands on his hips. "I can't believe you're playing his games. Though, you're looking right as rain, Pebble."

"I'm so glad the two of you are here. There is so much going on."

They both watched me, waiting for me to continue. I waved at a couch, but they just searched the faces of the people in the room, not moving.

"Fine," I said, my voice full of exasperation. "Chris, Andy, we have new pack members. Some are new wolves, some *will* be new wolves." As I introduced them to each person, Luna arrived from upstairs. Then Aunt Allison showed up.

Since Aunt Allison knew everyone, I didn't have to start the introduction over. Once everyone had shaken hands, they finally sat down.

"Thank you all for coming. I wanted you to come—"

It was then that Trista ran through the front door, breathing hard. "I am so sorry for coming in late. My class ran over, and then there was traffic." She shook her head. "I tried to be early, but it just wasn't in the cards." She cringed, shrugged, then dropped in the remaining recliner.

My head buzzed with the mixture of truth and lies she told. Considering she was a wolf and knew wolves could hear lies, I wasn't sure why she continued to cover things up. Maybe it was because her entrance into werewolf life was recent. *I wonder if she lied to her parents a lot. Little lies she didn't think mattered. Maybe it's just so much a part of her life she doesn't even think about it. Like the opposite of me who refuses to lie. I'll have to talk with her about it ... again.*

I sighed. "It doesn't really matter why you're late. The important thing is that you're here." Slowly, I let my gaze roam the faces of everyone in the room. These were my people, my wolves, my pack. Warmth filled me at the thought. "I wanted to bring you all together to discuss submissive wolves."

Trista shot up. "I'm not submissive. Why am I here?"

With an effort, I pushed down my irritation. Though Trista had a lot going on—we all did—I just wanted to get through this meeting. I raised my hands, signaling her to sit back down. "Yes, I know you're not a submissive wolf, however, my Aunt Allison, Chris, and Andy are. They're the heart of the pack. They have a connection to us, unlike my connection to you or even Conner's, once he learns what his is."

"Wait," Conner's brow knit. "I have a special connection to the pack?"

I chuckled, as did the three submissives who knew many of Jade's tricks. "You do. But we'll wait until tomorrow when Jade gets here to start epsilon school. I'm still over the moon that I have an epsilon wolf in my pack."

Chris and Andy gaped, and then Chris slapped his knee. "You said new wolf ... but an epsilon to boot? You needed to bring in two people, but you found a way to gift us a flying wolf and an epsilon, Pebble, all in under a week. What alpha has ever done that? Truly the best."

Happiness filled me. "You and your obsession with flying wolves."

He shrugged. "I can't help it. I'm just jealous."

Andy sighed, rubbing his husband's back. "Speaking of jealousy," he faced Conner. "I bet your parents are bummed you left. Have they started to offer you gifts if you return home?"

Conner's face glowed with his amusement. "Nah, they want me to be happy, get a good education, both at college and from your sister, and *then* return with all my new powers well-trained."

Howls and hoots erupted around the room. "Of course they do." I shook my head. "Anyway, we have three really amazing submissive wolves. By being connected to me, you are connected to them. When you have a really intense emotion ... I should say negative emotion, they will feel an echo of it. Don't be surprised if they call or reach out in some other way. They'll then help you as they can."

Luna's eyes narrowed. "More people playing in my mind?"

Chris snorted. "Not really. It's pretty rare that an emotion reaches us. We prefer when you reach out to us with the technology you all have. That said, the big emotions, big sads, usually get to us. Like when Pebble learned her parents were leaving, we received the echo. I'd been warned about it, so I didn't immediately call. Also, when it's Pebble, usually Allison takes point."

"Do you three have a group chat to determine who's going in?" I narrowed my eyes at them, suddenly realizing I'd never been approached by more than one of them.

Chris beamed at me. "Actually, we do. It saves on time and energy."

"Huh," I said intelligently.

Dayna tilted her head. "Is this a wolf thing, or do the other weres have it? I don't know if I've heard of the werebears doing anything like this."

Andy waved his arms out to the sides in a shrug. "Until Jade learned about her gym teacher, I didn't even know there were werebears, so I have no idea."

Chris leaned over. "Love, until we started dating, you didn't know about werewolves either."

"Well, that's true. But I've come a long way in the last twenty years."

Luna turned to me. "So, what, you want us to befriend these three? Isn't your aunt the one who threatened me earlier today?"

Both Chris and Andy swung to look at Aunt Allison, who just smiled. "I didn't threaten you, dear, I just gave you the low-down on the situation here. We need you to be your best self. Your angst and frustration have been bombarding us all week. Your priorities are all wrong."

"So, you *are* in my head." Her face screwed up.

"No, you're projecting. We can help you figure out how to be less ... loud, if you want."

"I ... yeah. I guess." Her anger suddenly shifted to confusion.

We spent the next hour and a half talking and getting to know each other better. In the end, everyone, including Luna, was having a good time. It was hard not to, with the submissives.

Once the three submissives left, I gazed at the others with a mischievous look.

"I have an idea."

Before I could say anything, Trista shot to her feet. "Hold that thought. I have to get to a study group tonight. Does your thought involve me?"

Disappointment bit inside, but I shook my head. "No, that's fine. Will you be back later?"

"I was thinking of crashing at my friend's place. Driving across town that late isn't my favorite thing to do. But I'll be back tomorrow." She came over and gave me a hug. "I'm so envious of your longer winter break. Soon we'll all be trying to figure out our classes." With a cheeky grin, she spun and headed for the door.

Knowing Luna would be judging me, I'd slowly breathed in while Trista spoke. She'd spoken more truths this time. She was busy and distracted and driving was definitely something she wanted to avoid.

I watched her go, then shook off my disappointment. "Okay, my plan." I gazed at the remaining new pack members still in the living room.

Dayna leaned back. "I don't trust that look, Pebble. What are you planning?"

"We need to bond. We've been spending this week training, but it's been disparate and stressful. We need a night to be teens."

Fern narrowed their eyes. "What are you thinking?"

"Follow me." I dragged the group to the basement. "Tonight we watch movies, lying on mattresses. We eat ice cream sundaes and pizza and just have a night of it."

Conner looked around the basement. "Are we going to have a slumber party?"

"That's the idea."

Dayna walked over to the bookcase. "Please tell me you know how to play Settlers of Catan and that's on the itinerary."

"It can be. Games, movies, food. It's *all* part of tonight."

I turned to Luna, expecting a snappy comment, but she just shrugged. "We should get into pajamas first."

It turned out Luna was the resident expert at Settlers of Catan. Fern had never played, so, the first round we had to teach them the rules. They did well, but we were all slaughtered by the goose queen.

The second round was much closer.

While we played, we enjoyed pizza and breadsticks. After Conner won, everyone else flopped on the mattresses while I headed into the kitchen. "We have chocolate, vanilla, and caramel ice cream. For toppings we have hot fudge, marshmallow fluff, chips, nuts, and butterscotch. I'm going to set it all out, and everyone can make their own."

It didn't take much to convince everyone and soon we all had huge bowls of gooey goodness. We sat on the couches, munching away at dessert. Dayna stretched out her legs and smiled. "Okay, Pebble, you said bond." My stomach clenched. Her smile was way too devious. "Let's tell stories with our ice cream."

Licking off their spoon, Fern narrowed their eyes. "What kind of stories?"

"Anything. Kid stories."

I squeezed my eyes shut, then sighed. If I was alpha, I should be willing to suck it up. "Okay, silly stories for a hundred."

Luna narrowed her eyes. "Is that a reference to something?"

Conner's mouth dropped open. "You don't know the TV game show, Jeopardy?"

She shrugged.

Before this could get out of hand, I waved. "Okay, when I was young, like five, I had just moved here." I quickly ran down the story of the Stones adopting me, figuring if they were going to be part of the pack they should know.

"Whoa." Dayna sat up. "I had no idea about that."

Luna smirked. "I did."

"Actually, so did I," Conner said. "But that story had been told around my pack for years."

I shook my head, and he stopped. The topic of my birth parents work partner, who they attacked and maybe tried to kill, wasn't one I was ready to face.

Fern shrugged and spoke up before the others noticed our interaction. "I think it was told around all the packs. The five-year-old girl found bitten and how long until the Wisconsin pack would have to put her down. My parents felt horrible about the situation, especially since the rumors went that your Wisconsin family cared deeply for you."

Warmth blossomed in me. "That part's true." I took a bite of ice cream. "Anyway, when I was young, everyone wanted to protect me, from the kids to the adults. I was well taken care of. One day, when I was in wolf form, I was playing monkey in the middle ... or well, wolf in the middle, with a few of the other kids." A smile flitted across my face as I thought about that day, and I chuckled. "So, one of the kids, Heather—"

Luna perked up. "That's who we had dinner with in Colorado, right? She had some funny stories about you."

I blushed but nodded. "Yeah, that's right. Heather threw the ball, and I chased it. I knew I should keep my eye on the ball, and I did, even while leaping to get the ball in the air before it landed. I slammed my nose into one of the supports of the tree house." The others in the room laughed. "I swear I saw stars that day."

"Okay, okay, my turn." Conner waved his spoon before dipping it in his bowl for more treat. We all turned to face him. "This had to be when I was a similar age to Pebble, maybe five or six, seven at the oldest, but really, not very old." We all nodded. "I was at the park with my family, and I saw a rabbit. For some reason I was convinced it was the Easter bunny, and I wanted more candy, chocolate to be precise. My parents were distracted so I got up and took chase. I lost my balance and ended up in a lake."

We all laughed. Dayna got out between chuckles, "Aw, that's hilarious. Did you catch your query? Did you get more candy?"

Conner giggled. "No. Another pack mate, John ... um, just John, he found me and pulled me from the water. When we got back to my parents, they explained that it was November, and that the Easter bunny didn't run around parks that time of year."

That got all of us rolling.

Fern rubbed the back of their neck. "I dated this girl back in middle school. Now, you have to understand that ... well—" They stopped. "I'm going to make a big assumption that since you're all wereanimals and have good senses of smell, you know more about me than I've said." They looked at me with a raised brow, and I nodded. "When we left Tennessee, I knew I wanted to transition, but at that time I wasn't sure how or what that meant. I had a friend and knew what she'd done seemed amazing, but ... I just didn't know."

I reached over and squeezed their hand. They quickly nodded then smiled. "I was in seventh grade and everyone started to date. There was this girl, she was beautiful. I was at her house after school, and we even kissed. I thought I'd die right then and there. She had to go to the bathroom, and I looked around her room. As much as I liked her, I loved everything about her room. It felt so much better than how mine was decorated. There was a dance coming up, and she had a dress hanging on the back of her closet. I went up to it and just gazed at it. I realized right then and there I wanted nothing more than to be able to wear the dress. My hand trembled as I reached out to touch it. When she returned she saw me. I guess her sister was trans and she recognized what I'd been trying to figure out. I mean, I knew, but just didn't know. She wasn't ready to date me, but we did remain friends."

A silence fell over the room, then Dayna sighed. "Okay, I have a story, but it isn't all poignant like that. Do I need to find a new one?"

Luna scoffed. "Do you have anything in your life that's poignant?"

Dayna glared then huffed out her amusement. "Probably not. Okay, when I was in elementary school I would always go up to trees and scratch my back, you know, like bears do."

Luna threw a pillow at her. "You did that a month ago on campus, dufus. You haven't stopped."

That got everyone laughing again.

"On my first run as a wolf," everyone turned to look at me, "first run here at pack house, I mean. Again, I was only five, and I darted away from my sister. I smelled chocolate and ended up with my nose in a strange kid's bag."

Conner covered his mouth to stop from interrupting me and Dayna's eyes widened. "Oh, no! Did you get caught?"

"No. Jade herded me back home and explained to me the pack boundaries. She also let me know we had plenty of chocolate in the house and I didn't need to take it from strangers."

Luna smiled, and it looked genuine. "Geese shifters learn to fly like most birds. We're dropped and told to stretch out our wings."

My eyes nearly popped out at the thought.

Gazing at us, Luna chuckled. "I know, but there's usually an adult who can catch us if we don't catch an air current. Anyway, the first time my mom took me up into the air, we were really high up. Don't get me wrong, I love the sky, and flying—now—but then, I mean, geese can fly high. So, we get to altitude, and mom drops me. Though I *know* I'm a bird, for some reason, my mind tells me I'm a girl, falling, with arms and not wings, and I freeze—"

As Luna tells the story, everything in me goes numb. I'm transported back almost nine years to when my sister's body transformed from bird to human, just as Luna describes, and almost died. All to save my life. It was the day I finally decided to hunt as a wolf, make my first kill, and because of that was almost killed.

That was the day my alpha mantle had been unfurled. I didn't realize it at the time, but my parents did. By accepting all aspects of my wolf, but having the ability to control her, I showed the power and precision to be an alpha. The only pieces left were desire and skill to lead.

A shiver traveled through my body at the memory of Jade and her near death. I didn't know if I could've survived the guilt. If I'd have died, she would've been livid that Sarah had let it happen, since her panther alpha had the ability to heal me. *I'm just glad we both survived.*

A warm hand on my knee shocked me and I jerked, realizing everyone in the room was staring at me. "I'm sorry, what?"

Fern's gaze is full of concern. "Are you okay?"

"Yeah, sorry, I'm fine."

Conner shook his head. "No, you're not. What happened? Where did you go?"

"It isn't a fun or funny story."

Luna clenched her jaw and narrowed her eyes at me. "Just talk."

And so I did. I started with the fear I had at killing furry animals and how long it took me to overcome it. Then how I almost died during my first kill. In the end, they had questions.

"Wait, I'll be able to heal people? That's why Allison asked about my desire to switch to medicine?"

I giggled at the wonder in his voice. "Yeah, that's right. Epsilon wolves have a million and seven tricks. You're going to be a magical wonder, my friend."

Before they could ask more, Dayna stood. "Okay, I know I started this, and it's been amazing, but I saw the Princess Bride over there, and with a belly full of pizza and ice cream, and a head full of gossip, I'd really love to move onto the next part of our evening."

For a few seconds I sat, clearing my mind of the tense memories of days both me and Jade almost died. Fern rubbed my shoulder and everything in me relaxed. They helped me up and we cleared the dishes as Conner and Dayna set up the mattresses and movies. Then we all flopped down under blankets.

Fern sighed with contentment. "I love this movie. I always wanted to be Buttercup ... and was also in love with Buttercup. Face it, I was confused as a kid."

Dayna laughed. "Not me. I swooned over Westley."

Conner shrugged. "It's the campy action. It's just a great movie."

Luna nodded. "I agree. Everything about the movie is perfect."

The buzz of contentment flowed through me, and I sank deeper into the mattresses as a movie we all loved played on the television. When it ended, I stretched, but didn't otherwise move, too comfortable where I was.

Dayna looked over the other movies. "What should we watch next?"

Conner yawned. "I'm tired. Should we all head back to our rooms?"

"No," I said quickly. "The point of this is to have a slumber party. Fall asleep to silly movies and just have fun."

Fern smiled. "I did enjoy the Princess Bride. I love that movie."

"Inconceivable!" Dayna proclaimed and Fern snorted.

Luna checked over the rest of the movie titles. "There are a lot of kid's movies here."

I made a small sound of disagreement. "Not all of them. There are movies for all ages."

She paused. "Oh! I haven't seen this in ... like, forever. I used to love this one. Would any of you mind if we watched the Neverending Story?"

"I'm in," Fern said. "I don't know if I've ever seen it."

Conner grunted. "I'm half asleep. I don't know if I'll make it to the end of the movie."

"You know I love that one," Dayna said, taking it from Luna and getting it set up.

We all lay back down as the movie started.

I wasn't sure if the others made it to the end, but I didn't. I really tried. But sleep claimed me as the joy and contentment of being with a part of our pack swirled around me.

Chapter 25 – Tell Us A Story

Heat infused my back as I woke up. I realized arms were wrapped around me, and I immediately thought of weekends in the basement with Heather, Hannah, Easton, Lilly, and Estrella—the kids of the pack—and the tension left my body.

From the time I was five and had been brought to Wisconsin from Illinois, the other youth always protected me. Waking up in the basement, wrapped in someone's arms, wasn't uncommon.

Wanting to purr, I curled back into ... Heather's? arms. Wait, she moved to Colorado a few years ago. It couldn't be her. My mind started to catch up with where I was. I wasn't with the original kids of my pack ... I was alpha, these were new pack members. I'd forced everyone to have a bonding slumber party the night before.

Wait, whose arms are around me?

The arms tightened and I relaxed further, the touch of pack overcoming my confusion for a moment. Since Mom told me about Tennessee, I'd been running, acting, and reacting. For the first time, my mind felt calm, like I was floating on a cloud. Not even the buzz of all the wolf emotions stung.

Eventually, I had to get up and go to the airport. Today would be amazing, but for a moment, time stood still, there was no stress, and I luxuriated in the feeling.

Around me, the others slept. It was time to start my day. Breathing in the calm one last time, I slowly blew out, then worked my way out from the cocoon of safety.

Once I could sit, I turned to see who I'd been cuddled up against and my heart skipped a beat. I gazed down into Luna's eyes. She smirked back. Softly, not to wake the others, she said, "Morning, sunshine."

"Morning." I smiled, then rose to my feet, uncertain how to interact with her.

Up on the main floor, I headed to my room and changed into exercise clothes, then stopped in the kitchen to grab a water bottle on the way to the barn. Once there, I started with a warm-up run to help me think. Not five minutes in, Luna arrived and joined me on the track. Then Dayna and finally Conner.

There was plenty of room for multiple runners. Something in me soared with joy. This was how it was with my family, people coming and going, doing their own thing.

After ten minutes, I shifted to weights. Conner followed me. "Can I join you? I don't have a routine and I'm not sure what to do with those, but I'd like to learn."

"Sure. I'm no expert and what's in the book was created for me, but I'm sure we can figure something out."

Dayna ran up. "I can help with the modifications."

"I may as well join all of you as well," Luna said, coming up behind Dayna. "You can modify for both of us."

"You know I can," Dayna said, her eyes twinkling.

I knew Luna was supporting Dayna, not me, but the four of us acting together, as a pack, felt good. We spent the next forty minutes working out our arms, shoulders, and backs.

When we finished, I wiped down the mats and headed to shower. Once I was clean and dressed, I went looking for coffee ... though, the scents coming from the main area of the house told me I wasn't the first, and I didn't have long to wait.

Conner had beaten me to the kitchen. He was making pancakes and eggs, and the coffee was already brewed.

I gazed at him as he moved around the room. "You are the best, you know that, right?"

He smiled. "Thanks. I like cooking, though I didn't have many opportunities back in Florida. Mom and several of the other pack members are great cooks, so I was usually delegated to watching, eating, and cleaning."

I bit back a laugh, not wanting to tell him that sounded like the perfect arrangement to me. Moving around him, trying to avoid getting in his way, I poured myself a mug of coffee. "Well, you're welcome to play in the kitchen whenever the feeling presents itself to you."

"Sounds great." He slid a plate of food in front of me as I sat. He'd made fried potatoes as well as everything else. It was a feast, and my stomach was excited to dive in. He leaned on the counter and asked, "What are your plans for today?"

Dayna and Luna came down and filled mugs with coffee. Conner handed them each a plate of food as I answered, dancing in my seat with excitement. "Jade's plane arrives at two. If Fern is up to it, I'd like to call their dad after we eat."

"I think I'm ready to face his wrath," Fern said, coming into the kitchen. "Gods, it smells amazing in here. Who can cook?"

Luna waved her fork. "Apparently, Conner. Though, so can Dayna, so we have a few options."

Fern nodded. "I can bake, but my savory creations never turn out as well."

"You're probably too precise," Dayna said. "You need to use some flare when using spice. Let your soul tell you how much of each ingredient to use."

Fern looked horrified.

Conner nodded. "It's true. Baking is a science, cooking is letting the ghosts of your ancestors talk to you and guide your motions."

I snorted. "That explains why I can't cook. My ancestors probably disowned me years ago."

The room got silent, and I shrugged. "Sorry, didn't mean to put a damper on things. I like the analogy."

Fern tilted their head. "So, you were adopted when you were five, right?"

"Yep."

"Will you tell us that story? You glossed over it when we were in the dorms, which I totally understand, and again last night, because it wasn't really part of the bigger story, but can you fill us in now?"

"You don't know it?" I ate some of the fried potatoes and considered Fern. "I thought you said all the packs were given a rendition of my story back then."

Fern shrugged. "I was five as well. By the time I would've been told anything, my family was leaving Tennessee."

"Yeah, I wasn't really given any details until a few years ago, and then just the basics." Conner added. "You know, you were adopted. When they found you, you were already a wolf. And ... well, the speculation in our pack is that your biological parents changed you. But, again, there aren't many details."

"Okay, that's fair. I don't remember much." I shrugged. "I was young. You know kids. Bad memories."

Luna leaned forward. "Don't, can't, or don't want to?"

My body deflated. "That's a good question. The memories of when I was really young are vague. I would be placed alone in a room for long periods of time. Sometimes with a TV left on, but not always. I remember those commercials that ran all day. I think it was that channel that sells stuff twenty-four hours a day or something. Sometimes it would be cartoons, but that was rare."

Dayna's eyes widened to saucers. "Your parents just left you alone all day?"

"I mean ... maybe? We're talking about memories that are twelve to fifteen years old." I sipped my coffee, the warmth chasing away the chill of the kid I used to be. "Anyway, my parents got a dog, no two dogs, but the dogs were never there at the same time."

Gods, the memories were muddled. *Did the dogs even have names?*

Conner rubbed my arm. "Were the dogs wolves? Did they try to introduce the wolves to you one at a time?"

His touch relaxed me, and the images tried to sort themself out. Inside my head, my wolf preened under his touch, happy with his words.

"Um ... yeah, maybe. I guess that would make sense. As a kid, the idea of a wolf was foreign, so my child brain just decided 'dog.'" My hands were cold as I rubbed my face. "Then, one day we were out in the woods. My parents had decided we needed to go to Chicago. We had only driven for maybe an hour, it wasn't very long into the drive, but we'd left at night. My parents were yelling, at each other, at me, at random cars they thought drove horribly. Then they pulled over to the side of the road and yanked me from the car."

I began to tremble. I couldn't breathe.

Conner refilled my coffee. "Are you okay?"

Nodding, I sipped a bit, but my voice was soft as I continued. "I remember ... um, ... I um, looked up to try to find a star. You know," I shrugged, "to wish upon, but it was cloudy. Then the moon poked out from one of the clouds. It was so pretty." My body tensed and I sucked in air. Nothing could hurt me ... but the memories. "Then, suddenly, there were monsters."

Fern came over and wrapped me in a hug. "Shhh. It's okay. The monsters are gone. You can cry."

I'm crying? Lifting my hand, I wiped my face and felt the moisture. I leaned hard into Fern, taking the comfort and calm they offered. "Gods, why am I still reacting like this?"

Someone else pressed in behind me, arms wrapping around my waist. "Childhood trauma can be as intense later on if we don't work through it." Luna sounded ... understanding. "Can you tell us about the monsters? They can't hurt you now, you know that. Not only are they gone, but even if they were here, you're strong."

I sniffled, trying to breathe in. My face was tucked into Fern's neck as Fern and Luna sandwiched me. I needed the contact and protection. "They were as big as mountains. One of them leapt towards me and I screamed, frozen in place. It bit my arm. The other slunk low and gnawed on my leg." My mouth went dry, and I tried to swallow.

Luna tightened her hold. "You're safe, Pebble. They're long gone."

As if her words scared away the nightmare locking my muscles, I could talk again. "The first monster ... I guess it was a wolf, probably one of my parents, gods." I shivered. "Anyway, it shook its head and attacked the second, getting it off me. Then they both ran. I curled up next to the car and cried, my arm and leg bleeding." I squeezed my eyes shut and pulled away from both my supporters.

I drank more coffee, the warmth reaching down to my soul, then laughed humorlessly. "You know, we, my parents and I, we made it almost all the way to Chicago. Then, someone else my parents changed without permission caught up with us. He didn't know that my parents had attacked me, so he left me by the side of the highway for the authorities to find. Andy later told me he hadn't been in a good state of mind and thought being raised by a werewolf would traumatize me. When the 'authorities'," I put quotations around that word, "questioned me, I told them about the monsters. By then I'd healed and had no scars, so no one believed me."

The others around the kitchen winced. Fern rubbed my arm. "Gods, you were five, telling the truth, and made to feel like your story was a lie?"

"Yeah. I started to believe them. Everything had happened so fast. The wolf attack, my parents being killed, being abandoned. It was so much. Eventually I thought that maybe they were right and there hadn't been monsters, I mean, I didn't have any marks on my body."

Luna snarled behind me. "You were five. That's an awfully big story to have made up."

A shiver ran down my back. "I know. I'm just really thankful that Hazel and River came and found me when they did. I can't imagine what my life would've been like otherwise."

Fern squeezed me with an arm over my shoulder. "Thank you for sharing. I know that wasn't easy. How are you?"

"I don't know. I've never told that story before."

Dayna came over to the counter to join the rest of us. "Why now? Why us?"

I shrugged. "I don't know. Maybe because it was time."

Fern and I decided to make the call to their dad in the office. I wasn't sure if Mr. Meadows would be more comfortable with privacy, but it was always better to land on the side of caution.

Once the door shut, I pulled out my phone. "As long as we're here, do you also want to call Hollis?"

A sad smile tugged at Fern's mouth. "I do, but I don't think that we should. We've both sent texts. She knows we're thinking of her. We need to give her time."

"I know, I just ... patience isn't always my best quality. When I started school back when I was a kid, she was always there for me. It wasn't easy going from my weird upbringing, to home schooling here with the pack, to finally being allowed to go to public school. I was awkward to say the least. She was always caring and understanding."

The scent of oranges filled the room. Fern understood what I meant. "Hollis has a knack for knowing what a person needs to hear. She really is an amazing friend."

"Which is why I want to run over there and make her understand. I didn't want to keep this secret—it was pack law."

"Which is why," Fern said calmly, resting their hand on mine, "you have to give her space."

"Okay, fine, you're right." I waved my fingers at Fern in a come-hither motion. "Out with your phone. It's time to call your dad."

There was a knock on the door. Because of the sound proofing, it was muffled, but I could hear it. I had to get up to answer it. Tanner stood on the other side. "Hey, what's up?"

"I was coming over to check up on things, and the ruffians downstairs said you were calling Ronald. I was hoping to sit in on the call." We both turned to Fern, who just shrugged. Their scent had been nervous before, so adding Tanner didn't change much.

Tanner sat next to Fern, who leaned away from the intimidating-looking man. They dialed and put their phone on the desk on speaker.

"Fern. Is there something wrong? Why are you calling?" Fern's dad sounded gruff and no nonsense. He also sounded distracted.

"Hi, Dad. There have been some developments. A lot has happened here, and I need to let you know about them."

"What developments? Is everything okay? Are you and that girl fighting?" He sounded exasperated.

"Well, kind of."

"Fern, what did I tell you? I need you to be safe, and for now, safe is in Wisconsin. You need to make nice with the girl. Can you do that?"

"Dad!" Fern barked out. "Listen." They set their jaw and glared at the phone as if daring their dad to say something. "You are on speaker right now. There are two other people listening in. I just thought you may like to know that."

There was a grunt. "Okay, it would've been nice to know that from the start. Who are these two other people?"

"One of them is Pebble Stone."

"That's one of your friends from college."

"Yes, but her full name is Penelope Stone, daughter of Hazel and River Stone."

The line went silent. I had to check the display to make sure we hadn't been disconnected. Then Tanner chuckled. "Hello, Ronald. It's been a long time. It's Tanner Billings. Do you remember me?"

"Good gods, Tanner. What in hell is my kid doing with you and the youngest child of the Wisconsin group leaders?"

I sighed. "Mr. Meadows, Pebble here. How much do you know about what's been happening in Tennessee?"

"As little as possible, Ms. Stone. I left that division of the company for a reason and have no plans of going back."

Squeezing my eyes shut, I wished I could look this man in the face and speak plainly. "Did you know that the Tennessee leaders were removed with prejudice over New Year's?"

"I did. That's why I agreed that Fern could head to your neck of the woods. I figured this location would become ... less safe."

"You know." I said, trying to keep the edge of frustration from my voice, "a heads up would've been nice. Just because I didn't know Fern was your child doesn't mean the unsavory lot who had been in Tennessee and came to Wisconsin didn't know. Even if I didn't know them, we would've set a patrol."

And even if you didn't think there was trouble here, it's always good to inform a local pack of these things. You know this. I locked my jaw shut before I said anything I'd regret.

There was a grunt. "Is Fern staying with you now?"

"Yes. For a few reasons, but safety is one of them."

"Thank you." He actually sounded sincere.

"Can I ask that you consider putting Tennessee back on the table? Things have changed there, and as the leader, you could change them more." *And if you say 'yes' my parents come home and I get to go back to being just a student.*

He growled into the phone. "I won't say 'no,' but do *not* get your hopes up, Ms. Stone."

"Call me Pebble. And thank you."

He muttered something low. I knew I'd gotten as far as I could on this phone call. I waved at Fern to continue.

"Dad, would it be okay if I came home for a day or two this week?"

"I don't want you taking public transportation or traveling alone. Who would you bring?"

"Um ... haven't decided."

"This is your home, but you're safer there, especially with everything going on. If you come, I want the leader, Tanner, or someone Tanner thinks can keep you safe traveling with you."

Tanner grunted. "That was the plan."

Mr. Meadows and Fern said their goodbyes, and Fern hung up.

Tanner smiled. "That went better than I expected. Not bad."

I gaped. "Really? I didn't think it went well at all."

Fern laughed. "He didn't hang up right away. So, yeah. Not bad at all."

Chapter 26 – Beware The Cobra Chicken

The car was peaceful as I sat in the cell phone parking lot waiting for a text from Jade saying she and Brooke had landed and were ready for me to pick them up. After my trip to Colorado and the cyclone of activity that followed, I hadn't gotten any of my normal winter break reading time in. Part of me hoped the plane would be late.

A notification popped up on my screen. *On the ground, meet you in five.*

I put down my phone and sighed. That was the few minutes of winter break I'd dreamt about. Then excitement filled me. *Jade's here!*

I pulled up to the curb and leapt out when I saw my sister and Brooke. With a groan, I noticed a slight glow of red around Brooke and green around Jade. *Of course, Jade is green. She wouldn't have it any other way!* For some reason, the glow seemed to dissipate once my mind had a fix on a person. I knew I had to figure it out, but with everything else going on, I kept putting it on the back burner.

Deciding that was where it belonged now, I tackled my family in big hugs, holding Jade just a bit longer than normal after all the emotions from this morning. Warmth and love swirled around us, then I pulled away. "Okay, bags in the back, and let's go."

Jade sat up front and Brooke slipped into the back. "So, Pebble, how are things?"

"I mean, it's not the relaxing winter break I'd hoped for. Hollis may never speak to me again, and Fern is apparently going to be a werewolf one day, but besides that, it's all upside-down and backwards."

Brooke chuckled. "So, status normal for you lot."

Jade shook her head. "I'm going to need coffee and ice cream, I can tell. Let's start with the new friend ... Fern?"

"Okay, what about them?"

"Werewolf?"

"Oh, yeah. The attack." As I drove, I filled them in on the major points from the week. I ended with the one pack member they wouldn't meet today. "I don't think Trista will be around much. With school being in session, she's not around a lot, though she's living at pack house."

Jade groaned and Brooke chuckled. "Welcome to leadership, mini-Jade. It's like the idiot wolves come out of the woodwork ... they smell an opportunity, even when there isn't one."

Looking in the rearview mirror, I grimaced at Brooke. "They're the ones that created this. Three of their people have fallen. We don't know how many more there are."

Jade gazed out the window. "And you don't know why."

"I don't. Mom and Dad are trying to pick up a lead in Tennessee. I just worry that all the lone wolves are here."

Jade reached over and rubbed my leg. "You know the house is well-protected. As long as everyone is being smart, the pack should be okay."

The touch of family relaxed me. "That's part of what the meeting will be about tomorrow."

Behind me, Brooke flopped to the side dramatically. "A pack meeting? Really?"

The snort escaped me before I could stop it. "How could I not? Everyone wants to see both of you. Moreover, Jade knew. I can't believe she didn't tell you."

Jade chuckled. "You're acting like the kids back there, love. And I wasn't sure you'd come if you knew." She turned her smile on me. "I'll get to meet Trista tomorrow, then I'll know all of the new pack members. Maybe figure out why Julez doesn't like her."

A stress I'd been holding relaxed. "Yes, that will be great."

"Just remember," Brooke almost purred from the back, "no Oscar shakes."

Jade's eyes got wide. "But I can have Tanner's, and his were my first love. Oh! And I can go into the kitchen here." She shimmied in her seat.

That set us all off again.

In the last few minutes of the drive, I told them about Hollis. Losing my first real friend, my best friend, the person who'd always been there for me, hurt. They both tried to give encouraging words, but we all knew only time would tell.

There wasn't much time to discuss it more before I pulled into the driveway. Once parked, I helped them with their bags, breaking the news that they'd be staying in the basement. Once they were settled, we met the others in the living room where I introduced Jade and Brooke to the new members of the pack.

Luna tilted her head, narrowing her eyes. "So, you're the swan. I've been meaning to ask, which side of the family do you get that from? I'm assuming your mom since your dad didn't give any indication of being a shifter during the few days he was here with us."

After gaping at Luna, Jade snapped her mouth shut. Then she smiled. "Which of my parents are shifters?"

"Well, yes. Pebble is adopted, so I understand why she isn't a shifter, but she told me you were. It's a hereditary trait, so, which parent?" Luna's scent was turning minty with her frustration. I could almost feel her thinking my sister was an imbecile.

Brooke walked up and took Luna's hand. I was certain Jade had filled her in on the issues I'd been having with the goose shifter and Brooke was protective of anyone she considered hers. "Hi, I'm Brooke. You haven't been pack long enough to be asking these questions. Sorry. Maybe in a few months ... or years. But not yet. It's been less than a week since you were bitten."

Luna's face scrunched up. "Who are you?"

One of Brooke's eyebrows raised. "Are you dim? Do I need to use smaller words? I do believe I introduced myself. I'm Brooke."

The tension rose, and as fun as a throw-down between these two would be, it wouldn't improve the situation.

"Stop." I didn't say it loudly, but I added a little force behind the word, letting my mantle drop a bit, and releasing some of my alphaness.

They both turned to stare at me. Brooke beamed at me with approval. "Nicely done. You're learning fast. Did your power only touch the two of us?"

A warmth filled me at the compliment. My new recruits didn't think to give them, the adults were distracted with everything going on, and Luna liked to critique. Hearing a positive felt like a treasure.

Nodding, I confirmed, "Yeah. I've always had pretty good control of my wolf abilities."

Luna, on the other hand, looked annoyed. She opened her mouth then shut it, mouth tight, apparently at a loss for words.

"Brooke, was it?" Dayna leaned forward, elbows on her knees. "I like you. It's not often someone leaves my cousin speechless."

Jade chuckled and moved around the room, ending near Dayna. "So, Dayna, you're the bear." They shook hands and Jade nodded to herself. "Yep, they're both in there.

Conner gasped. "Wait, you could read that with just a handshake?"

"Yes, young padawan. And once I'm done with you, so will you." She waggled her eyebrows. Her head swung back and forth, taking everyone in. "Okay, ladies first I think." She headed over to Luna, who still had a petulant look on her face.

The two shook and a shiver went down Jade's back. "So, that's what a goose shifter feels like ... good to know." She nodded at Luna. "Thank you." Then she turned. "Nonbinary next?"

Fern sat in the recliner with their legs curled under them. "But I'm not a werewolf."

Jade went over to them and knelt. "But I was told you'll be joining the ranks of the furry in March. Do you mind if I confirm?"

"Not at all." Their hands were fisted in their lap, but they slowly extended one. It trembled slightly as if they feared Jade would take away the hope Conner had given.

Jade knelt and took Fern's hand. The process always took only a second. But Jade narrowed her eyes and stayed there for almost a full minute. Brooke and I exchanged confused looks.

Finally, Jade looked up. "Conner, can you come over here? I'd like to confirm something." She hadn't let go of Fern. Conner shrugged and went over and squatted next to Jade. She slid her hand into his, effectively connecting all three of them. The rest of us watched as the three of them stayed like that for almost five minutes.

Worry crashed into me as I waited. It never took this long. Brooke pulled me into the love seat and began regaling us with stories of the babies and how they were ruling the California pack's Werehouse.

Finally, with a goofy grin, Jade released them and stood. Both Fern and Conner had dazed looks on their faces, as if they had no idea what had just happened to them. "I think we should get some food—preferably some coffee—then come back in here, and talk."

"Why?" I asked, still nervous, though Jade wouldn't smile like that if she had bad news. "Is there something wrong with Fern? Are they not going to shift in March?"

"Oh, they'll shift all right. It's just ... Fern will be another epsilon. There are three of us here, and I'm curious as to why." Jade leaned in and sniffed Fern's arm. "Is this what I smell like? It really is relaxing.

Shock rocketed through me at her words. *Three epsilon wolves? How is that possible?* I gaped, then felt Brooke push me towards the kitchen.

Brooke sashayed over, then made a production of sniffing each of the three of them. "No. You each have a different calming smell. Maybe it's regional. Conner is eucalyptus and citrus, Fern is more of a deep woodsy scent, and you, love, are pine trees and a river."

After that, coffee was made and Dayna dug out a package of muffins. We all headed back into the living room and got comfortable.

"Okay," I said, sipping my coffee. "There weren't any epsilons, and now there are three. Do you think there's something you all have in common?"

Jade shrugged. "I can't imagine what it is. I'm from Wisconsin, Fern was born in Tennessee, and Conner is from Florida. There really isn't any commonality there."

"You two have alpha parents," Fern said, "whereas my dad was never an alpha."

Brooke narrowed her eyes. "But he could be, right? That's part of what's going on right now. He's like," she looked at Jade who mouthed 'Tanner,' then she continued, "Tanner. Alpha-light."

"I guess. He just always seemed to avoid it."

Luna paced the room as if she had too much energy to sit. "Maybe it's more fundamental? I was bitten, but all three of you are natural wolves." She paused and looked at Jade. "Wait, are you a natural wolf?" Jade nodded with a shrug. "Okay, so the question is, can an epsilon be bitten, or do they have to be natural? And what about your parents?"

With a sigh, Jade shook her head. "I don't think that helps. I know that Conner's parents were both bitten, but I have one each."

Conner shook his head. "No, my dad was bitten, but Mom is natural. Our Moms were best friends. They took out that rogue that created all the other wolves that have shaped our lives."

"Gah!" Jade said, slapping her forehead. "That's right. We both have one each."

"I have one each as well," Fern added.

Dayna laughed. "Could that be the connection?"

Conner leapt to his feet. "Oh, my gods. That's it!" He kissed the top of her head. "You're a genius."

"What?" Dayna gaped at him. "What did I say?"

He ran off, returning with the ancient book I'd lent him. Jade's mouth dropped for a moment, then her hands started to animate. "I know what you're going to say. But let me think." She continued to tap her fingers in the air. "Fern, which of your parents was bitten?"

"My dad, back when he was in college in Georgia."

I shook my head. "That was around the same time my parents were in college in Florida." I stared at Jade as puzzle pieces connected in my head. "You don't think ..."

Her face lit up. "It would make sense."

Luna stopped walking and balled her fists. "Okay, you two have to finish your thoughts for the rest of the class to follow."

Conner sat, cradling the book in his lap. "You two think that the same rogue wolf that bit my dad and River also bit Fern's dad on the way south."

A grin spread on my face. "I do. Lone wolves and rogue wolves are rarely very strong. The idea that they could create an alpha level wolf is unlikely. But one wolf that was powerful enough to create a bunch of other powerful wolves ... well, that makes a lot more sense."

The scent of citrus surrounded Jade as her excitement built. She pointed at the book. "I can't remember the exact line, but I know which one you're thinking about. I've wondered about that for years."

With reverence, Conner opened the book. "It's right here. *Created strength mixed with natural power will bring pack balance.* It has to mean a bitten alpha mating with a natural alpha can make an epsilon wolf. It's in the section that has the most stories about epsilons."

"The book talks about a time when there were more epsilon wolves." Everyone turned to me. "I bet, at one point, before the packs became as strong as they are now, there were more powerful lone and rogue wolves. Today, most alpha wolves are natural, and come from other alpha wolves. If there were strong rogue wolves, or more alphas in general, we'd have more than six packs in the US. With fewer really powerful wolves, the epsilon wolves all but died out."

Luna shook her head. "But the alphas are the ones who bring new wolves into the pack. You are the one that bit me and Dayna. Why aren't the alphas creating more alphas?"

I tapped my head. "Wolves have an instinct or premonition. Mine happens to be stronger than most, but all wolves have it. They know what a pack needs. If a pack is strong and doing well, alpha level wolves aren't what it needs."

"Then why aren't there any other alpha level wolves in Tennessee? Didn't any new wolves get created there?"

"I don't know," I said, "but my guess is no."

We all just sat, eating our muffins and letting the information set in. Finally, I gave Jade a wicked look. "You know, now you have to write that book. I mean, you only have three kids, are a doctor, and have a second job on the side. You have a ton of time."

Jade wrinkled her nose at me, making a funny face. "Gods above, Pebble. You're absolutely right. Nothing but time."

Fern shrugged. "As we work together, I could take notes and write something up. I'm not the best writer, but I'm not the worst."

Glee infused Jade. "You'll write the book? Wait, no, you already said you would, no take backs."

A smile tugged on Fern's face. "Yeah, sure, but I warn you—I'm more of a science person."

Conner shrugged. "So am I, but I'll help. We'll get our alpha to help as well. I mean, that's part of her job, right?"

I groaned, and both Jade and Brooke laughed. Brooke bumped into Jade. "Why didn't you try that with Bevin? Make him do all the work?"

"José would've killed me, but besides that, great idea."

We finished our coffee and muffins, then Luna approached Jade. "I've never seen a swan shifter. Are you interested in a flight?"

Jade froze in her seat. "Um ... maybe not right now."

"Was it something I did?"

Slumping, Jade shook her head. "I just can't imagine choosing to fly with a cobra chicken ... I'd never live it down."

Chapter 27 – Reality Check

The cold air pricked my skin, but I couldn't refuse the chance to run with Jade. I'd mentioned it was January in Wisconsin, but she countered that it was almost forty degrees today. An unusual warm spell. And since I was being mocked by someone who lived in California, there was little I could say in argument. So we ran.

"First, I organized my thoughts for today's meeting. Then I wrote some notes for a call with the alphas. I figured it's time I initiate a call with all the packs."

Next to me, Jade grunted, but didn't comment.

"You don't agree?" A cold shiver ran down my body as I thought about her disapproval.

"I didn't say that, I just wouldn't want to do it myself."

I shook out my arms to dissipate the nervous tingles. Thinking about her opinion, I couldn't say I didn't agree. "Between the wolves attacking and the sudden influx of epsilon wolves, I figured I need to start talking to the other packs around the country. I can't just share information with Mom, Dad, José, and Bevin."

"Why not?" Jade struggled to keep a blank expression, breaking into a fit of giggles.

"Why not, indeed," I retorted. "So, I have a meeting, and then a meeting. I even sent out emails to all the leaders. The call will be at eight."

"Well, sounds like you're going to have a thrilling day. I can see why you wanted this job." The sarcasm dripped from Jade's words like hot fudge from ice cream.

"Eh, you know, it pays well, and then there's all the prestige."

We both laughed as we ran in silence for a few moments.

"How do you think Mom and Dad are doing down in Tennessee?" Jade asked.

"I haven't talked with them much. From what I understand, that pack is a mess, the alphas were," it took me a moment to figure out my words, "particular."

Jade snickered. "Nice diplomacy. I see why they tagged you for this leadership role."

"Ha! Anyway, from what I understand, not only are they looking for a new alpha, they're reprogramming the wolves to be less docile and hostile, if that makes sense."

Focusing on the path, Jade's face scrunched up as she thought. "Like passive-aggressive? Did they have that many dominance fights?"

"It was that or do what the more dominant wolves did." My body recoiled at the idea of how that pack ran. "So, Mom and Dad are trying to restructure if they can." After a few steps my voice dropped. "I miss them."

"I know. You're doing an amazing job, by the way. I'm really proud of you. So are the others. Even Luna, if I'm reading things correctly."

I stiffened.

Finally, Jade asked, "So, do you want to talk about Luna?"

"Not really, but sure."

"Have you spoken to anyone about her?"

"I mean, not really, maybe a little. I just—" I huffed. "I don't know what to say?"

Jade gazed at me, concern in her eyes. "Pebble, this is your life, your future. Have you slowed down enough to decide if you're happy?"

My head started shaking before she stopped talking. "Have I slowed down? When? I swear, in the last week, when did I have time to breathe? What are these words 'slow down'? Do you realize what's even happened this week? Much less this month? I can't believe how much I've done since finals, and that was barely a month ago."

"That's my point. You've been reacting to everything and not stopping to really let your situation sink in. If you don't make a decision for yourself, you're going to end up in a situation you may not be happy with."

I could almost feel my wolf's claws digging into my soul. She wanted me to listen to Jade. *But you're pushing me to Luna. Are you having second thoughts?*

A pressure built in my chest, a heat, and I wanted to scream, to howl. If I were in wolf form I would have.

"Do you know how unfair it is that you can speak with your animals?"

Jade snorted. "Do you think it's helpful? Do you think they make any sense? It just means I get to communicate, and it still makes no sense."

I grunted. "Yeah, I guess."

"So, tell me about Luna."

I took a deep breath, thinking as I ran. "She's intense. It's one of the first impressions I had of her. She's also loyal to those she believes are her people."

"Hmm. That's very goose-like."

"Is it now? Funny, that."

"I can't believe you ended up with a goose-shifter," Jade laughed. "I can't believe there *are* goose shifters."

"I can't believe *you* refused to fly with her. You're scared of her in goose form."

Jade huffed. "No, I'm not scared of *her*. I'm just convinced you or Brooke will video the escapade and send it back to the California pack to be used against me. Now, stop changing the subject."

We got to the turnaround spot and started back towards home. "Fine. When Luna forgets to be mean, I like being around her. She's smart and caring. I think she could be a strong addition to the pack and a great leader." We ran for a bit longer as I sorted my thoughts. "When I see how she acts towards 'her' people, I think if I could be in that category, she and I could be a dynamite team. I just don't know if I'll get into that category."

"Give it time. Like you said, it's been a week. I can't imagine being told that I'm to mate a wereanimal I barely know about. It's practically an arranged marriage."

I snorted. "I hadn't even thought about it like that. And she's so independent." I shook my head. "Not that I think marriage is in our future. Just ... co-leadership."

Jade shrugged. "All I'm saying is, sister mine, don't over analyze. Remember, the first full moon run changes things, you know that."

Muscles in my back tensed. I wished something about all of this was easy. "We did go out on a run already."

She growled low. "Have you forgotten everything? That wasn't a full moon run. It wasn't with the entire pack. You can't come to any conclusions until after Tuesday. You know this, sis."

As we ran, I thought about her words and knew she was right. Part of me wanted to slap my head. The other part knew I'd been doing too much to think things through soundly. A new thought popped in my head and, with it, a bit of joy. "So, you're going to become a teacher, huh? Train my two epsilons?"

The bark of amusement from Jade scared a flock of birds from the nearby trees. "The other packs will be both happy to not have your rogue wolf issues and salivating to get your new wolves."

"Oh, they'll be able to dream all they want, but Fern and Conner are mine!" Glee shot through me at the good fortune I'd had with most of my new wolves. Such a mixed package. "And I have a werebear, so my pack is becoming as diverse as the California one."

"We could have a bear, I'll have you know." Jade said, narrowing her eyes at me.

"Only if said werebear wanted three animals, and I don't think you want the government to know that's possible."

The grapefruit scent of Jade's joy at our banter filled the air. "Until you have a panther, I think we still outrank you."

"Wow, the gauntlet has dropped. I see what you've done." Jade's smile was infectious. "Okay, enough about me and my pack, tell me about my nieces and nephews. The five terrors of the California pack."

"Oh, the triplets are running around. Bini was the first to walk. We all thought it would be Esperanza, but she was the last, watching her brother and sister tottering about. Soren and Lilly are babbling back and forth, and Lilly is eyeing the triplets. I don't think it'll take her long to figure out the walking bit. They all miss their Aunt Pebble."

"I know! I really wanted to come to visit this winter break. Hopefully over the summer. Either I'll go down there, or you can bring them here. Either way, I will see those kiddos."

"That you will."

We ran for a bit longer. Then Jade asked, "So, you decided to move back home because Trista is living here. You don't trust her?"

"It isn't that. It's just ... she's new to the pack. I don't want her to feel abandoned. I know this is the first time she's been with a pack, but she's never around and hasn't learned what it is to be a werewolf. She still speaks in half-truths. I'm assuming it's because that's what she did before, but I could be wrong. I don't know, she's hard to read. So ... I just want to be around."

"People tell half-truths all the time. I hear it in all the non were-people I meet. The only people I can speak with and not expect half-truths from are at Werehouse."

I smirked. "I knew you'd understand. But I still think I should be around more if she's using the pack den as her main residence."

"Living at home isn't the worst thing but consider spending some time in the dorms. The pack den is close to campus, but not that close. It'll be much more convenient to not have to drive in every day."

"Julez hates her."

Jade scoffed. "So you said. I haven't met her yet, but I'll try to see if I can get a feel for her in the next day or two."

"Thanks, Jade."

As we got to the end of the path and cut across the yard to home, it occurred to me just how much I'd needed this time with my sister.

Chapter 28 – The Circus

The room bubbled with sound, movement, and excitement. Alone on the stage, I could feel everyone's emotions both internally and as a pressure on my skin. The scents battled, some people knew what was going on, and they were nervous, apprehensive, and stressed while others were just hopeful and curious.

My head buzzed with all the people. I spent a few minutes reinforcing the barrier. I wasn't sure if having everyone close or just their excitement was the reason, but my head hurt.

When my parents had given me the pack, there had only been seventeen members. Then Luna and Dayna joined. Now, we had Conner and eventually Fern, unless they planned on switching colleges. With Jade and Brooke in the meeting room, the space felt oppressive. Having two epsilons around helped. We'd had big meetings before, but the topics for the day weighed on me as well.

Before I'd entered, Tyler had pulled me aside. During the week, he'd been in contact with Dad, his boss at Stone Security, Dad's business. They'd been working the IT side of the investigation. I now had one more item to add to my agenda.

"Hi, everyone." Those words were enough to cut through the chatter and quiet the conversations. It was an odd feeling to have so many people shift from light conversation to full attention on me, and it made my skin prickle.

As I gazed around at all the faces of the people connected to me, I saw how everyone sat in twos and threes, depending on the size of the couch they were sitting on. Before I continued, Trista came in the back with a sheepish smile, waved, and sat in the rear near Hannah. *At least she has someone else in the pack she gets along with.* "We have a lot to discuss, but I feel nothing will get done if I don't let Jade and Brooke come up here and give an update on their kids and Owen's babies first."

That got the laughter I'd expected.

I stepped to the side and let the two take some time to regale everyone with a few stories of the five babies.

Chris shot to his feet. "That's all well and good, but when are you bringing them here? Don't think we won't charter a plane and bring the whole pack to you if you don't. I want to meet the babies before they can shift."

Clare smiled wide. "Wait, can they shift? Do you know what they can shift into?"

I glanced at Conner and Fern who both looked shocked at the question. I don't think it had occurred to them that being epsilon and being able to predict if someone was a wereanimal would extend that far.

On stage, Brooke threw back her head and laughed. "Gods, don't ask her. Jade doesn't have a poker face and Bevin has threatened everyone. No one can find out before the kids, and none of them have asked."

"So she does know." A glint came to Tanner's eye.

Jade shook her head. "I think that's our cue to skedaddle." Reaching over to Brooke, she dragged her wife from the stage.

Andy snickered. "You even sound like a parent. 'Skedaddle.' I don't remember you using words like that when you lived here."

The warmth of pack love filled the room as I made my way back to the center of the stage. "Okay, now that we've done the really great part of the meeting, we're going to move to the bad stuff."

Everyone shifted in their seats. Piper raised her hand. "How bad? We haven't heard anything, Pebble. Should we have been told?"

What she meant was she and Julez had a baby, and they wanted to know if Spruce was in danger.

"This is me telling you, and everyone. There wasn't a need to get the news out sooner. I've been in meetings, first with my parents, then with Tanner, Clare, and Allison. We all decided it could wait. I want to start at the beginning. A tourist was attacked last semester ... last fall."

"We know about that," Julez said with a sigh. "That's old news. And yes, I agree, that was on the east side of town. Didn't Tanner take—"

I gave Julez a hard stare and she stopped talking. "This will work better if you let me talk. There are a lot of things we need to cover today." A bit of my power slipped the confines of my mantle, but I took a moment to rein it in. "If we don't want to be here until tomorrow, you'll wait until I open up the floor for questions."

In my mind, I felt Jade reach out to me. '*What?*' The word snapped out.

'*You're doing great, even with the power slip. They need to remember who you are. Just breathe.*'

The connection was gone.

As my pack sat stunned from the show of my power, I quickly explained about the body Aunt Allison had found and the second body on Willy Street. When people started to ask questions, I held up my hands and moved on to the night I went out with my friends.

"At first I thought that they were after me. But a few things clicked as I discussed the evening with Tanner. First of all, they didn't attack me, they went after my friends, Hollis and Fern. Second, we didn't take a pack car, we took Hollis's car. And third, as I approached, the men said something about only wanting Fern."

Estrella raised her hand. "What are we missing? Why would they want your friend? And how does Hollis's car fit in all of this?" José's sister had always been clever.

"To understand that, you'll all need to know who Fern is. Fern?" Fern joined me on stage. Together we told their history.

Uncle Jackson's mouth dropped. "You're Amy's kid? I remember when Amy was here in college. Hazel went to Florida, but I stayed here. She was only in the pack for those four years, but she was great, we got along. I remember we stayed in contact for a few years after that. She went to grad school in Georgia, though she said she always wanted to return to Tennessee, maybe run the pack. She told me there was one other wolf who was as strong as her that she worried would become alpha before her since your mom left the state for school."

After a moment Uncle Jackson blushed. "I'm sorry. This is your story. It's just that I've wondered about Amy all these years. She told me she met someone, but back then it was harder to keep in touch. And then Allison came into my life and, well, I got distracted."

A wave of amusement flowed through the room.

Fern smiled at my Uncle. "I'll tell mom, see if she remembers you. If it's okay, I'll give her your contact info. I bet she'd love to hear from you."

"I'd like that." He beamed at Fern.

"There are a few other things I'd like to mention about the attack," I continued. "First of all, Dad and Tyler finally got images of the attack on the Tennessee wolves. Though there weren't cameras in the alley, the building across the street had some, and with some of their technology wizardry, they got copies. From what we can tell, the attack on Hollis and Fern was the same. The one difference was the man who put a knife to Fern's neck didn't cut. With the alphas, there were four men, and they did. Then they threw them both down the alley to be mauled, covering up the knife wound."

Clare growled low. "So, they were the same people?"

"That's what we think."

Chris's face was a mask of fury, something I'd never seen before. "But why? What is the point of attacking the alphas of Tennessee and then coming here? I don't understand."

"I don't either, but that's what we're going to find out." I held up my hands before anyone else could react. "I know you're all really upset, and we can vent and fume later. Right now, Tanner, Clare, Tyler, and I are coming up with plans, as are my parents. But there are more things we need to discuss."

Aunt Allison gazed at me sadly. "Is one of them the fact that your friend Hollis was bitten?"

"Yes. Hollis was tested and there's no sign of a wolf. But I'd like to do another one. She's angry that Fern and I kept secrets from her. I haven't been able to get a hold of her, but I may need to push the issue. I really want to confirm that she's still a norm."

"Wait." Julez's eyes were the size of saucers. "What do you mean 'Hollis was tested'? Do you mean Jade tested her? Because I can't see not being confident in your sister." Her eyes narrowed as if things were falling into place. "If not her, who? Who administered the first test that you aren't confident with?"

"Well, now we move on to the next item on the agenda. We have a few new members of the pack. You all know about Luna and Dayna." They waved, but didn't move to join me, which was fine. "Fern will be joining the furry ranks in March, determined and confirmed." I held up my hands. "But we also have Conner." I waved him up. "Conner comes to us from Florida. He is Rory and Tilly's son. His first run was in December, so he's very new."

All around the room people had small reactions. I let them take in the news. "When Conner arrived, he told me stories about how he always seemed to calm the wolves around him, even before he found his paws."

A stillness came over the room, and then Jade snickered. I grinned back at her. "Like Jade, and eventually Fern, he is epsilon."

There was no stopping the reaction of the group of wolves this time. I had to let the shock and talk run its course. Then, slowly, the three of us explained what we'd discovered about where epsilon wolves came from.

Smirking, Fred, José's dad, leaned forward. "So, Conner, how many times have you passed out learning how to use your new super powers?"

Conner blushed as the room erupted again.

"Who's going to write the book?" Chris demanded.

With a sheepish grin, Fern raised their hand. "I'm not great at writing, but I can take a crack at it. I figure I'll be starting from the beginning, having to learn everything."

Chris's face lit up with joy as a grapefruit scent filled the room. "Good. We need someone to get all this stuff down. Maybe *you'll* learn something you can teach Jade."

Jade groaned. "Please, no more!"

Once the commotion settled, I signaled Dayna to come up. "We have one more item on the agenda."

There was a tension in the room. We'd already covered so much.

Dayna waved. "Hi. I know I'm new to the pack, less than a week furry. That said, I'm going to start a local food challenge. I want us, as highly sensitive werewolves, to find the best of everything, from cheese curds, to pizza, and everything in between in the area. I'm hoping we can get a page on our website where everyone can vote."

The amusement ballooned in the room as I leaned into her. "We don't have a website."

Her mouth gaped open. "What do you mean we don't have a website? Even the luddite bears have a website!"

In the back, Tyler waved his hands, trying to control his laughter. "I'm on it!"

Chapter 29 – Questions Answered

When I opened the doors, the scent of lasagna, garlic bread, and baking pies filled the room. A collective groan of appreciation came from most if not all of the wolves in the room.

During the meeting, several of the pack non-wolf partners had cooked a meal. The close-knit group warmed my heart and filled my belly, once again.

I stood back and waited, letting the others get food and find places to sit. Once everyone was settled, I got myself a plate and sat at the counter. Trista sat next to me. "That was an intense meeting! I had no idea so many things were happening this week. No wonder you seemed so busy."

"Sorry if I wasn't as attentive as you'd hoped." My smile was a bit forced. I knew she was hurting with so much happening back home, but I'd been scheduled just about every minute of the last week. I'd given her the time I could.

"Oh, no. That's not what I'm saying. Classes were busy and I wasn't even around that much. I mean, thank you for getting me situated in a room here. It really takes a weight off my shoulders."

The lasagna was amazing, the scent filling the air all around us. I took a few bites, rebuilding my energy after a long day ... and it was barely noon. "Of course. You're pack. But, have you actually stayed here every night? I'm trying to think if I've seen you here all that much."

A blush colored her cheeks, and she scrunched up her face as if embarrassed. "Yes and no." She waved her hands. "I love that I have a place here, but it's really far from campus. One of my friends who lives closer to Madison College is letting me crash on their couch once or twice a week, so I don't always have to drive back and forth. It saves on gas money."

As always, her words were a mix of truth and lie. It was like talking to a norm. When we weren't surrounded by the pack, I really had to sit her down and discuss this habit.

"That makes sense. Everything is so expensive." I touched her arm, trying to let her know I wasn't mad. "And, Trista, you don't have to hide that. It's your life. You can decide where you stay."

She blew out a big breath. "Okay, good. I didn't want you to think I wasn't appreciative. I really am. I just want to have all my options available."

"It's fine."

My phone buzzed, and I pulled it out. *Owen is facetiming with the kids on my laptop. Living room.*

I put my phone down and turned, seeing a bunch of people crowded around Jade. Chuckling, I took another bite of food.

"What's so funny?" Trista asked.

"Oh, Jade just asked me to come see her in the living room." I held up my phone and shook it before putting it back down. "I'm just going to quickly finish my last few bites first. There are so many people wanting some time with her, I figure I have a minute."

Flipping her hair, Trista gazed over her shoulder. "Yeah, you can finish that, talk to your sister, then go for dessert—the best part of the meal."

"Now you're talking."

We smiled at each other, and I bet my eyes sparkled with mischief as much as hers did.

Once I finished my plate, I left my mess to clean up later and headed to the living room. I didn't think the call would take that long. Space was made for me on the couch.

On the screen, Owen sat holding two babies. I gasped. "Oh, my goodness, are those my niece and nephew?"

His smile lit up his face. "About time you showed up, sis. And yes, they are. They want to meet their favorite aunt."

Jade huffed next to me. "Favorite?"

"Of course. Who can compete with Pebble?"

That made Jade and Brooke snort. "Fine."

"I really miss you, bro. I can't believe I missed my trip out there. I know! Fly here for your birthday."

His eyes widened. "You remembered my birthday? Does that mean you got me a gift?"

A hand appeared from offscreen and slapped his arm. Sarah's voice came over the line. "What kind of question is that?"

Owen looked over the screen. "It's the kind of question a brother asks his now alpha sister."

I laughed. "There may be a gift I can send back with Jade and Brooke. But only if you promise the kids won't get any bigger before I get to see them in person."

He threw his head back and laughed. On his lap, the two kids jerked in surprise. Sarah appeared, taking Soren. She looked into the screen, "It would be nice, wouldn't it? Hi, Pebble! It's nice to see you."

"You too, Sarah."

Behind the couch, movement caught my attention. First, Andy and Chris walked past, waving at Sarah and Owen and the kids, then Aunt Allison and Uncle Jackson.

I figured everyone in the pack would find a reason to pass behind and ogle at the screen.

Lilly began to fuss, and on their side, Quinn, one of the California pack, came to collect her. He narrowed his eyes for a moment, searching the faces on our side, then smiled. "Hiya, Jade. Hey, Pebble." Then he left.

Bevin popped into the screen with two of the triplets and everyone in the pack repeated their need to see him and the kids.

Jade tapped my shoulder. "Why don't we let Brooke take over here? I need to speak with you for a moment."

I shrugged. "Talk to you soon, Bevin."

"Of course, call whenever you need to ... though we'll talk later tonight, right?"

"Yep, at eight."

Brooke took over the call, letting everyone in the pack see the kids. Jade led me to the office. "Why here?"

"We needed some privacy."

A sense of dread filled me. "Okay, why? Is something wrong?" Everything had seemed to be going so well.

"What do you know about Quinn?"

I scratched my head, thinking. "Wasn't he originally part of the Dynasty? You met him and his twin at college. Then, when the Dynasty started killing people, Quinn decided he didn't like the direction his people were taking and jumped ship, joining all of you?"

"Yeah, that's it, more or less." Jade paced the room. "The Dynasty was a small interwoven group of families. They acted a lot like a cult. Jerry was their leader."

"Okay, I know all that. But all of you took them down years ago. Why are you bringing this up now?"

"Because, Pebble. Quinn recognized Trista. She used to be one of the kids of the Dynasty."

Thank you for reading Yugen!

Please leave a review <u>online</u>.

Check out my <u>website</u> to find all the links to my socials and find information on my next series!

Coming Soon:

- A new dystopian fantasy series: Chameleon

    - Ivy is alone in the world, trying to survive without people questioning her magic. Petra lives with her dad, though after her mom was caught lying by the government, his reprogramming meant he'd never be the same. After meeting at work, can the two trust each other enough to share their biggest secrets? Are they strong enough to fight for better lives for themselves?

About the Author

Huckleberry Rahr is a mathematics instructor at the University of Wisconsin-Whitewater. She spent many years teaching math around the Midwest and in Papua New Guinea with the Peace Corps. Her parents  instilled a love of reading from a young age.

She grew up with lesbian moms who had a huge collection of women authors with heroines as the protagonist. Her favorite genre was fantasy and science fiction, that is, until she discovered urban fantasy. What her mom's library lacked were books with characters that looked like her family: diversity in background, gender identity, and sexuality. She decided if she couldn't find that series, then she would write it.